Praise for
Carolyn Wall's astonishing debut novel
SWEEPING UP GLASS

"This **EXTRAORDINARY** debut novel ... is filled with arresting images, bitter humor, and characters with palpable physical presence. The fresh voice of that clear-eyed narrator reminded me of Scout in Harper Lee's *To Kill a Mockingbird*. I literally could not put it down." —*The Boston Globe*

"A **RIVETING** story full of intrigue." —*The Oklahoman*

"Wall gives her heroine a **POWERFUL** voice in this **HAUNTING** debut." —*Kirkus Reviews*

"Carolyn Wall is a **BRILLIANT STORYTELLER** and this book is a wonderful read."
—MARTHA BECK, author of *Steering by Starlight*

"Carolyn D. Wall has created an engaging character in Olivia Harker and a complex and densely interconnected community in Aurora, Kentucky. Her evocative prose recalls the regional style of such authors as Flannery O'Connor, Harper Lee, and Eudora Welty." —*Mystery Scene*

"**A REAL STUNNER,** with plot and characters the like of which you've never seen." —*MLB News*

"**HIGHLY RECOMMENDED** for all collections."
—*Library Journal* (starred review)

"This is a perfect little book, like a head-on collision between Flannery O'Connor and Harper Lee, with a bit of Faulkner on a mystery binge. **I LOVED EVERY PAGE** of it."
—JOE R. LANSDALE, Edgar Award winner

Sweeping

A Novel

Up Glass

Carolyn Wall

Delta Trade Paperbacks

2009 Delta Trade Paperback Edition

Copyright © 2008, 2009 by Carolyn D. Wall
Reading group guide copyright © 2009 by Random House, Inc.

Published in the United States by Delta,
an imprint of The Random House Publishing Group,
a division of Random House, Inc., New York.

DELTA is a registered trademark of Random House, Inc.,
and the colophon is a trademark of Random House, Inc.
RANDOM HOUSE READER'S CIRCLE & Design is a
registered trademark of Random House, Inc.

Originally published in hardcover in the United States
in a slightly different form by Poisoned Pen Press in 2008.

Title page art from an original photograph by Kinsey Christen.

Wall, Carolyn D.
Sweeping up glass / Carolyn Wall.
p.   cm.
ISBN 978-0-385-34303-9 (trade pbk.)—ISBN 978-0-440-33850-5 (eBook)
1. Widows—Fiction. 2. Grandparent and child—Fiction. 3. Mothers and
daughters—Fiction. 4. Depressions—Fiction. 5. Mountain life—Kentucky—
Fiction. 6. Hunters—Fiction. 7. Kentucky—Rural conditions—Fiction. 8.
Kentucky—Race relations—Fiction. 9. Domestic fiction. 10. Psychological fiction.
I. Title.
PS3623.A35963S84 2009
813'.6—dc22   2008048080

Printed in the United States of America

www.randomhousereaderscircle.com

BVG   9   8   7   6   5   4   3   2

Text design by Virginia Norey

This book is for my father,
who listened as if my words were absolute
and my voice could save a nation.

Acknowledgments

My eternal gratitude goes to the Dead Writers Society for their suggestions and for listening while I ranted. Thank you, Rafael, for your fine editing, and gratitude to all the folks at Poisoned Pen Press. Most of all, my undying love and appreciation belongs to my children, all, and to Gary for being the best spouse a writer ever had.

1

The long howl of a wolf rolls over me like a toothache. Higher up, shots ring out, the echoes stretching away till they're not quite heard but more remembered.

There's nobody on this strip of mountain now but me and Ida, and my grandson, Will'm. While I love the boy more than life, Ida's a hole in another sock. She lives in the tar paper shack in back of our place, and in spite of this being the coldest winter recorded in Kentucky, she's standing out there now, wrapped in a blanket, quoting scripture and swearing like a lumberjack. Her white hair's ratted up like a wild woman's.

I'm Ida's child. That makes her my ma'am, and my pap was Tate Harker. I wish he were here instead of buried by the outhouse.

Whoever's shooting the wolves is trespassing.

"I'll be out with the boy for a while," I tell Ida.

I've brought her a boiled egg, bread and butter, a wedge of apple wrapped in cloth, and a mug of hot tea. She follows me inside and sits on her cot. Ida's face is yellowed from years of smoke, her lips gone thin, and her neck is like a turkey's wattle. Although there's a clean nightgown folded on a crate by her bed, she hasn't gotten out of this one for almost three weeks.

Pap once told me that when he first met Ida, she was pretty and full of fire. She rode her donkey all over creation, preaching streets of gold over the short road to hell. She still calls daily on the Lord to deliver her from drunkards and thieves and the likes of me. Last summer, she sent off for Bibles in seven languages, then never opened the boxes. It's dark in Ida's shack, and thick with liniment and old age smells. Maybe it's the sagging cartons, still unpacked, although my Saul moved her here a dozen years ago. Then he died, too.

"I can't eat apples with these false teeth," she says.

"Will'm saved it for you."

"Pleases you, don't it, me stuck in this pigsty while you and the boy live like royalty."

Royalty is a cold-water kitchen behind the grocery store. Will'm sleeps in an alcove next to the woodstove. I take the bedroom. Here in the cabin, I've tried to better Ida's life, bring a table, hang a curtain, but she says no, she'll be crossin' soon.

"I'll be out with the boy for a while," I repeat.

"I'll ask God to forgive your sins, Olivia."

Ida's not the only thing that sets my teeth on edge. I worry about the way folks come for groceries but have no money. Most of the time, they take what they need. Will'm and I write everything down, and they pay as they can—sometimes in yams or yellow onions, a setting hen when the debt gets too high.

If Pap was here, he'd tell me everything was going to be all right.

"Hurry up if you're going with me," I tell Will'm.

Damn fool's errand. I put on my big wool cape and mittens. I have Saul's rifle.

Will'm brings the toboggan from the barn. He's wearing a

pair of old boots and so many shirts that he looks like a pile of laundry. I can barely make out his dark gray eyes through the round holes in his wool cap. I know what he's thinking, just like Pap used to—some injured thing might need his care.

I'll be forty-two next year—too old and thick-legged to plow uphill through snow that makes my hips ache. I should be home in my kitchen, warming beans from last night's supper. Behind me, Will'm pulls the toboggan by its rope. We haven't gone far before my fingers are froze, my toes are numb, and I realize I've misjudged the light. Where the snow lays smooth and clean, we stop to get our breath. It's darker up here among the alders and pine. I set the lantern on the toboggan, strike a match, and lay the flame to the wick.

Below, to the left, lights blink on in Aurora, and a car or two winks along in the slush.

"Another shot!" Will'm says. "*Gran?*"

I hate it when he looks to me like that, like I can fix every damn thing in Pope County. "Will'm, this winter they'll starve to death anyway."

But I don't mean that, and he knows it. Shortly the hunters will go home to their dining rooms where they'll drink rye whiskey and eat hot suppers. Past the alder line, the last of the silver-faced wolves are curling up, hungry. They're the only wolves recorded in Kentucky, and tonight a few more are dead.

In a clearing, we come upon the two males. Will'm stares at the round dark holes in their flanks. Their right ears are gone. A small gray female has crawled off under the brush, and she lies there, baring her teeth. She's been shot, too, and her ear cut away. The blood has run from the wound, filling her eye and matting her fur. There's no sign of the ears.

These aren't just any wolves. The silver-faces have lived peaceably on Big Foley for sixty-five years. Then a week ago, a male was shot and his ear cut off. Will'm and I found the wolf, and finished him off. Today, the hunter was back, and he brought others.

"Damn," I say. "This one's had pups, winter pups."

"Don't shoot her," he says.

"There's lead in her haunch, and she's near bled to death."

"We'll take her home."

What I'm really thinking is—*I know who did this.*

"Back off from her, boy." I lay the gun to my shoulder. "Halfway down, we'd have a dead wolf on our hands."

Will'm says, "But she's not dead *yet.*"

Confound this child. I ache with the cold. More snow is likely, and when it comes, it'll cover our tracks and the sheer rock faces. It would be right to put a clean shot between her eyes. But also between her eyes is that fine silver stripe.

I wonder if Will'm's likening himself to the cubs. Time's coming when I'll have to tell him about Pauline, although he's never asked. He hasn't yet learned that all God's creatures got to fend for themselves, and the devil takes the hindmost.

"Well, give me your scarf, boy. We'll muzzle her good and tie her on the toboggan."

"I could sit with her," he says, grinning.

"You could not. You'll walk behind and keep your eyes open. Now do as I say, or we'll leave her here."

"Yes'm."

"And there's not God's chance she's sleepin' in the four-poster, or under it, either. And if there's no change by morning, I'm putting her down."

It's tricky without a rope. I pull, Will'm steadies. More than once the wolf slides off, and we stop to rearrange, and trade places. God love me, every day I understand myself less. I'm so tired that the wolf and the boy and Ida run together in my mind till I can't think who's who, or which needs me most.

2

We lay the wolf in the kitchen, on a blanket in the corner. It would be wrong to put a sickly thing in our rattrap of a barn where she could be found by a hungry bobcat—or seen by Ida if she stepped out her door. The wolf breathes ragged, and her eyes are closed. Will'm's scarf still softly binds her snout—the kind of loose muzzling I've seen Pap do. Blood seeps from the place where her ear once was.

I stack kindling in the stove and light it. Fetch a dish of navy beans from the cupboard and dump them in a pan. With a teaspoon I slide some onto her tongue, but she rolls her eyes.

"We've got chores to do," I say, getting up.

Will'm stands in the middle of the kitchen. A yellow bulb hangs over our table. "But if we don't stitch her up, she'll lay there and die."

"Sometimes that's the way of things."

"Like Wing Harris's wife?"

My head snaps around. "Don't you talk to me about Wing's missus."

"Everybody knows she gets more feeble every day."

But I won't hear it. "Get out there and bring in the wood while you've still got your coat on."

Potato peelings lie in the sink, and I scoop them up and put them in my pocket. I kick at the snow that's drifted under the back door and turned to slush on the porch. Take the buckets from their nails and bang ice from their bottoms. Will'm stumps out after me, and down the steps. I wish he hadn't said Wing's name.

When we were young, Wing and I had not a secret between us. But for over twenty years, we've crossed the street to avoid each other. Now we share only howdies at Ruse's Cafe.

All in all, I have a crazy ma'am who owns a hundred dusty Bibles, a leggy boy with a too-soft heart, and no man to bed down with. And an Alaskan silver dying on my kitchen floor.

Out in the dark, Will'm works the ax from a log. "You think we could at least sew up her ear?"

Damnation. Years ago, Ida buried Pap by the boarded-up privy. Since then, I've trod over him ten times a day. I pass over him now on my way to the wellhouse. Pap was a self-taught veterinarian, and a truly loved man, but there's not so much as a stick to mark his grave. Someday I'm going to move him to the hillside near Saul, and set a real marker.

For near thirteen years, I was married to Saul. When he died, I paid Junk Hanley a dollar to come up and lay a flat paving stone that said Saul Cross was a beloved husband and father. Not that I loved him all that much.

My boots break through the dark snow crust, and chunks of ice cling to my skirt. I push the door open, set the lantern on the ground, dip feed in one bucket, fill the other with potatoes. I cut down a string of onions. In the morning, I'll take stock of the bins and shelves in our store, line up the last cans of lima beans and baking powder. If folks don't start paying their bills, I may not be able to order again.

I let myself into the goat pen, throw the peelings to them, use a hoe handle to crack ice on the water trough. It's so dark out here, I can just make out the squatness of Ida's cabin and the donkey tethered in her sideyard. In spite of Ida carrying on about her supper, I'm sure she's eaten it and fallen asleep with her pipe lit. One of these days she's going to burn us to the ground, and when she does, I hope she takes the donkey with her. Across the yard Will'm splits kindling.

I chip through the ice on the shallow pans, too, but the half dozen hens would rather die of thirst than budge from their nests.

Will'm follows me inside, shrugs off his coat, and sits letting snow melt from his boots. I set the potato bucket under the sink.

Hell. Maybe I've brought the wolf home as a favor to Will'm—or because of Pap, whose old clinic still lies under this kitchen. I haven't been down there in years, nor do I want to go now. But I bring the lamp from where it hangs on the porch. Will'm's eyes grow round when I take the keys from the hook and open the cellar door.

My boots make hollow sounds on the stairs, but the floor at the bottom is hard-packed earth. There's no electricity, and as Saul would have said, it's moldy as molly hell down here. No wonder Saul stayed out of the place, mildewed and spun with cobwebs and dust. Saul said Pap needed his head examined, damned near living down here with his beasties, and the rest of the time running the still in the toolshed.

It's the first time in years this room has seen light. It smells bad, like things died and rotted here, although Pap hardly ever lost a patient. The rot is in the tunnel he built from the cellar to the shed. It kept him from trudging through four feet of snow just to get to his still. Now both ends are boarded.

I look around at the bunks of old straw, the table running the length of the room, rusty wire cages and carriers with bent handles, buckets, a pitchfork and shovels, crates, a pair of broken lanterns. Seeing the long caged runs and water bowls, I have a minute or two of bone-deep sickness. It's not Pap's memory that I fear under this house.

"A body could die of the damp down here." I select from a shelf a dusty brown bottle and other things—long-nosed scissors and a pack of curved needles—then we go up the steps into the light. I lock the door and slip the keys back on the hook.

From my sewing basket I fetch white thread, tear squares of clean cotton for bandages and long strips for binding. The chloroform has lost its strength, but it's all we have. I pour three drops on a rag. We wash our hands with hot water and soap, then sit on the floor. When the gray's as far under as I can get her, I cut the matted hair from her haunch. She jerks and twitches, and her eyes roll white while I shave a patch of fur and dig in the wound. My face feels painfully tight, and my eyes water something terrible.

"Who d'you think did this?" Will'm says.

I withdraw my fingers. In my palm is the metal shot. I pour peroxide in the wound and watch it boil. Spin off a length of thread, snap it with my teeth, and hold the needle to the light. Curse under my breath that my eyes aren't what they used to be. I show Will'm how to draw the edges of the wound, and while he pinches her skin between his fingers, I take a half dozen stitches. We do the same with the ear, cleaning blood from her eye the best we can. She flinches and whines. Under the men's britches

I'm wearing—plus the cotton dress, cardigan, and longhandles—I'm damp with sweat.

Will'm offers to say a prayer over her.

"You do that," I tell him. "And while you're at it, pray for the hunters. I'm going to make them sorry they were born."

3

I have nothing to give the wolf for her pain. It wouldn't do to crush up a Lydia Pinkham's or a Carter's liver pill, and I dare not chloroform her again. I'll ask Dooby, the pharmacist, what will help her to heal—if by morning she has not torn the kitchen to pieces and eaten us in our beds. She breathes thready and light, and her eyes, when she opens them, are yellow and rolling with fear.

God help me if she dies in the night, and it be upon my head. A good Samaritan, after all, is not always a beneficent thing. Folks die every day in the name of love.

Between the kitchen and the grocery I have hung a curtain. The only bedroom is in the front of the house, separated from the grocery by a door. I fear for Will'm, sleeping in his kitchen alcove with nothing but eight feet of space and another hung bed-sheet between him and the gray, so we take our supper and sit in the middle of my four-poster. I love this high-ceilinged room with its feather mattress bed, an old wardrobe, and a cricket rocker. What used to be a closet now contains a toilet, a cracked mirror, and an electric light. No matter that we have to come through the grocery and the bedroom to get to it.

I tell Will'm about how my pap could soothe a jackrabbit with a leg so busted the bone stuck through. In our nightshirts, Will'm and I tear bits of bread to dunk in our bean soup, and we talk about Ida, and the gray, and what we will do in the morning.

"Gran?" Will'm says. "Her pups'll die without her, won't they?"

"If they haven't already."

"Think we could go up in the morning and look for 'em?"

"You've got school, and even if we found any of them alive, she's too bad off to nurse them."

"We could make up some way to feed them."

"No, we could not."

Daylight will tell us whether the mama wolf lives or dies. And Lord help us if Ida rises from her bed and wanders over in the morning looking for her tea and oats.

I tuck the boy in beside me. We lay in the dark looking at each other. Toward morning, I drift off till something brings me hard awake. I shove my feet in boots and wrap myself in a flannel robe. I move through the grocery and peek around the kitchen curtain. Bits of gnawed rope lay on the floor, and bloody strips of sheet. Blood streaks the linoleum and the windowsill. Glass has exploded out onto the snow. The gray is gone.

"Sweet Jesus."

I open the back door and go through the porch and down the steps, mindful of the ice. The sky is leaden and holding its breath. Bloody tracks lead to the shed and around, past the iced-over pickup and out to the barn. And there's the gray—one leg stretched out and lying on her side. From under her belly a circle of blood spreads dark on the snow. Twenty feet away, Ida stands in her nightgown. Pap's old Winchester is at her shoulder, and her head's still thrown back from the force of the shot.

4

I want to kill Ida. It's not the first time.

When I was thirteen, Dooby told me something about her I wish I'd never known.

When I was first conceived, it was Dooby's pap down at the pharmacy that sold Ma'am the powders with which she tried to empty her womb. The first child she spat out like an unripe persimmon, but the second was me, and I would not go. I clung to her dark inner lining until she grew round in the belly and was sick most of the time from the bitter German beer the doctor ordered to make her gain weight. Later folks told me I was delivered sputtering, squalling, and already starved.

In the months that followed, while Pap ran the store and doctored dogs and cats, Ma'am lay dying of this or that. Her nerves, she said, were frazzled at the ends like burnt matches. Although I squealed like a nest of mice, she would not take me up, nor change me, nor feed me, until Pap, coming from his work, snatched me out of my crib. He stripped off my diapering, soaped me, and rinsed me till I was fit for company. He fed me all the supper I could hold, and although he rocked me into the night, he could not stop my crying.

The racket was too much for Ma'am, and even though Pap

tried to put me in the crook of her elbow, she wouldn't take me, but preferred to sit rocking an empty blanket. In short order, Ma'am slipped into an abyss from which no one could save her. She walked the length of the house, wrung her hands, and cried, causing the last of our customers to speak in low voices. They wouldn't have come at all, but they loved Pap dearly.

Sometimes Ma'am vomited into a bucket in the kitchen. Most of the time she lay in the big four-poster while a succession of ladies from Aurora came and went with covered dishes. Pap brought her the bedpan and changed her sheets, for she would not set her feet on the floor nor raise her head. Doc Pritchett gave her powders and enemas, liver tonic and sulfur with sugar and molasses, but nothing worked. She would not even swallow soup, and she was no bigger around than a stick horse. Finally, Pap sent for a doctor from Buelton. He came one Saturday afternoon, applying an assortment of poultices to Ma'am's belly and chest, and finally leeches to the palms of her hands. Nothing helped.

Shortly thereafter, Pap gave up trying and hitched the neighbor's horse to our wagon, for our mare was old and in need of being put down. He wrapped Ma'am in a blanket and laid her gently in back, with pillows around her so she would not roll. They say I stood on wobbly legs at the door of the grocery, and watched them go off down the road. Nobody remembers if I cried or not.

What came after, I remember well.

Folks came to shop. They bought packets of yeast and slices of cheese, rhubarb in summer, sweet potatoes, and cans of yellow waxed beans. There was only Pap to wait on them, running up and down the stairs with me under his arm. Time went by, one day melting into the next like warm candle wax.

Folks we'd known, and a number we didn't, came to the store

and stayed to visit, to pat me on the head, and to remember, suddenly, that they also needed a pound of headcheese or two ham hocks. Pap tore off sheets of butcher paper and penciled signs for the front window—three bundles of collards for a nickel, six eggs for a dime. We took in money. I scrapped with the chickens for their eggs, and every morning I milked the goats. Pap brought home three more nannies, and twice a week he sent the warm milk to Mrs. Nailhow, who made cheese and kept a portion for herself. We sold the cheese for an outrageous eight cents a pound. Before I went to school, I knew the grocery business backward and forward.

We were also the unofficial postmasters. From a small metal box I sold penny stamps. A man in overalls and a blue cap came Monday, Wednesday, and Friday mornings, delivering letters that I sorted into bundles, for I'd already learned the names—Sampson, Ruse, French, Andrews, Phelps. Harker, that was us. I knew which were bills to be paid to the dairyman. At six, I could tuck the money into an envelope, address it, and drop a penny from the cash register in the box for a stamp. In all that time, there was never so much as a postcard from Ma'am, and that was fine with me.

One century became another. Pap initiated me into the world of home doctoring—the mysteries of mange and foot rot, and the damage a motor car could do to a slow bluetick hound.

Finally, our old mare stumbled and broke an ankle. Pap dug a hole and shot her at an angle so that she'd fall right in. Then he set a fire of leaves and sticks, and stunk up the air with her cooking. He covered her bones with loam, and for years, cornstalks planted there grew ten feet high. Pap bought a cantankerous mule by the name of Sanderson, and we hitched her, braying and bellyaching, to the wagon. Evenings, we delivered groceries, and picked up sweet hominy at the Daymens' farm, watermelon and pumpkins from the Sylvesters'. Early mornings, we hauled bales of hay from one field to another. Pap was a good hand at turning a dime.

I went with him nights when he carried brown jugs to the outlying farms, and I kept watch by the road while men came for a trade. We raked in haunches of rabbit, fresh vegetables, apples, and tomatoes. We piled them in bushel baskets in the store—and we ate like kings.

After school, I ran the grocery. Coloreds came on Wednesdays; whites bustled in on Tuesdays and bought up stuff like it would be a month before Thursday came around.

Miss Dovey was one of our Wednesday shoppers. She was black as night and so bony you could have scrubbed clothes on any part of her. She kept her hair in a rag, and under her long dress she was barefoot, like most of her kin. She shuffled in one morning while I was sitting on the floor, trying to stitch two hankies together. I had just uttered a swear word my pap had forbidden, when she looked over the counter.

"What in the world you doin' down there, Miss Livvy?" she said. Her glasses were thick as Mason jar bottoms and the same celery-green.

"I'm tryin' to sew a dress for my dolly, Miss Dovey," I said. "But my thread won't stay still."

She took my work in her hands. "Hand me that needle, and I'll show you how to knot that thread."

And she did, the two of us sitting cross-legged on that wooden floor, her instructing me in the ways of gathering and hemming, lining up edges, and sewing on buttons. I often had to scramble up to box groceries and make change. The coloreds finally collected in great numbers to watch. I remembered my manners and jumped up, saying, "You-all stay here, and I'll get refreshments."

They were trapped while the daughter of their horse doctor, whom they worshipped near as much as God, went off to the kitchen. I slathered butter on bread while out in the store they counted out change for salt and rice they didn't need. I cut my sandwiches in tiny squares to make them go further, and they nodded and praised my buttering.

When the rest went home, Miss Dovey took her leave. At the door, she paused to lay her hand on my head. Coloreds did that. Once I asked Pap why, and he said it was a blessing.

In the months that followed, I sewed up rag dolls, hemmed baby gowns and aprons. White ladies admired the fine stitching. While I watched the store and showed off my handiwork, Pap went downstairs to check on his patients. Every time I passed the cellar door, he was whistling, and I don't know which of us was happier.

But then there were the funerals—solemn, silent Sunday morning burials that, oddly enough, preceded colored church. I guessed the time was convenient, folks being already gussied up and planning to fry chickens for their dinners anyway. First Lacy Settle's boy dropped, then her oldest nephew, and before we knew it, two fellas who lived in shacks out along the river. The caskets were plain, the eulogies mournful, and those young men went to heaven without one note of a song. Standing in line to drop a clod of dirt in the hole, I loudly asked Pap if they'd come down with some disease that was catching, and why we weren't shouting our usual halleluiahs. It was the only time I ever recall Pap putting his hand over my mouth.

From Sunday to Sunday, Pap also kept his still fired up, and I learned the value of a brown glass jug. He never allowed me a drop of corn liquor, nor did he drink much himself. On occasions when he and a half dozen men sat around our yard on up-turned crates and passed a jug, they included me in their conversation until Pap sent me squarely off to bed. Even as he wound slowly into drink, singing and waving his arms in story-telling, I forgave him for any sin he might be incurring. He loved me, and he could do no wrong.

Pap and I took turns with the wet wash and the scrubbing. Old Miz Prince from near Buelton brought us a half bushel of tomatoes for Pap's delivering six puppies. Her brown dog Bessie was too old for a litter, and the birthing was twisted, the poor dog panting, and Miz Prince apoplectic. Afterward, Pap and I peeled tomatoes for two days and made chili sauce with onions that we spooned on everything.

For the most part, I was in charge of the kitchen, frying up peppers and boiling greens, making gravy from flour and lard. Although my corn cakes were flat and my biscuits came out like lumps of coal, Pap choked them down with a smile that went clear to my feet. He was as handsome as a moving picture star, and he had charm enough to give away. I wonder now that the ladies didn't fall at his feet while Ma'am was gone—or perhaps they did, but he had the grace to keep it from me.

5

For as long as I can remember, Junk Hanley had been bringing his mammy to our store on Wednesdays. One day he said, "Mr. Harker, we beholdin' to you, and it'd be an honor, sir, to sweep yo' steps."

Even I was smart enough to know what that meant, but to say it would only remind us how poor we all were. We did, after all, have a lot of steps.

"That'd be fine," Pap said. "Fact is, I been looking for a sweeper, couple times a week." Then he twisted his lips, like he was working on a harder thought. "Need wood cut on the hill, too, hauled down for selling, and other things—tater patches turned in spring."

For all that and more, Pap would pay him a quarter a week. Junk's grin was as big as a melon slice.

I knew the stories about Junk, and I loved them.

Aunt Pinny Albert said when Junk was a baby, his mama dropped him on his head, accounting for why his skull was back-flattened and he walked with a sideways shuffle. His head was shaved clean as an onion, and his eyeballs were great white marbles that he mostly kept shuttered. He had a bent-up ear and a crooked nose, and every button on his shirt was a different color. He came from the only literate family in Pope County.

Junk's daddy was a collector of scrap metal and old rags but his grandpap was a newspaperman in the War Between the States, and then in Glover County for twenty more years. Ida said newspapering was a white man's job, and it was a sin for him to be in possession of its paycheck. I like to think both coloreds and whites sat on their porches reading his penny paper. I bet they nodded their heads and said, "That Hanley sure can turn a phrase."

When he was young, our Junk went off to the Army. He was shipped up north to Three Mile Flats where he learned to march and salute and scrub outhouses with a toothbrush. Before long, the Army delivered Junk north to Euclid, Montana. There, he met up with black-faced men from all over the country. They rode in saddles and brushed up on their shooting. After a while they headed south into desert country where they engaged in one of the last Apache battles on the western front.

Only a few men in Junk's battalion could read and write. In the one letter he sent home, Junk penciled that he harbored bad feelings about shooting the Indians. Then one day Junk received a letter meant for somebody else. It was a sad good-bye from one Miss Jackson of Falsette, North Dakota. She signed it "Love Alice," Junk figuring "Love" was part of her name.

He politely wrote back. Turned out Love Alice was colored, too. They fell head over heels in love, right off. When the skirmish was over out west, Love Alice hitchhiked down from Falsette. She met up with Junk in Omaha, where they were married by a traveling reverend in the back of a pool hall. They settled down for a honeymoon in the storeroom. In exchange for a cot, they scrubbed floors and dishes—which Junk had become quite a hand at—waxed the bar and chalked the pool cues. They ate soda crackers and sardines for breakfast, lunch, and supper, and sent a postcard home. They signed it: Junk and Love Alice Hanley.

Sudsing kettles across five states, they made their way to Aurora and settled down with Junk's mama and a truckload of kin, including Aunt Pinny Albert and her two bowlegged sons, in a three-room house on Rowe Street. They were quiet and respectful, and they went to church regular.

Love Alice herself was no bigger than a sparrow, lighter of skin than her husband, with a freckled nose that spread across her face. When she came to live in our town, she was a married woman of thirteen, and I loved her right off.

Like others on Rowe Street, the wood on the Hanleys' house was rotting. In winter, the windows were boarded, and in spring the boards were ripped off for the breeze. The front and back porches sagged with useless things, and in summer the youngsters chased ribby dogs around the dirt yard, running ass-naked like the day they were born. Whenever I passed by, the oldest child delivered a *whap* to the little ones' ears. I suspect he wanted them at attention or maybe on their best behavior, but they just stood watching me, their thumbs in their mouths and their skinny businesses dangling below. Then they smiled with teeth white as milk.

For the most part, their mamas and pappies worked as maids or janitors. But jobs were scarce, and as time went by, more and more young colored men left town. Aunt Pinny Albert kept her bowlegged boys at work in a laundry, and her three sisters cooked and cleaned for families in Buelton. Others worked farms farther away.

Finally, Junk's brother, Longfeet Abram, won a rusted old bus in a poker game. On good days, Longfeet carried his neighbors and kinfolk to their jobs and back, and they pitched in for the gasoline. But the bus was cantankerous, and it belched and backfired and smoked something fierce. Longfeet parked it in the shade of his pappy-in-law's—the Reverend Timothy Culpepper's—place. Daily, he'd open the hood and climb up inside, tinkering with one thing or another.

Like most folks around here, the Hanleys and the Albert sisters raised corn and tomatoes behind their houses. They bought their flour, bacon, and coffee from us. Once a month, the relief truck set up on the shoulder of the highway, and folks lined up for brown beans and rice, tickets for a quart of milk from the dairy, and packets of seed corn. When they were sick, they doctored themselves. If consumption hit, or influenza, they were carried out to Doc Pritchett's place where they sat out by the gully and waited their turn.

It was in that gully that Love Alice lost her baby, its life running down the insides of her legs so that before she could even cry out, she was squatting in a puddle of her own dark blood. I wondered if my pap could have saved her baby, but when I said that, it made Love Alice cry harder.

One old house at the end of the road was their place of worship—the Rowe Street African Methodist Episcopal Church—and they met there not only on Sundays, but other nights, too, eating out of covered dishes and praising God with a vengeance. On summer nights, their singing drifted down to us. They prayed for Longfeet Abram who was in jail, for the soul of Love Alice's baby, and I'm sure they prayed for us, too.

Meanwhile, it was good to have Junk around. He came in the afternoons and chopped wood or helped tend the store. He'd hang onions, and fill the barrels with red beans or dried northerns. Most of the time, Pap was downstairs nursing some sick thing, and I'd go to the kitchen to slather jam on two pieces of bread. Junk was partial to persimmon, which Miz Leona Abernathy had sent down as thanks for curing her cats of the stomach upset. Junk and I sat on the grocery counter—by then we had a big bronze cash register that clattered and clanged when I pushed the buttons—and ate our bread. And we talked about everything.

Sometimes Aunt Pinny Albert sent fried pies and tarts as thank-you's for the dippers of peas that were too much for us, and an occasional hank of embroidery cotton that I threw in the box. I'd have given away every blessed thing we had, and from time to time, Pap sat me down and explained about the cost of Ma'am's doctors, and her hospital bill.

Then one day Junk's mama sent word—I could accompany them to their Wednesday church meeting if it was all right with Pap. I let down my braids. Pap dragged a brush through my curls and tied them with a ribbon. He told me I was the prettiest girl in ten counties. He was the only one who'd ever said that. When Junk came for me, I put my hand in his, and we set out up the hill, me in fresh-ironed overalls, an eyelet shirtwaist, and a big white bow on top of my head.

Miz Hanley was waiting on her porch. Her navy blue dress bulged at the seams, and her face was so tight it seemed her cheeks needed letting out. Her hair was short and curled tight, and her gloves had most of the fingers worn through. A handbag was over her arm. She said she'd sent Love Alice on ahead with the covered dishes, on account of us taking so long. Then she gave Junk a look, and he moved smartly, with me running to keep up.

"Your pappy been all right, Miss Livvy?" Miz Hanley said, her breath coming in puffs.

"Yes'm."

"He a fine, fine man." She put a hand on my back. "Don't you ever let no one tell you different."

"No, ma'am."

She looked at me sideways. "You ever set foot in a church?"

I had not. My ma'am, in her earlier days, had worn my pap smooth out with her circuit-riding ways, and he never took to religion after that.

"Well, you jus' keep your wits about you, and be the lady your pappy raised you to be."

I looked at Junk, but he was apparently working on keeping his own wits, and anyway, we had come to the steps of the big white house they called the church. Ladies with pretty faces and gentlemen with their hats in their hands stood about on the porch, saying howdies, and everyone smiled at me and touched me like I was made of glass. We went inside, Junk ducking his big head to clear the door, and we stood to one side while the ladies bustled about setting up chairs and laying out forks. Boards had been laid on wooden sawhorses, and the whole thing was heavy with platters of food.

The Reverend Culpepper, a small man with frizzled white hair and a big voice, raised his hands and bowed his head, and I held my breath while he asked God to deliver this bounty to our bellies as he had delivered Jonah to the belly of the whale. He asked that we find faith with every mouthful of collards and fatback. A-*men.*

The eating commenced. While Pap and I had never gone hungry, this was more food than I'd ever seen. Miz Hanley took up a plate and asked me did I want chitlins and boiled taters, and would I like a chop or a slab of mealed catfish, a chicken leg or ham hock. I nodded yes, and also accepted greens boiled with vinegar, pickled watermelon, and peas with fatback. I ate corn pudding, Love Alice's sweet potato pie, and creamed wild mushrooms. Miss Dovey, who taught school in the front room of her house, brought me a wedge of chocolate cake, which I shoveled in while balancing a bowl of blackberry ice cream in my lap.

Then supper was over, and the ladies began to clear away dishes. The men drifted out to roll cigarettes and sip from paper bags they'd hidden under the bushes. Junk sat with the other men, and after a time Love Alice came out, too. My stomach hurt, and I told her so, but she had a smile on her face as big as Kentucky, and she said this here was family, all right.

"Your real family's in North Dakota, Love Alice?"

"Till they all died," she said.

My belly had set up a rumbling, and I clutched it. "You got *nobody* left?"

"Don't know about my mammy. How old you, O-livvy?"

I burped. "Ten."

"All right, then, I tell you about my pappy, yes ma'am. He work at the general store, bustin' up crates. One day he laying a new porch on the place. A white lady come by, lif' her skirt to step on that porch. He look away quick, but it too late. She let out a scream, say my pappy look up her dress. Say he gonna rape her for sure. Pap say he do no such thing, but the store owner come out, and other men, too. They push him around, thinking what to do."

Another burp. "Oh, Love Alice—"

"When he didn't come home for supper, Mammy say—go on, Alice Lee, and see what's keepin' him. You want to hear this, O-livvy?"

"Yes."

"Well. They behin' the livery, got my pappy's hands tied. They sling a rope ov' a sycamore tree, take three men to lift him."

I could feel my mouth open.

"Then they let go. He jerk and he twist."

"What'd you do?"

"I go back and tell my mammy. She say to fetch her pocket-book. Then she go out the door. I never saw her again."

I wanted to tell her how sorry I was, but I couldn't find words. I touched my sore belly.

"Come on now," she said. "They fixin' to start."

We went inside and found our chairs with the family. I thought about what it would be like to see my pap killed. I'd heard somewhere that when folks were hanged, their eyes came out of their sockets and hung down on threads. I sat not saying a word until, without warning, my innards cramped, and in the next instant, everything I'd eaten came up—all down the front of Junk's mama's dress and her shoes and the mended stockings of several ladies sitting nearby. Junk took me up in his arms and carried me outside where, behind the hedgerow, I groaned and wept in mortification.

Afterward, in the big room where they held the service, I sat leaning against Junk's mama, whose arm stayed around me. Her dress was damp from scrubbing, and she smelled of soap and lavender water, and her bosoms were like great, soft pillows. I wondered if other ma'ams were like this—or was it only the colored ones. I let my eyelids slip down while the Reverend Timothy Culpepper prayed on and on. He said God was among us, yessir and *yessir*. We were all his children—he pronounced it *chirrun*. Let the rejoicing begin. Then the music commenced, filling cracks in the floor till the whole place throbbed like a hurt thumb, and I knew this was what we could hear down the wash. It thrilled me to my bones. There was foot-stomping and hand-clapping, folks smiling and shouting halleluiahs right and left. Even after I grew up, I never knew the word rapture to be anything other than this.

Later, leggy as I was, Junk carried me home while I slept with my face in his neck. It was late, but Pap met me at the back porch, lifting the lamp so Junk could clear the doorway and set me down. I hoped Junk would say nothing about what a shameful showing I'd made. But there was something different about Pap's face, so that I tried to come awake and get my feet under me.

"Olivia, honey," he said. "We got a telegram from the hospital in Buelton. Your ma'am's coming home at the end of summer!"

I shook my head.

"We've got to start getting ready for her."

It was not possible. This woman who called herself Pap's wife belonged in Buelton, where she could not touch us. Well, as long as I lived I would neither love her nor call her my ma'am. Pap had betrayed me.

I twisted away and ran down the back steps to the garden, where I flung myself down. My face to the wet earth, I prayed that Junk's mama would claim me first. I begged God to let me eat chitlins without throwing up—to flatten my nose and kink my hair. I asked it in the name of the potato garden with its turned-up plants and rubbery stalks. I asked in the name of sliced green tomatoes and cucumbers, summer squash and pickled watermelon. In the name of the Reverend Timothy Culpepper, I prayed to be colored. *Yessir*. Amen.

6

Love Alice was Junk's wife, first, last, and always. I wondered what Miz Hanley thought about her son having brought home a child bride.

When she could, Love Alice met me in town. One of our favorite things was to press our noses to the windows of Dooby's drugstore, French's Hardware, and other places along Main Street. We were doing that one cloudy day when she heaved a sigh and sat down on the sidewalk. I sat, too.

"Something wrong?" I spat on the toe of my boot and rubbed it with my finger.

Love Alice was barefoot, the soles of her feet being a lighter brown than the rest of her, almost pink—and her hands were, too. Her heels were thick and yellow with calluses, the way the heels of Pap's hands were from plugging whiskey jugs.

"I plumb wore out, O-livvy," she said.

"Miz Hanley makin' you do all the work?"

"Oh, it ain't that." She giggled. "It's that Junk man. But I shou'n't tell you thangs—what a man do to a woman."

It struck me then that Love Alice was privy to secrets only married people knew. "My pap's told me everything," I said.

"All of it?"

"I've seen dogs," I said importantly.

She leaned so close I could make out each freckle. "Well," she said, "when a man climb on a woman—that got a name."

"What name?"

She lowered her voice even further. "Mountin'."

"Mountain?" I said.

"Yes'm. When a man do his bidness."

I had never got ahold of why this occurred, nor, until now, had I known its name. "How come a man's got to?"

"If he don't," she said, "he'll puff up like a toad—"

"Love Alice Hanley, you're making that up."

"I ain't, either," she said. "You seen them ol' men what sits in front of Mr. French's store? Fat as pigs? Well, you can bet yo' life they ain't mountin'."

"Junk tell you that?"

"I figured it out my own self. You want to hear this?"

I did.

"Well, it build up all day, but a man got to hide it. Won't do fo' him to go around, his trousers pooched out. I as' Junk what a man do if he don't have a woman to come home to."

I was not sure I wanted to know. My pap had no woman—but this chance might never come again. "What did he say?"

Love Alice giggled. "He say a man take hisself out in the woods and do his *own* bidness."

I couldn't imagine. Old man French was unmarried and skinny as a hoe handle. "How?"

"I as' the same thang. Junk show me his hand, curl up his fingers. I say yessir, that'd do it all right."

I wondered why nobody had revealed this to the geezers who slouched on Main Street in their tipped-back chairs. Then they wouldn't have to leave their trousers unbuttoned, or suffer bellies like ripe watermelons.

"Anyway," Love Alice said with a sigh, "Junk think 'bout me, out there inna field, mm-hmm, but he wait. Some nights we barely get through our supper fo' he take me in the back room—leavin' his mama at the table, fit to bawl."

"Why's she upset? She's done it, too—or she wouldn't have Junk."

"Well," Love Alice said. "Maybe it hard to think of her boy all growed up."

I wondered how a man the size of Junk Hanley could do *anything* with this girl who was no bigger than a toothpick. I bit my lip. "What's it like, Love Alice?"

She twisted her mouth, finding the words.

Junk had sat eating bread and jam with me. I wished we weren't talking about him.

She drew back her lips. "The first time I kep' my teeth—so. 'Cause it hurt like anythang. But when Junk seen the blood, he got weepy, say he never gonna do that again."

A dozen pigtails bobbed up and down. "But I say, *Mm-hmm, husband, you comin' at me again.* An' sure enough, the next night—"

"Oh, you poor thing."

"O-livvy, sometime he big around as a syrup jar!" She shrugged. "I get used to it. Amazin' what a man can do, and later on—"

I sat there blinking.

"Later on," she said, grinning, "it like too much pecan pie."

"Really."

Love Alice laughed. "Oh, here come ol' Mr. French." She

jumped up and pressed her back against Dooby's window, her eyes on the sidewalk.

I'd seen Love Alice do this a hundred times. When I'd told Pap how much I hated it, he said to let things be.

"Love Alice, after you lost that baby out at Doc's, how come you never had another one?"

She sighed. "I'z no more'n seven or eight. Takin' a shortcut home. A white man I never seen before, he come outa the field, and he throwed me down on this dirt road. I was so little I fitted in a rut. After, I was all swole up, purple and bleedin'. Mammy said she like to lost me. Doc said sumpin' was tore real bad. Now I ain't ever gon' have babies."

I was angry with the whole world for making Love Alice lie down in a rut. It was then, through the window, that I saw Dooby's sparkling soda counter, the stools that spun.

"Love Alice, come on in and have an ice cream cone with me."

She shook her head.

"Don't you like ice cream?"

She put her hands behind her back.

"I'll treat you. My pap'll pay for it."

"You know Mr. Dooby don't allow it."

"That's a stupid rule."

"Don't matter." She wagged her head and the pigtails flopped around some more.

"Well then, I have somethin' to say to Mr. Dooby."

"Oh no, O-livvy!"

But I'd already marched into the store with both my chin and my backside in the air, and I stood where Dooby was unpacking boxes in the middle aisle.

"Mr. Dooby," I said. "How come you don't let coloreds in here?"

He took cans of snuff from the box and lined them up on a shelf, just so. "They can come in, Olivia. They just got to come around to the back door. Then if there's no white folks shopping—"

"Mr. Dooby, that's not very Christian."

"You and your pap do the same thing. Coloreds shop one day a week. They get what they need. I fixed Miss Dovey's medicine for her backache this morning, and powders to help her sister's gout."

I was embarrassed that it was our rule, too, and I was spoiling for a fight. "Well, I'd like one ice cream cone for Love Alice, and one for me, please, and put them on my pap's bill." I had never done such a thing before, and Pap would tear me apart.

"Can't do that, Olivia," he said. "We don't serve coloreds from the soda fountain. You know that."

"Then I would like two cones for myself, Mr. Dooby. One chocolate and one strawberry."

"Olivia—"

"You won't let me have two cones in case I give one to Love Alice," I said.

"Yes, ma'am, that's right."

I dropped my chin and watched him from under my eyelids. "Then I guess I'll take just one."

"All right, then." He sighed like grown-ups do when a child tries them mightily. "Chocolate, is it?"

I climbed on the stool and watched him open the carton, dip the frozen stuff into a cone. I tried not to think about Pap's bill at the end of the month.

"There you go, Olivia," he said, handing it to me with a paper napkin.

"Thank you, Mr. Dooby." I got down. Then I went out the front door and gave the cone to Love Alice. I looked back through the glass to make sure Dooby was watching.

Love Alice got up and stood looking at the thing, till it began to melt and run down over her hand. I smiled at her, showing my teeth, then turned and walked away. At the end of the block, I looked back. She was standing right where I'd left her. Then she stepped into the road and dropped the cone. With her bare foot she ground it into the iron grate. It sucked the breath right out of me, and it came to me as I stood there, that if there were such a thing as honor, Love Alice possessed more of it than I ever would.

I wanted to run back and put my arms around her, tell her I was sorry. Wanted to rush into Dooby's store and beat him with my fists. But all I could do was hide around the corner, lean my sorry face against the sooty bricks, and wish I'd never been born.

7

Every July Reverend Culpepper took his flock down to Captain's Creek for fried chicken, buttered corn cakes, and renewal of the spirit. The creek itself had happened by accident.

A long time ago, our town was discovered by Frank and Aurora Solomon, who steered their boat down the Capulet River, probably meaning to catch a fish for their supper. They built a dock so they could tie up their boat, and a shack for bad weather, and pretty soon folks came behind them, setting up houses and opening shops. Then one night by the light of the moon, Aurora packed up their things, and they moved on in search of some other place where nobody was.

Over the years the Capulet sprouted arms and legs. Now folks from Aurora picnicked in the elbows of those creeks, their babies playing in the shallows, toddlers catching minnows. Reverend Culpepper used Captain's Creek for baptizing. This was an event I had never witnessed, but by the grapevine I'd heard that more people drowned than came up saved. In the first place I wasn't sure what salvation was, except that the Lord Jesus was involved. Maybe He came out of the clouds and spoke to the Reverend in a voice the rest of us could not hear.

I'd once seen a picture of a courtroom in a book, with the

judge seated high up in front, and the guilty man standing before him in chains, pleading for mercy. I wondered if baptism was like that, and if each man went before the Lord—or the Reverend—and stated his case. And if, in this life, baptism was the only chance he got to do that. I asked Pap if I could go down to the creek and watch. He said to mind my manners and not get in the way.

In an elm grove I crouched behind a tree, not because I wouldn't be welcomed, but because the possibility of them seeing me and tossing me in the river threw me into a panic. I could not swim well, and I didn't want to die. I wondered, too, about the fat folks, if the handlers would have trouble hauling them back up. And if they drowned, did those people float downstream and wash up, sanctified, at somebody else's picnic?

While I considered this, the ladies spread blankets, and set babies to roll, gurgling and half naked. Like a normal Sunday afternoon, they passed drumsticks and melon slices. Old men sat on folding chairs under the trees, spitting seeds and roaring with laughter. They drank lemon water from paper cups, smoked brown cigarettes, and slapped their knees. I watched children play stickball and wished I could join them.

Miz Hanley saw me. "Miss Livvy, child, that you?" she called from her place on a quilt where she was surrounded by grandchildren, bowls of mustard potato salad, and jars of sweet pickle.

I was taught better than to turn and run, so I stepped from behind the tree. "Yes, ma'am, Miz Hanley. It's me, Olivia Harker."

"Well, come on down here, and let us see you."

"Yes, ma'am."

"Junk," she said, "fetch this young'n a plate. You hungry, child?"

"Yes'm," I said, although I couldn't have eaten, my stomach

doing flip-flops and being more scared then any previous moment in my life. But these people loved me—Junk, and Love Alice who was playing chase with the children and making them squeal. They would not let anything happen to me. Still, I wished I knew how to swim.

I sat down next to Junk's mama, and two little babies crawled in my lap. I touched their fuzzy heads and stroked their backs. Their skin was smooth and cool, the color of chocolate melted in a pan. Although I could have gone on touching them all day, Junk shooed them away and laid a paper plate on my knees.

"You just happen by, Miss Livvy?" he said. He was taller than Pap, and bigger around than any six oak trees. His hands were the size of Easter hams that hung in the Buelton butcher shop.

"I—"

"It's all right if you was or wasn't," he said, his voice slow and kind, his face wide with smiling. Junk knew me better than I knew myself.

Nobody said it was time to get started, but a man in the shade began to hum, then another, harmony sliding between trees, rising and falling. Some closed their eyes and held out their hands like it was raining, only it wasn't. Their sound was like warm water washing over me, which reminded me of the river and made me anxious again. I set my plate down.

The Reverend lifted his head and prayed in his loud, rich voice.

Once when Pap and I were delivering an animal to a Methodist preacher in Buelton, we'd driven up to find the doors standing wide and the preacher leading his congregation in prayer. Pap, with the hound across his arms, nodded off his hat and elbowed me to do the same. We stood on the bottom step till the preacher finished a prayer that was so soft it floated out to us like a whisper. No one even said amen. Then we sat on the porch and scratched the hound's ears till the service was over.

The Reverend Culpepper was nothing like that Methodist man. He cried out to God on behalf of those on the riverbank, and he cried out to me. So in love with the rise and fall of his voice was I that I missed the words. I peppered his prayer with my own amens.

Then folks began to crowd into the stream, some with babies in their arms, and a man stepped up to help the Reverend while the rest went on singing, *Shall we gather at the ri-ver*... Sinners folded their arms. The Reverend pinched their noses and laid them back. When they came up, they were radiant, like the sun when it bursts through a cloud, like they'd been handed a fork and a strawberry pie.

I wandered down to the sandy creek. The little ones who'd been in my lap were being submerged, folks crying, *Praise be to God,* and, *Thank you, Jesus,* the babies coming up with surprised looks on their faces. When one burst out howling they passed it around for wet-sounding kisses and let it suck on somebody's thumb.

"Junk," I said, wading in, "how come these little'ns got to be baptized, when they aren't old enough to have done any sinning?"

"It gets 'em ready for life, Miss Livvy."

"How does it do that?"

"I can't rightly say, 'cause it sure don't bring in no dollar bills." He laughed at his own joke, the sound rolling from his belly.

"Have you been baptized, Junk?"

"Many times."

I could see they weren't dunking folks far under, just enough so they could say they were river-wet. I could make out their faces below the surface. Another came up spitting, and the brothers and sisters laughed and patted him on the back and wrapped a towel around him. Offered coffee from a flask.

"How do you know when it's time to get baptized?" I said.

"Oh—when things get too heavy."

"Well," I said, "if you've got a worry as big as the world, is that a good time?"

"I reckon so. 'Scuse me, Miss Livvy, I got to take my turn helping now."

The singing thinned. Folks were moving, gathering up plates.

"Reverend Culpepper," I called, the water to my waist. "I want to be baptized."

"Why, Olivia Harker," he said. "You got your daddy's permission?"

"I do, sir," I lied. Another thing for which I must ask forgiveness while under water.

"All right," he said. "Then we'll ask Jesus to wash away your troubles."

I nodded.

A man I did not know put his hand on my back.

"Fold your arms," said the Reverend. "Take a breath, and hold it in."

But as I felt myself going back, I had more thoughts than moments to put them in. What if they let go, and I drifted to the Capulet and on to the sea? What if I never saw Pap again? They laid me down, and water came in through my nose and mouth, thick with weed and the slickness of bodies. I swallowed and gagged and tried to open my eyes, but they were swimmy and burning. I kicked and flailed and struck the Reverend a blow that knocked his glasses away. If he blessed me, I never heard, but I felt Junk's hands lift me out of the water.

I came up streaming and wiping at my eyes and my hair, my face twisted with the probability of tears, and colder than cold. I was mortally embarrassed at my behavior, at spying on them and being here in their river, and when I had my feet under me, I wrenched free and waded ashore, making for the trees. But roots stuck up through the ground and tripped me, so that I went down on my face and lay there, humiliated. Mercifully, no one came to help me up. I would not cry. I lay there, with my fists clenched, willing them all to go home.

"Miss Olivia?"

"Go 'way, Reverend."

He sat down beside me, grunting, his knee bones cracking. "Miss Olivia, you all right here?"

"Yessir."

"I see you got your ear to the earth."

"Yessir."

"You hear it talkin', do you?"

His saying that surprised me, for I did hear something, I always had—roots shifting and stems uncurling, the popping of seeds like things being born. It was only when the wind blew lightly over my wet self that I remembered where I was. "I hear it," I said.

"Well then, there's your proof."

"Proof of what?" I did not want to look at him. I'd dealt him a mighty blow, and I wondered if he'd found his glasses, or if he'd have to go around squinting for the rest of his life.

"Some folks are born of the water," he said. "Olivia Harker was born of this earth."

"You can't make me feel better, Reverend. I made a pure fool of myself, and everybody knows it." I buried my face in my arm.

There was a tender place on my cheekbone, and my knee was beginning to smart.

"No, ma'am, they don't," he said, his hand on my head. He let loose a fistful of dirt. "In the name of this earth, I baptize thee Olivia Harker, renewed by the lovin' Father, the blood of His Son, and the Holy Ghost."

I waited to see if I would feel any different.

"Your sins have been forgiven, Miss Olivia."

I turned my head. "Reverend?"

"Yes, ma'am?"

"What's the Holy Ghost?"

"Why, Miss Olivia," he said, "when you put yo' ear to the ground, that's what you hear."

The Reverend drove Miss Dovey's wagon, with all the children inside and me among them, hugging the backboard. Behind us, folks walked arm in arm, carrying folding chairs and empty baskets. They looked tired and happy and full of something I hadn't found.

They let me out at the crossing, and I walked the rest of the way. Pap was working in the cellar, the light slanting up the stairs and across the kitchen floor. There was a covered dish on the back of the stove, reminding me of the plate of fried chicken I'd left on Miz Hanley's quilt.

"That you, Olivia?" Pap called up.

"Yessir."

"Light a lamp, and I'll be there directly."

I went into the alcove and pulled the curtain, unbuckling my wet overalls, unknotting my laces. I hadn't even thought to take off my shoes before I'd stepped into the creek, and I hoped they wouldn't dry two sizes smaller. There was a time when I'd have run downstairs to tell Pap what I'd seen and heard, but this day was so private I couldn't even think of it myself. I didn't wait for him to come up, but pulled a clean nightgown over my head, crawled into bed, and turned my face to the wall. When he came to check on me, I pretended I was already asleep.

8

It was my secret hope that when Ma'am came home, she would decide she'd been happier in Buelton, thank you very much, and instruct Pap to hitch up the donkey and take her back. If things didn't turn out that way, I would go live with Junk and Love Alice until Pap came to say that Ma'am had fallen in a bar ditch and drowned.

In August, my birthday came. Pap and I went down to Dooby's and sat at the counter, where we ate chicken sandwiches and vanilla ice cream from fluted dishes. I was still mad at Dooby, and would not look at him. Then Pap and I walked up to the Ridge and stood on the lip of the bluff, listening to Grandpap's wolves call down the night.

Pap was tall, with long arms and legs and a bony face. He was magic, could look a thing in the eye, and it'd settle right down. One time a half-grown bear ate out of his hand.

"Listen, girl," he'd say.

I loved this story.

"My pappy first saw 'em in the Alaska sun, stretched out, cleaning their paws, caring for their young. Then it came upon him that he either had to stay there or bring 'em home with him."

"Why didn't he stay?" I asked on cue.

" 'Cause me and your grand were here, and he loved us more."
Pap looked at me. "The way I love you. So he built cages—and he
covered them with brush. Put in meat and watched 'em all winter
before he caught a male and a female."

"And he was careful to never look them in the eye," I said.

"That's right. Hitched up mules, hung the cages on poles.
Hired a half dozen fellas and lit out for the south. You won't forget that story, will you, girl?"

"Nosir."

"There never were any wolves in Kentucky before these, but
they did all right. That first spring, there was a half dozen pups
with silver snouts. Nothing can happen to 'em—you understand?"

I did not. I knew only the things that had befallen me—chest
colds, the pox, scarletina, and mumps. But in those days there
were a number of things I didn't understand—like how a soul
separated from a body when it died. When old Mr. Sykes passed,
I hung around the doorway of his bedroom, my pap sitting with
his missus at the end. Thought I'd see God reach down, siphon
off Mr. Sykes' soul, like skimming grease from a stew. But all that
happened was his jaw sagged open, and Pap reached over and ran
a hand down his eyes so he'd quit staring at the ceiling.

If I couldn't fathom death, I was even more confounded
over conception and birth. I found the colored girls to be a
pure wonder—on Sunday playing hopscotch with me, and on
Monday they had bellies round as melons and two babes sucking. I suspected, therefore, that they married secretly and early
and took more than one husband. I wondered where they kept
these, and what would happen if these gents met up at the dinner
table one night. I inquired about that, and about other things,
too. I learned that boys who took care of their own business

would most certainly go blind. I also heard that if a full moon co-incided with a girl's monthly bleeding, she might burst into flame. It was spread around school that big bosoms were the mark of a hussy, and if a girl looked into a hand mirror six nights in a row, the young man of her choice would come calling. I knew for a fact that all the popular girls took up their mirrors five nights in a row and then giggled and whooped over whether or not they would carry it through, for fear there'd be a mistake and the ugliest boy around would show up. I heard that if a boy kissed a girl using his tongue, she would find herself in the family way, and I passed that news on, adding my personal but disjointed belief that the same would occur if a boy peed in a bottle and left the jar overnight under a young lady's window. Finally, my teacher, Miss Reingold, sent a note home to Pap, saying I'd been giving out unsuitable instruction.

Pap, she said, ought to ask a neighbor woman to advise me on what a young lady should and should not talk about—and to make sure my information was correct. It was *her* job, Miss Reingold said, to teach me to add a column of fractions and find England and Scotland on the map, to know the correct spelling of Mississippi, the capitals of New York, Virginia, and Vermont. She taught me to sing "America the Beautiful" and that young girls should at all times carry clean handkerchiefs in their pockets.

In the end, I took the note, climbed the hill to Miss Dovey's house where she instructed colored kids in her front room, and sat on her porch step until she let out school. Some of 'em, running out with their books, said, *Hey, O-livia.* Then Miss Dovey took me inside and read the note, and she told me about things like keeping clean rags for times of bleeding, and to say no if a boy wanted to take me behind the barn or raise my skirt or touch me in private places. I remembered what Love Alice had told me about her uncles, and I wondered how old Miss Dovey was when a man first lifted her skirt.

She said, Lord, where was my mama when I needed her? I loved Miss Dovey's voice, and under different circumstances I could have listened to it for hours, but today I wanted to crawl in a hole. I knew about the couplings of hounds and horses, and where baby rats came from. Thanks to Love Alice, I even had a name for it. I vowed that none of this nastiness would ever happen to me. I kept my eyes on my shoes and prayed for the heat to run out of my cheeks. I said, *Yes, ma'am* and *No, ma'am,* and sat hunched on the stool until she fetched me a sugar cookie, patted my head, and sent me home.

9

That same summer before Ma'am came home, a vague itching settled in my chest, which Love Alice said was a sure sign of growth, and with a piece of string I checked its measurement nightly—afraid my bosoms would sprout too early, or too late, or not at all. Love Alice's bosoms were small and round and perfectly shaped, but I could never be that lucky. Although I loved heavy breasts on Junk's mama, and on Mrs. Dooby and her fat widowed sister, I was afraid mine would come on too soon, and by winter I'd own a chest that would topple me over. It was one more thing to fret about.

Meanwhile, working alongside Pap in the cellar was grand. At the bottom of the stairs, two lanterns hung on nails. His doctoring charts were tacked to the wall with big masonry nails. A pair of thick black books lay open on his bench. Day after day, I held rabbits and possums, raccoons scared spitless, while Pap splinted paws that were mangled in traps. It was then that I came to hate hunters—not the ones who took home a hare or a pair of squirrels for the table, but the ones that shot a thing and left it wounded.

Pap tended animals that belonged to the Simpsons, Mr. French, the Daymens, and the Sylvesters. He fixed up Doc Pritchett's cats and pulled Mrs. Nailhow's calf. Up and down the valley he mixed pastes and poultices, ointments and powders. In exchange, he brought home poke salad and green peas for shelling, sweet corn, and once a leg of wild turkey.

Pap and I ate almost no meat, for we couldn't afford to buy it. But we did have chickens, and Pap was a master at wringing their necks. Aside from that—and a sampling of salt pork for working on somebody's mule—we ate vegetables and fruit and yellow corn cakes. Mostly it was cabbage soup with onions, and flat bread for dunking. Potatoes roasted with sage and rosemary. Molasses that we spread on hotcakes like butter. We loved rhubarb boiled with white sugar and wild honey on our oats, and we drank milk fresh from nannies in the yard. When it came to eating, we were two of a kind. But in other things we had our differences.

Pap was the quiet one—I was the talker. Folks often said, "Hush up, Olivia. Don't yap so much." But he listened. Sometimes he'd put down what he was doing and look right at me till I was through. Like maybe he believed I had something to say.

In preparation for Ma'am's arrival, Pap began to whitewash the house—five gallons that he'd gotten for pulling a foal—and although the bare wood showed through in a dozen places, and our roof still sagged from years of snow, I could tell he felt grand.

I, on the other hand, would not help. Pap could not make me. I argued and stomped. For the first time ever, he sent me to my bed to think things over. With the covers pulled to my chin and the sun not yet set, I thought it over, all right. Ma'am's leaving us had been a mercy. And even if she had bosoms like Junk's mama, I didn't want her back.

From my bed in the alcove, where I had drawn the curtain, I heard Pap in the kitchen, pouring water, stoking the stove. I smelled corn bread warming, heard the rattle of dishes. I listened to him eat his supper, his fork stabbing the plate, and I hurt all the more. After a time he pulled back the curtain and stood there with a square of corn bread and a cup of milk.

I sat up. "Miss Dovey says Ma'am's a loony bird."

"That's foolish talk."

"She says that's why you never went to visit her. And if you haven't seen her, how do you know she's getting better?"

He came in and sat down beside me. "Her doctor says so."

"I don't want her here, Pap. I like it being just you and me."

"I remember," he said, "when she was young and pretty. Full of spunk. Olivia, why do you hate her so?"

My shrug was the truth. I did not know.

"Well, I need her to help out," he said. "Keeping this house and the clinic and store and watching after you is one hell of a job."

I felt my face tighten. "I want more corn bread."

"She'll be home in three weeks. I need you to be kind to her when she gets here. And there's no more corn bread."

I licked crumbs from my palm. "Then can I have a dog?"

"What?"

"If I had a dog, I'd feed him every day."

"Olivia, please . . ."

Across the kitchen, the window was now dark. I laid down in my bed, and turned to the wall. It was enough to study my face every day, making sure I looked like Pap and not one bit like her. I could not take her in the flesh.

"If I had a dog, I'd call him Spot." I pulled the quilt under my chin and closed my eyes. I pretended Pap had gone away, too, that I was alone and fixing to starve but nobody cared.

Pap got up and I heard him pull the curtain behind him.

I lay looking through hot tears at the cracks in the wall plaster and listening to Grandpap's wolves call down another night.

10

It was September. School had commenced, and in two more weeks, Ma'am would be home.

On Tuesday afternoon, as had been our custom all summer, Love Alice and her friend Mavis Brown came to call. We made tea from hot water and milk, them remarking that the house looked spanking new with its whitewash outside and double wax on the floor. I lifted the iron burner so we could toast bread over the fire, and we sat at the table with our cups raised and our fingers crooked.

"Miss Harker," Mavis Brown said to me, "I'll have anudder spoon of sugar in my tea, uh-huh. This a nicer eatin' joint than Mr. Ruse's."

Love Alice hiccupped. "How you know that, girl? You ain't ever been to Mr. Ruse's place."

I said, "Everybody who's *anybody* has been to Ruse's."

I had not seen the back door open, nor Pap come in. He must have caught my words because he stood staring at me like I was somebody else's child.

"I'm sorry."

Pap hung his coat on a porch nail.

"How you, Mr. Harker?" Love Alice burbled.

He sat down at the table, poured tea into a saucer, blew on it, and drank. "Fine, Love Alice. You? And Junk?"

"We well," she said, showing her big white teeth.

"I've got deliveries to make, Olivia," Pap said. "I won't be long."

Here was a chance to repair the damage I had done. "Take us with you! Please, Pap."

He shook his head. "Not to the Phelpses'."

"We'll stay in the wagon, and we won't be any bother."

"Olivia, I got to put my foot down over this."

"But—"

"Them Phelps boys are mean as whipped weasels. In fact, to-day I'm cuttin' off their supply. What goes on out there—" Pap got that pinched look on his face like he'd said too much. "I'll be back in a while."

Soon as he'd gone out, I said rudely, "You-all got to go, now."

"Uh-oh, O-livvy," Love Alice said. "You up to sumpin'."

"I'm gonna hide in the wagon. You can come."

"Not me," Mavis said, backing out the door and down the steps. "Us ain't allowed to go out there."

In the end I hunkered alone between two bales of hay, under the old woolly blanket Pap used to cover the jugs. Pap licked the mule lightly.

I had once asked him how he knew the number of jugs to de-liver. He told me to pay attention—a man might ride by our house, take off his hat, and wave it three times. "It's a sign, Olivia. You got to learn to read the signs."

With me bouncing along in the back of the wagon, we headed east to where the hills evened out. I knew a few things about the Phelps boys. They were a lot like their land—gone to seed and thorn since their pap had died. I never knew their ma'am, but I'd seen the old man. For a while, his three sons hung around Ruse's Cafe.

But then Ruse's boy took sides with the Phelpses till Big Ruse throttled him with a flapjack turner and locked him in the outhouse. The Phelps boys had a good laugh over it, but after that, they left Little Ruse alone, and kept pretty much to themselves.

Then one day old Mr. Phelps went and died, and the two bigger boys turned mean, James Arnold being barrel-chested, bragging, and always the leader. Alton was in the middle, smart-mouthed and hateful. Booger was the baby, puffy-eyed, white-faced, and light in the head. He walked hunched over, with arms hanging like a monkey's, and the other two beat the living tar out of anyone who made fun of him. Booger quit school after the third grade because his teachers couldn't do a thing with him. One day the sheriff came to get the three from school, and none of them ever came back. A few weeks later, we heard that their ma'am ran off with a traveling salesman.

Today, I wanted a close-up look at Booger. We angled in at a falling-down gate, and drove up to the big house. Pap whoa'd the mule, and I heard him call, "Hey in the barn!"

I turned back a corner of the blanket, and peeked out at James Arnold Phelps in his overalls and no shirt. He was as big across as he was tall, and his beard was matted with food and twigs. He asked if Pap had brought the drink.

Pap climbed down, and when he flipped back the blanket, uncovered the corked jugs, and saw me there, fire came to his eyes, and I feared for my life.

"Looks like you boys got into it early," he said, but his eyes were still on me.

James Arnold's lip curled like a dog that's been trifled with. "Yessiree, Mr. Harker. These is hard times."

"Well," Pap said, lifting out the jugs. "Drink up, boys. These two are on the house."

James Arnold shook his head. "Two ain't gonna do us, no way. How many jugs you got in 'at wagon?"

Alton came out of the barn. Alton wasn't near as big as his brother, but he swaggered even when he was standing still. "I hear you refusin' to sell us whiskey, Mr. Harker?"

"I am, Alton," said Pap. "You boys drink half the night, and then go scaring the hell outa folks. Last week you ran old Bristow's horse flat to death. Took my shovel up there, and helped bury him—Bristow had that animal a long time."

Alton grinned at his brother.

Pap shook his head. He turned to climb up on the wagon seat.

But James Arnold was fast for his size, and he fisted Pap's jacket and spun him around. Slammed him hard against the wagon so that his hat fell off. James Arnold put his face close to Pap's. "We ain't gettin' no new supplier, Mr. Harker," he said. "You cut us off, and we're gonna tell the sheriff over to Buelton that you're crankin' the meanest hooch in these parts."

Pap said, "Sheriff likes my liquor, too, boys. Tell him what he already knows, and see if he don't bring a federal marshal to your barn on a Saturday night."

I clapped my hands over my mouth and heard Pap draw a breath. "I'll leave you-all now. You got things to take care of—your daddy's ranch, your brother Booger—how's he doin' any-way?"

James Arnold drew back his fist, and he hit Pap hard across the cheekbone. I saw Pap's head snap around sideways, and if James

Arnold hadn't put a hand flat on his chest, Pap would have gone down. A wide red gash had opened on his cheek.

"Booger's dead," James Arnold said between his teeth. "Drank your fine corn liquor, Mr. Harker, then went and shot hisself, that's how he's doin'."

Pap put up a hand to touch his face, and I threw back the blanket and leaped to my feet.

Alton Phelps grinned in that toothy way dogs sometimes do when they're dying. "Well, lookee here, what we got in this wagon."

I clenched my fists. "Filthy pig men!" I shouted. "You-all got pig faces, an' you're wearin' stinkin' pig britches!"

Alton came around and gathered me up by the overall straps, his breath and his bad teeth sour in my face. "Little girl," he said, grinning, "your mama let you talk like that?"

"My ma'am don't live with us yet."

"Olivia," Pap said. "Don't say any more."

"Well," Alton drawled, "seems I heard about her. 'Em crazyhouse whores set a man on fire. When she comes home, girlie, you tell her Alton Phelps be up to pay his respects."

I couldn't collect spit fast enough, but delivered a gob to his eye so that he yelped and jerked back and I near fell over the side while he wiped it away with the heel of his hand.

"Little bitch!" he swore at me. "Who d'you think you are?"

"I'm Olivia Harker, and you're nobody!"

"Wrong, girlie. I'm Alton Phelps. And this here's my brother, James Arnold Phelps. You'll want to remember our names. Devil sure knows I won't forget yours."

Then Pap head-butted James Arnold, knocking the wind clean out of him.

Alton came between them slow, like he was thinking things over and was no longer in a hurry to settle this hash. He brought out a square of scarlet cloth and wiped his face with it. "Well now, Mr. Harker, you goin' to sell us more jugs? To help ease these troubled times?"

Pap shook his head slow. "I am not. But I'm real sorry to hear about Booger. I know you boys loved him. If I can help with the burying—"

James Arnold said, "Already done. Hard goddamn ground, boy's half gone to dust." He lifted Pap by the shirtfront and said, hot in his face, "I know what you're doin' around here, Harker, and I want you to stop." Then he hit him again.

I heard Pap groan, but he got to his feet. Picked up his hat and slapped the dust from it. With great effort, he climbed up on the seat and pulled the hat low. Hawed the mule and eased the wagon around the barn. I stood in the back, staring down Alton Phelps till he disappeared in shadow.

"Sit down, Olivia," Pap said at last.

Then we lumbered onto the road and drove back the way we'd come.

After a while Pap said, "We get home, you'll need to take needle and thread to this cheekbone—"

"Yessir. Pap, what happens in their barn on Saturday night?"

He took out a rag and held it to his face, looked at the blood. "Olivia, you heard things you shouldn't have. I need you to forget we were ever here."

11

The week before Ma'am came home, Love Alice leaned across the table and chirped, "I never said this to you, O-livvy, but I'm goin' to tell it now. Sometime I know thangs."

"What things? Like times tables and stuff?"

"No," she said in a whisper. "Stuff I oughtn't to know—like when a body's goin' to die. Or if some woman's man is slippin' around."

"You're making that up."

"It ain't right, I know," she said. "God gonna punish me. Gonna say, *Love Alice, you can't come into heaven 'cause you peeked in folks' heads an' you know they secrets.*"

I shook my own head till my braids danced. "Love Alice, nobody knows what other people are thinking."

"You ought to believe me."

I held my teacup in both hands. "Then what'm I thinking right this minute?"

Love Alice tilted her head so that her freckles slid downhill. She looked like a robin listening for worms. "You thinking 'bout your mammy. You goin' to have heartache, an' I'm sorry for that. God's own grace, O-livvy, it'll be a long time befo' you happy."

"You're just saying those things 'cause I told you about Ma'am coming home."

She shook her head. "You scared a her, and she ain't even here yet."

She was right; I was afraid. Not only of Ma'am, but scared that maybe Love Alice really could see the future. I was glad to hear Pap's footsteps on the porch.

"And, O-livvy," Love Alice said in a whisper, "someday you goin' to have a little girl of yo' own."

"Not me, I'm never going to marry. I'm gonna stay right here and work with Pap till I'm an old, old lady."

Love Alice smiled sadly. "Yo' little girl, she have hair like the sun. An' you goin' to call her Pauline, uh-huh."

12

On a hot Monday afternoon, Ma'am came home. She rode in a fancy buggy that Pap had hired. He had baked her a lopsided brown sugar cake from eggs I gathered in our henhouse, and he talked of building an indoor privy. There were fresh-laundered sheets on the big four-poster. And he planned to give her the new mule Sanderson for her own. He would buy her a saddle if she wanted one. That day, we closed the store early and put a sign in the window, but nobody needed telling.

Pap met Ma'am on the road, and lifted down her carpetbag. She took his arm, and he led her up the long walk and the steps, into the grocery where she stood looking at the shelves of canned goods and pickles. Golden curls were piled on top of her head, and her body was slender and curved like a willow branch. Then she spotted me peeking from behind the curtain. Pap went to the kitchen to make coffee.

She came right to me—I was almost as tall as she was—and said, "Filthy, that's what this place is. Well, I'll never work a single day here. And you—you stay clear of me. Don't do anything to get on my nerves. No laughing, no crying, no raising your voice."

In the kitchen, I could hear Pap setting out cups and cutting cake. Ma'am ran a finger around the edge of the potato bin, like what dirt she found there was my fault. Then she studied my face. "You're so plain," she said.

I knew then that whatever illness had befallen her, it had not been bad enough.

Pap called us to coffee, but she declined and took to her bed for a "stretching out."

I tried to tell him, said, "She's too fancy, and anyway, she doesn't like us."

But he laughed in a tinny way, and told me to go ahead and start supper. We'd leave her alone, and she'd settle in. He went down to the cellar where he made not one sound, and I wrapped the cake in a cloth and put it in the larder. Then I washed a cabbage with salt to kill the bugs, and took great comfort in whacking it hard with the butcher knife. I threw the core to the goats and went off to the outhouse, banging the screen door three or four times. The more noise I made, the better I felt. But my belly was tied in a knot.

I cut up a potato and a scrap of yellow pepper, added a handful of green peas, and stirred up beaten biscuits that I set to rise. Went out to sit on the back porch steps and shaded my eyes, looked out across our place, past the dried-up creek to the first slope of Big Foley. I wondered what Ma'am would say when she heard the wolves howl—or if they knew she was here, and were right now up there, tiptoeing around.

Before long, I announced loudly that supper was ready. Pap came up first, looking anxious around the mouth, and he straightened the forks and set out salt and pepper shakers. The bread turned out decent. Ma'am didn't come, and Pap and I stood looking at each other until I marched to the bedroom door and knocked lightly. There was no answer, so I turned the knob and looked in. The curtains were drawn so there was not one bit of light to see by, but I heard Ma'am say in an aggravated voice, "What is it?"

"I've got supper on the table."

She sighed and sat up. Put a hand to her back like the bed had given her an almighty crick.

Pap was at the table when she came in, but he jumped up like he was on fire, and pulled out her chair. He tucked her into her seat, brought the dish towel, and laid it in her lap. When I set his soup on the table, he gave it to her, cut open a biscuit, handed her a knife, butter knife he called it. I brought two more bowls.

Ma'am took one look at the cabbage soup with fresh peppers and peas, and she curled her nose. "This is a sorry enough welcome supper."

"Ida Mae—" said Pap.

"I should have known she wouldn't be handy in the kitchen. Swear to God, children do nothin' but set the nerves on fire."

I waited for Pap to tell her cabbage soup was his favorite, and the bread the best yet. But although he moved his mouth, no words came out.

"Well," she said, "you can't expect me to take over the kitchen. I've forgotten everything I knew about cooking, and I don't care to learn again."

"Olivia will do better," Pap said, looking at his bowl.

I stumbled from my chair, turning it over and upsetting my milk glass. I didn't know which of them I hated more. "I didn't make it for you, you crabby old loon!" I shouted. "I made it for Pap on account of he likes it! I wouldn't cook for you if you were starvin' on the steps of hell. I don't know why you came back here anyway. I hate you—and I hate that damned ol' donkey, too!"

It was far more than I'd meant to say, but I guess some dams needed to be broken.

She flew out of her chair and jerked me by the arm. She was amazingly strong, bending my head over the sink, shoving a bar of lye soap in my mouth. I came up, gagging and wheezing, pleading for Pap to make this stop. But he just sat there, looking at his supper and saying nothing. In his need to keep the peace in his household, he slid sadly from my grace.

I spent the night in my alcove, with the curtain drawn, listening to her sobbing and Pap promising her the moon. He would tear down the still, stop his doctoring, and pay more attention to the store so that she would not have to. He'd take on more of the cooking—she needn't turn a hand.

She sobbed on, whining and whimpering about being stuck out here in the boondocks.

Pap told her he would get a loan from the bank and buy a car so that she might take frequent trips into Buelton. He would see to it that she lived a life of comfort. He spoke to her as if she was that pretty young thing that he remembered, and I realized then what had happened—my birth was the cause of her nervous condition. I wondered, in those whispered moments, if he apologized for my plainness.

Later, I heard him lead her off to bed. A few minutes later, he rustled around in the kitchen, groaning and shifting things so that I knew he'd bedded down on the floor. It was then that I decided to call her Ida, and although I prayed nightly for God to take her away, he never did.

Sometimes, in the weeks that followed, I envisioned Pap and me moving our things to the cellar, where Ida could not touch us. We would cook our dinner over a candle flame and bathe in the tub he used for surgeries. We'd tend to our patients and never have to see Ida again. If we were lucky, sooner or later, someone would come down and tell us she was dead.

For the most part, I ignored her. On Saturdays and Sundays I made paper patterns for fancy aprons and sun bonnets, cut fabric I'd taken from the store, and stitched them up. Early mornings on my way to school, I'd carry them to Dooby's where he let me line my things up in his window. My business was booming, but Pap's was something else. As time went by, fewer wounded things came to our house. Folks seldom called him to deliver their breech calves or bind up a wound, and we missed the greens and fried apple pies. Daytimes, he minded the cash register, but even that wasn't the same. Folks hurried through their shopping and cast anxious eyes on the kitchen curtain.

That fall, Pap brought back a man who installed electric lights in the grocery, one in the bedroom, and a dangling cord for a bulb over our kitchen table. He ran a roll of black wire from our house to one of the electric poles that had been put up along our road. Pap gave him four boxes of groceries, and signed an IOU for the rest.

After school, I minded the store and did my stitching there or under the kitchen light while Pap went up the mountain to cut cordwood that he delivered in the wagon. It brought us a dime or two. He came home after dark, ate whatever I'd left on back of the stove, and slept in his blanket on the kitchen floor.

From my cloth I cut spike-roofed houses and round red apples, and stitched them onto bleached muslin. I sewed gingerbread boys on dish towels and embroidered their eyes and mouths. Twice a month, on Sundays, I went around Aurora collecting scraps. Angus Sampson's wife, rolling up toweling for my bag, said I was the prettiest sheeny man she'd ever seen.

Food was getting scarce, and there was an electric light bill to pay. With so little business, we could not order more canned goods or tooth powder, and we stopped taking from the dairy-man and lived on goat's milk. At the end of the week, there were few coins left over to drop in the kitchen drawer. In the dark of night, men sometimes came to our back step, asking for a bottle of Tate Harker's swill, but Pap wagged his head and warned them off. But he could not resist going out on a call when a horse bruised a hoof or a calf insisted on coming into the world by its hindquarters. These trips to the country brought us summer squash, melons, and ripe tomatoes, which, he said, would help restore Ida.

I carried my lunch to school in a tin—bread with no butter and a salted boiled potato. In summer a peach or an apricot. Nobody else was any better off.

Before long, Pap and I ate corn cakes and brown beans five nights a week. Ida stayed mostly in her bed, picking at yellow waxed beans and hard-boiled eggs that Pap ordered me to send in on a tray. She curled her nose at everything and drank mostly weak tea with a bit of sugar. Fruit, she said, blistered her tongue and overworked her kidneys. Meat made her blood dark, milk tied up her bowels. She complained that her legs cramped, and her head pounded. She was in danger of collapsing. When Pap questioned her, she called him an ass, and screamed for me ten times a day, just to tell me I'd gotten on her nerves. We were, she told us, the reason for her demise.

Doc Pritchett, examining her, said there was nothing wrong, and no death was imminent. She should, in fact, get out of bed and find something to occupy her time. Ida called him a quack of the first order.

13

Finally Ida asked Pap to find her a Bible, for which he paid ninety-five cents at a store in Buelton, and she began to read aloud. But the scripture was heavy, running over me like a logging wagon. The beatitudes affirmed I was going to hell. One day I said so. Ida put on her coat and, taking a bread knife, ventured out on the narrow length of our land—as far as the first incline, where she cut a switch from a green willow tree. Thereafter, she used it to whip me regularly in the name of the Lord.

I fervently wished she'd climb on Sanderson and ride off preaching to somebody else. Meanwhile—if she lashed me for my cooking one more time, I was going to put her eyes out with a fork.

Christmas morning, Pap killed one of our last three chickens, and I stuffed it with bread and baked it, gizzards and all. I made custard with eggs and a little sugar, and threw the shells to the chickens, which made me think about how all things come around. That, after all, must be why Ida'd come home.

Pap stayed in that day. Mid-morning, while Ida was in the outhouse, he slipped me a sweet red apple and two spools of thread—one silver, one gold. I had never seen anything so beautiful. In the afternoon, while we sat at the table and burned wood in the stove, the precious thread rode in the pocket of my apron. Pap and I recalled funny Christmases and other holidays from years gone by while Ida held her Bible and looked off out the window. I fetched the pair of lace hankies I'd been stitching, sat working them by the light of the bulb, and for a while things felt almost good. It was the closest the three of us had ever been.

And then, in January, it was Ida's birthday, and Pap was treating us to supper at Ruse's. I suspected he didn't trust me to cook that night, and he was right not to. A pinch of nightshade, sprinkled on her potato, would've put Ida away forever.

She and I were to meet Pap at the cafe at six o'clock, him coming from the settlement of Lansing.

Several large families lived there, growing their own food, raising and butchering hogs so that they seldom needed to come to town. When they did, however, and we'd pass one of them on the street, Ida'd call loudly, "Would you *look* at the weight of that woman. Good Lord!"

Tonight Pap was out amongst them, delivering a stubborn litter of kittens. He told me later how Mrs. Nailhow had wrung her hands and wept, three or four of the children bawling with her.

But at five-thirty in our kitchen, Ida was ready. She wore her best cream-colored linen, with a bow at the collar and pearl buttons at the wrist. Her hair was rolled back on both sides and hung in a wheat-colored froth down her back. She had not gained a single pound in the time she'd been home, and was as fine-boned as a bird.

She shoved me into the closet Pap was converting to a toilet stall, and put me in front of the mirror. I was as tall as she was, my hair was thick and coarse, a red-brown color. Ida said it looked like I'd been dipped in red ink and left to dry in a nor'easter. She rolled it in her hands now, and stuck a comb in the back. Then two more to hold it, and turning me around, she pinched my cheeks. Then she looked down.

"Olivia Harker, you get out of those trousers, now!" she said. "Young ladies do not wear men's britches under their skirts."

Ida jerked up my dress and unfastened my britches as quick as that. I held on to them and pulled free of her hold, but in another instant we were on the floor, she tugging on my trouser legs, grunting and swearing. I ripped the bow from her dress, and we tumbled around the bedroom—me whacking my head on the footboard of the bed, and Ida yelling, "Dammit, Olivia, you are a heathen child—act like a lady for—*my goddamn birthday!*" To be so little, she had a mighty wrath, and she rolled on top of me, pinning my legs. At which moment I slapped her good.

But she had me by the hair, and banged my head on the floor. I heaved her off, and we lay glaring and red-faced, breathing heat into each other's mouths. My trousers may have been tangled around my knees, but her hair had come loose, and two buttons were ripped from her dress. Somehow, all that struck me as funny. I'd given as much as I'd got.

"I will wear my hair down," I said.

"The trousers come off."

"I'll freeze to death."

"You will not freeze. I'll give you stockings to wear."

"I hate stockings," I said.

But I got them anyway, skinny-legged brown things with ribs that bristled and pinched at the crotch. She changed into a brown plaid dress that hung a size too big on her, but it didn't matter. Ida looked like a picture in any damn thing. She fluffed out her hair and tied it with a brown grosgrain ribbon. Now she was the child, and I the old woman.

In silence, we pulled on our boots, coats, scarves, and mittens, and we trekked down the road toward Ruse's in the early dark. We were late; Pap would be waiting for us.

"You will not mention this to your father," she huffed, her breath forming clouds.

"Why?" I said. "Are you afraid he'll think you've gone crazy again? That he'll send you back to Buelton?"

We turned to cross the stone bridge, and she snorted. "If I were you, young lady, I'd watch my step. There are places for disobedient children, homes for unruly girls. They sleep on bare mattresses and get bread and water to eat. They work their fingers to the bone and are beaten every day of their lives."

It was an icy night, and the road slickly polished. I kept to the side, where the snow had been thrown by traffic and my boots found purchase. "I never heard of such a thing."

She looked at me. There was still a slight imprint where my hand had laid into her cheek. "Your father and I have talked about this. Believe me when I tell you—you are on the edge."

14

We crossed over to Main Street where the lights were on in Ruse's window. There was no one out—not a single horse, nor a wagon. When we pushed open the door and went in, we were the only customers. Ida pulled off her cap and put on a sunny expression. "Mr. Ruse, are we too late for supper?"

Ruse, the elder, looked up from behind the counter where he was reading a newspaper. "You're sure not, Miz Harker. Olivia. You two go on and take a seat, and I'll bring you a menu."

"Thank you, sir," Ida said as though she were a fine lady and he had offered to carry her across a river. I wanted to gag.

The cafe was L-shaped, the remaining space being taken up by the barbershop next door. Mrs. Ruse stayed pretty much in the kitchen while her husband presided over a counter with seven stools, and five wooden tables with chairs. Each table held salt and pepper, a sugar bowl, and a small covered dish of Mrs. Ruse's homemade chili sauce. There was a high glass counter by the door, and a cash register where Ruse rang up bills owed and sold Chiclets and peppermint patties wrapped in waxed paper.

Ida chose a table by the window, as if she wanted to be seen by any passers-by. She sat smoothing the front of her dress, in case Big Ruse hadn't noticed the shape of her.

He brought two glasses of water and menus. She laid a hand on his arm. "Can you tell me, please, what time it is."

"Six-thirty," he said, blushing slightly. I guess he wasn't used to being touched by any woman other than his missus.

I shook my head and studied the menu.

"How are you, Olivia?" he said.

"I'm guess I'm fine, Mr. Ruse. I'd like—"

But Ida shushed me with a flutter of her hand. She looked up at Big Ruse and smiled. Her teeth were so white I could have read by them.

Ruse smiled back, curving the bottom half of his face. He looked plain silly.

"I'll have a cup of coffee while I'm makin' up my mind," she said. "And milk for the girl."

She had taken to calling me "the girl" lately, like she had forgotten my real name. I knew what I wanted to eat, but as often happened when Ida was around, no sound came out of my mouth.

When Ruse came back with our drinks, Ida laughed and patted his leg with her menu. "It's my birthday, and my husband was bringing me here as a treat—but it seems he's been detained. I think, dear Mr. Ruse, that we'll go ahead and order."

"No problem, Miz Harker," Big Ruse said. "If Tate don't make it, he can settle up later. And I'll include a slice of pie for each of you as my birthday gift."

"Why, aren't you the sweetest thing," she said, smiling.

If Ida kept this up, her face would crack, or I was going to throw up on the table, one.

"Well, what do you recommend?"

"Turkey pie's done to a turn, Miz Harker. Fix you up with two a them."

"I want beefsteak," I said, because that's what Pap would have ordered. "Cooked lightly, please. Red inside."

Ida waved her menu. "The girl doesn't know what's good for her. We'll have two helpings of turkey pie."

I watched through the window, praying Pap would come. But he did not, so I looked around, although I knew the place like the back of my hand. On hot summer days, Big Ruse often had set a glass of cold water in front of me on the counter. He was also famous for his biscuits and honey, which Pap had sometimes treated me to on Saturday mornings. I knew his son, a few years older than me and homely as dish soap. His first name was actually Cornelius—no wonder he never used it. We called him Little Ruse.

Just now, Little Ruse was scuttling around, wiping off tables, filling salt shakers, and unable to take his eyes off Ida.

Wedges of turkey pie came, with thick gravy and a biscuit on the side and pats of butter. And so did Mr. French, and Mr. Andrews who had just closed his barbershop. They sat together, ate slabs of chocolate cake and drank coffee, looking in our direction and talking in low voices. I hunched over my plate. Ida sent them smiles that were both brilliant and quivery. I spread butter on my biscuit and stuffed half in my mouth.

Little Ruse wiped the table next to ours. "Hey, Olivia," he said. I could hear his mama in the kitchen, banging pans and spoons. "Hey," I said around the bread.

He grinned at me, and Ida saw it. She put down her fork. "Olivia Harker," she said, "I won't have this boy makin' eyes at you. If you are doin' anything a-moral with him . . ."

I was mortally embarrassed. Little Ruse, with his flapping-big ears and his quarter-of-an-inch haircut, darted away to the kitchen. I did not see him again that night.

"Oh, Mr. *Ru*-use," Ida called, and he came with the coffee pot and refilled her cup.

I wished with all my heart that Pap would show up. Then I could have a bite or two of his steak, and he would tell me about the Nailhows' cat, and the news from the settlement. I hoped there was somebody out there to give him a ride. Otherwise, Pap might not be home for a long time.

Ida had her hand on Big Ruse's leg. "Goodness, I admire a man who runs his own business. It takes such courage." To my astonishment—and probably Ruse's—she hooked his leg with her hand and pulled him close so that she was talking directly into his belt buckle.

Ruse kept looking off to the kitchen. I wondered what he thought about Pap's wife playing up to him. But Ruse obviously was not thinking at all. His own flopping ears had turned red as Christmas bulbs, and his eyes were coming out of his head. I couldn't wait to tell Love Alice that I'd seen Big Ruse nearly breathing smoke with his need to stick his business into Ida. If Love Alice was right, he'd blow up into a toad any minute. I wanted to crawl under the table.

Ida looked up at him. "Here I am talking on and on. If you're ready to bring our pie, Mr. Ruse, I'd love it if you'd join us."

I never heard his reply. I jerked my coat from the rack and ran out of the cafe as if wildcats were after me. I had witnessed Ida whoring with Big Ruse, and I would never come back.

I was no more than two steps into the road when a shiny new truck came roaring along under the streetlamps. Through the windscreen I could see Alton Phelps' face, and I guessed that was his brother, James Arnold, with him. They fishtailed on the ice, and by the time they opened their doors and fell out, I was miserable over not having run for my life.

Too late, I dodged.

But Alton was already reaching for my arm, and he slammed me up against the truck. "All right, girlie," he said, sounding like his tongue was too big for his mouth. "You go on and leave us alone with Ida Mae now. We'll fetch up with you when it's time."

I wrenched free, cut between buildings, and set off across the field. Before long, the stumpy ice slowed me down, but at least I could no longer see, or be seen from, Main Street, the dark hotel, or the bakery with its kitchen light on. It was bitterly cold. After a while, my boots filled with snow, and the wind whipped so fierce that it froze my ears. They hurt clear to the middle of my head, and I clapped my hands over them, but my fingers already ached like rows of bad teeth. I was not going back to Ruse's for my scarf and mittens. Instead I would find Pap, and when I did I'd tell him what happened.

But I could not remember which was the turnoff to Lansing. After a while, I began to cry with the cold. The cold wind howled. I longed for the trousers I'd given up in the fight. Worse, I could no longer feel my feet, and before long fell into a deep snowbank. Whimpering for Pap, I spotted faint light far away, and I cut through a field, struggling over the frozen stalks of last summer's corn, and sinking into blown drifts.

Finally I just lay there and closed my eyes. If I was going to die here, I hoped Pap would find me and be sorry he'd ever brought Ida home. But there were three sets of lights, and one of them not too far off. I hobbled along, hearing dogs bark and fearful of being eaten alive. It was likely dogs would drag my bones off for burying, and then nobody would know how I'd suffered at all. Maybe they'd have an all-out search with great weeping when they found me. If that happened, I hoped it was not Big Ruse who found my frozen body. On the other hand, if he did, maybe he'd remember what a fool he acted on the night of Ida's birthday, and be mortally sorry.

On my knees, I slid down an embankment and across a creek where the ice was jagged but did not break under me. Then I made my way across a yard and knocked on the first door I came to. Mrs. Nailhow opened it.

I fell into her arms. Then Pap was there, the cat's blood on his shirt, and he carried me to her sofa and laid me down. Mrs. Nailhow took off my boots and stripped away my torn stockings. My legs were clotted with blood, and burned like fire. My hair stuck out in frozen spikes and Pap cautioned her not to touch it, for fear of it breaking off. She set to rubbing my feet, and several of the Nailhow children rubbed, too, until I cried out with the pain, and I stumbled to the kitchen to where Pap sat on the floor beside the poor mewling cat.

Poor thing, she was worse off than I. Pap had muzzled her and bound her paws so that she could not claw him. With one hand he kneaded her swollen belly, and with two fingers of the other he probed inside her.

"How one cat can have so many ass-backward kits—" he said, looking at me, but not seeing. He was thinking about Mrs. Higgins' innards. He'd rescued three kittens already. If I'd been the fourth he'd have seen me better, and bandaged my hurts. He laid the kittens beside their mother.

Suddenly I was embarrassed by my bare and wounded legs, and I pulled my knees up under my skirt so Pap could not see the mess I was.

"I count two more," he said. "Gotta take 'em slow, or she'll bleed to death."

I suspected Pap hadn't remembered Ida's birthday dinner at all, and I was not going to mention it. He'd hear about that soon enough. I wondered if, by now, Mrs. Ruse had come out of her kitchen and beaten Ida to death with a frying pan. Sitting there in the warmth of the Nailhows' kitchen, it occurred to me, further, to ask Pap about this home for wayward girls. But I held my tongue. And I watched the cat. One thing was sure—if having babies amounted to this, I'd never let a man have his way with me. He could keep his trousers buttoned. And it was all the same to me if he swelled up and exploded all over Pope County.

15

One night toward the end of winter, Pap came home, banging his boots on the porch and shouting for Ida.

"Lord love a duck, Tate Harker, what's the matter with you?" She came out of the bedroom with a wool shawl around her and her hair mussed from sleeping.

"Put your coats on," he said, looking from one of us to the other. "Come on out and see this."

"I can't see nothin' in the dark," she said.

But Pap shooed us down the steps and around the house, and there, pulled up against a snowbank, was a pickup truck. Its front end was beat in so bad, it looked like the Phelps boys had used it to pound out their meanness. Only one headlight worked, laying its beam crookedly across our yard. The passenger door was roped shut.

"Sweet Sonny Jesus," said Ida. Then her hands flew to her face. "Look what you've gone and made me do—taking the Lord's name in vain. This thing is an abomination."

"No, it isn't," Pap said, running his hand down the fender. "It's just been rode hard."

"Well, I will not ride in it—do not ask me."

"I'll ride," I said, and I got in on the driver's side.

He ruffled my hair.

"It's the devil's machine!" Ida shouted after us. "And the ugliest one I ever saw!"

Pap loved the truck, and was prouder than anything when he drove to town, or out to a farm to pay a call. He was still selling firewood and again peddling moonshine on the sly. After that I grinned ear to ear when we rolled into a yard, the window wound down and my elbow stuck out like I was the Queen of Sheba.

For a long time, Ida would not ride, but after a while she put on her coat and instructed Pap to back the truck out onto the road. Then she climbed in and sat up straight as a rake. The county had cleared the highway of snow, so with me in the middle, Pap drove us up north to Paramus and back. He was smiling so wide I thought his face would split. By then he'd lost two teeth on the right side, but it did not spoil his handsomeness, and after that we drove into town on Saturdays and parked in front of the cafe while Ida shopped. I sat in the truck and looked at the empty buildings up and down the street. Then Ida would come out, and Pap, who'd been watching, would trot up from the hardware on the corner, and we'd arrange ourselves on the seat and go home. We did this week after week while the icicles melted from our eaves and the grass came up thick and green in the yard.

By early summer I was begging Pap to let me get behind the wheel of the truck. In the matter of driving, Ida was the opposite, and it created a constant argument between them. Then one morning, she tired of the fight, buttoned on her sweater, and took the truck out by herself. She came home in a fume.

"Tate Harker!" she called from the top of the cellar stairs. "I nearly kilt myself, and it's all the doing of that infernal vehicle!"

Pap came upstairs wiping his hands on a rag. "God sake, Ida, I got a pair of sick piglets sleeping. What have you done?"

"Your truck near did me in, is what!"

Pap looked out the kitchen window. "Where've you parked it?"

"I didn't park it nowhere," she snapped. "It parked its own self in the ditch over to French's place."

"God sake," Pap said again. He took his coat down and shrugged into it. "You get Henry French to bring you home?"

"I did not. I don't want folks knowing Tate Harker turns his wife out in a killin' machine!"

Pap swore loudly, words I'd never known to come out of his mouth. It was a four-mile walk to French's. He never let her drive again.

On one cold night, he and I went off to help deliver a litter of puppies at the old Sampson place. I'd heard that Mrs. Sampson was deaf and that she and her mister never spoke but made signs with their hands, which I was anxious to see. We drove with the windows down and the chill wind blowing the dust from our brains, as Pap said. He smelled wonderful, like horse liniment and starched cotton.

The Sampsons' was a shotgun house with a high, sloped roof. The front room led to the bedroom, and past that was a tiny kitchen with a covered slop bucket, a table, two chairs, and a round-bellied stove. Squatting on the floor, we brought eleven puppies into the world. Seven of them never even took a breath. Mrs. Sampson brought me a rag to wipe my hands, and while Pap cleaned up the bitch and set the newborns to suckle, I wandered out in the dark yard to watch Mr. Sampson dig a hole. He threw in the dead pups and covered them with dirt. Stomped the earth with his boot, then looked me square in the eye and said, "Too much is always a bad thing."

It was more than I'd heard him speak in the years I'd known

him, so I figured his words were mine to keep. I followed him inside and wondered if God looked like Angus Sampson with his white hair and beard. Pap collected his hat.

"Tate," Angus murmured at the door, "you want one of these y'ere pups for the girl, you're welcome to it."

I nearly fell over with joy. I looked to Pap with my heart in my throat.

Breathless with the promise of a dog, I chattered on about nothing and everything. A dog of my own. I bounced on the truck seat, thinking up names, and asking how long I would have to wait.

"Till it's time, Olivia," Pap said.

"How long will that be?"

"A while yet, when it's weaned from its mother."

We were almost home when he laid a hand on my shoulder to settle me down. Neither of us saw James Arnold Phelps until we were on him. In the light of our headlamp, his eyes opened wide and his undershirt lit up. James Arnold put up both hands, and then he was gone. Tires plowed through the snow. We skidded toward the ditch, then rolled end over end, so that I slammed into the dashboard and the roof, then again, tangling with Pap. After what seemed a long time, I crashed through the windshield, and slid face-first out on the icy road. For months, the only sound I could conjure up was the shriek of Pap's brakes—and Angus Sampson's warning that too much was a bad thing.

16

I woke in a black tomb of a thing, with my head sticking out. I wondered, vaguely, what my body had done to be so incarcerated. Mostly I slept, occasionally sliding into consciousness. Wrapped in this contraption, I knew only the steady hum-suck of experimental machinery and the whisper of shoes on linoleum. Sometimes a voice. I recall opening my eyes, once, to a flurry of people shining lights in my eyes, beating fists on my chest.

All I wanted was for Pap to come and tell me this was just a dream, and that he was now taking me home. But my only attendants were people in white coats. At the time, it worried me that I couldn't call up Pap's voice. Still, in that moment before sleep, I caught a glimpse of his face. But then came the headlight and James Arnold Phelps' eyes. I wanted to ask what had happened to Pap, but I was afraid. So I struggled against sleep until I could no longer hold on, then staggered through the shattering of glass and bone and metal once again, and finally drifted off.

I hurt in uncertain ways, but when it gathered in my legs or my chest, or I screamed in a sudden rush of pain, ladies in white dresses came running. They clucked their tongues, and laid their hands on the machine that tried to do my breathing for me. In my worst moments, they worked something into the corner of my mouth with a dropper, and I slept.

Other times I lay looking at the ceiling. I was wired and taped, with tubes running in and out, and glass bottles suspended over my head. My throat was as dry as meal. Next to my bed was a straight-backed chair, and I often woke to find a nurse sitting there.

Eventually I was moved to a bed where I lay between cold cotton sheets. My left hand and arm were bound to a board, but my right hand was free. As the days went by, I discovered that my head was bandaged, with slits cut for my eyes and more holes for the tubes in my nose and mouth. Thick gauze was wound about my jaw and mouth.

In time, my fingers found the heavy metal halo that circled my head and seemed to be bolted through the bandages to my jaw. It was then I knew I'd been hurt bad. I could not open my mouth nor turn on my side. I was being fed through a rubber hose taped to the roof of my mouth. Later they brought me milk shakes with a straw, but I did not drink.

Because I'd been so long in the iron box, my right leg had healed wrong, and, under anesthetic, had to be broken again before it could be set right. Now it was bent at the knee and trussed up on a rope like a butcher-shop turkey.

Now and then, Ida came. She'd stand there in her coat, her handbag clutched to her chest. She said little or nothing, and neither did I as I drifted off, and when I opened my eyes, she was gone.

Eventually, my leg was lowered and the cast cut away. It took two doctors, an orderly, and a flock of nurses to dismantle my head contraption, and at last I was free to turn stiffly at the neck while they stood there clapping. I had a headache most of the time, but I seldom complained. There was, in fact, nothing I wanted to say, and no one I wanted to say it to. Then they cranked up the head of my bed, and I saw, through the slits in my gauze, that I was in a long narrow hall with twenty or thirty beds on each side. This was the Indigent Ward, someone told me, for people who could not afford to pay. I was too tired to stay awake and too slept-out to sleep. I was cold all the time.

Two weeks later, they eased me into a straight-backed chair for a few minutes each day, then for a long half hour. I imagined I looked bad in my wrappings, but without them I was sure I would look worse.

Then one day, a young man brought a wheeled cane chair. He lifted me into it, trundled me down the row, and set me in front of the window. When the nausea passed, I was surprised to see that winter had ended and forsythia bushes were a yellow blur. By now I knew that Pap was not coming.

Doctors came. They spoke of jawbones, readjustments, and corrective operations. They took me to a small room with a soft light, and unwound the bandaging—first from my forehead and then around my eyes. I put up a hand and felt not the long, jagged gashes I'd expected but a raised line over one eyebrow and another at what would have been my hairline. While they stood there admiring their work and talking, I scratched my scalp where they'd shaved off my hair. They told me it would grow back.

One day I heard Ida in the hall, shouting that we had no money for more operations, and the nurses murmuring soothingly. Afterward, Ida came and sat on the edge of my bed, which I took to be as loving a thing as she'd ever done. Around the tube and from between my teeth, I said awkwardly, "How long ha' I been here?"

"Months," she said. "For God's sake, Olivia, you're skin and bone, and they won't let you out of here until you eat."

"I'm not hungry."

"Well, they won't leave those tubes in there forever, missy. And then we'll see who starves."

I drew a long breath, and without looking at her, said, "Pap."

She opened her pocketbook, dug around for something, and closed it with a snap. "Your pap is dead, Olivia, and don't go making a scene or it'll take that much longer to get you out of here." Then she got up and walked out the door.

A month later they removed my tubes. With a pair of canes, I was now expected to walk to the lavatory and sponge myself down each morning. They said I was lucky to be alive, that I'd cracked several ribs and compressed my breastbone, which had made it impossible for me to breathe on my own. My right leg had been fractured in three places, and I lost three back teeth and shattered my jaw.

I went twice more to the operating room where the old bolts were removed, and I was fitted with new ones below and behind my ears. A new set of wires circled my face. It was summer when the doctors removed the rest of the wrappings—and left them off. My hair was about two inches long; my cheeks felt as if they had been pulled tight and pinned at the ears. My jaw hurt, like a perpetual toothache. Three back teeth were now porcelain, attached to a narrow bridge that fit the roof of my mouth. With my fingers I located more scars, a thick one along the left side of my jaw, and another at the corner of my mouth, turning my bottom lip slightly downward.

Ida came with a mirror, held it up so I could see. She said, "That's what the wages of sin look like."

The woman in the next bed slammed a fist into her pillow, and for a moment I thought she was going to rise up and beat Ida senseless. I never bothered to ask which sin—I knew what she meant. I had killed my pap.

In late summer the doctors cranked my mouth open by loosening things one hair's breadth at a time, straightening my teeth with wicked bits of hardware and making porcelain ones to fill the spaces. It was over in October, the last bolts taken out while I was under yet another anesthetic, and when I was able to eat rice pudding with a spoon, Ida came to get me in a different pickup truck. She wore a new winter coat and hat, and never said a word while she drove. I looked out at the countryside and realized I'd missed almost a year. To show for it, I had a wooden cane, a limp, and a new smile I never used.

I was surprised at how grim our place looked, how empty the grocery. The floor and drainboard were crusted with food and filth, and there was not one clean dish in the cupboard. I wondered how Ida had paid for the truck and her clothes, so I asked.

"That," she said, "is none of your business. Don't think you can give me trouble, girl, because I've kept this place going on my own. Lord knows I deserve some relief. And if you must know, your pap's buried out there in the yard. Next to the outhouse."

"Folks came to the burying?"

"Not a soul. Goes to show what kind of man he was."

"Is there a marker?"

"There is not."

It was a long time before I learned that my chatter that night had also killed James Arnold Phelps. I discovered his grave in the Methodist cemetery. I hadn't known the Phelpses were Methodist. In fact, I was hard-pressed to remember a single religious, or even Christian, thing about them.

Next to our outhouse, Pap's grave had long ago grown over,

the grass now withered and brown. And the sky looked like snow. Then, too, came the promised dog—ten months old, the owners driving up in their Ford, and bringing him to me at the back door. I hid my wounded face in his fur. But Ida said we could not take it, could not afford another mouth to feed, and finally they got back in the car and drove away. I hated her, and I told her so.

17

I had lost most of the seventh grade, but my teacher thought I was bright enough to catch up. However, my jaw with its thick white scar and my turned-down mouth were a fright, and no amount of kindness could change that. I let my hair grow out, and it fell over my face. I seldom looked up.

Even with my studies, working in the store, and keeping the house, I found time to sew. I cut squares from scraps of cloth and stitched them together. Evenings, Ida's rantings gave out early, and when she went to bed I stole away to Junk's house where his mama taught me to fill quilts with beaten batting and back them with muslin, to knot the corners with embroidery thread.

After hand-me-downs had been passed through all her grand-children, Miz Hanley gave them to me for scraps. I made a half dozen quilt tops, each a more complicated pattern than the last—overlapping circles, diamonds, and one-inch squares. When they were finished, they looked like something I'd wanted to say but hadn't found words for.

I cleaned out the chicken pen and shoveled goat leavings, but I could not stand the sound of Ida's voice. I was careful not to look at her, either, for her unmarked face was more than I could bear.

Sometimes she stomped and fumed and threw things—the kitchen spoon, the hairbrush, the milk bucket. I'd wake in the night, clutch my belly, and rush out to the yard to vomit up my anger. Still, Ida never touched me. I wondered if she was afraid of my put-together body, that if she back-handed me, some expensive piece might come loose and fly off. Then one stormy night when she'd had enough of my sass, she took me by the arm and dragged me to the cellar. She lit a kerosene lamp, went back upstairs, and closed and locked the door.

"Best learn not to back talk, girl!" she called through the door. "Else you'll rot down there!"

At first it wasn't so bad, being among the long dog pens and things Pap had held in his hands. I fancied I could smell him, and hear the way he crooned to a sick thing. But then I recalled how much he'd loved Ida and how bitter she'd been, from the time when I was no more than a seed.

After a while the oil burned away, and the lamp went out. The damp settled in, and my empty stomach rumbled. I felt along the tabletop and found a wire door. Crawled inside and curled in the farthest corner of the pen. I woke sometime in the night, thinking spiders were crawling up my arms. I clawed till my hands were sticky and my arms burning where I'd torn away skin. I wanted my pap, and I cried till I was sick.

In the hours I was down there, I had soiled my underpants and vomited on my jumper. All I wanted was for Ida to look at the damage she'd done, and I think the sight of me frightened her. Or maybe it was the way I smelled. Over the weeks, my skin became crusty with rash. I stumbled through the days stinking of myself and my shame, my hair in braids as stiff as dried wax. For every night she dragged me to the cellar, I came up the next morning hating her ten times more.

I woke one morning to a great racket overhead. Then doors slamming, and cars starting up.

Ida came down. "Damn niggers," she said and shoved me ahead of her up the stairs. She stripped me naked, and washed me down while I stood in the middle of the kitchen with my eyes closed against the light. She shoved a jar of melted lamb's tallow at me, told me if I wanted to, I could spread it on my arms. After that, we never talked about the basement room. The cellar door stayed locked, and it was a long, long time before I spoke to her again.

Grudgingly, Ida settled down to run the store, and I worked there after school. We closed at six o'clock, when one or the other of us would heat something on the stove. We ate in silence. In the evenings, I did my homework and sewed. On Saturdays, I ordered, stocked shelves, and manned the register while Ida took to her bed. On Sundays we were closed. It was a routine neither pleasant nor unpleasant, it simply was.

Often on weeknights, men I didn't know slipped in through our porch door and headed straight for Ida's room. Occasionally Alton Phelps came back through, buttoning his trousers, but for the most part Ida's gents left after I was asleep. On only one occasion did he ever speak to me.

One Friday night I was frying onions and flour-dusting a bit of beef for the skillet when Phelps' hard body pressed me to the stove. With him suddenly against me, I could feel his sharp heat and smell his breath.

"Little girl, you got something I want," he said.

My hand closed over the skillet handle, but I could feel him grinning.

"Oh no," he said, "I got Ida for the business." And he laughed and jumped back, for I guess he saw the skillet coming.

"When I'm ready, I'll want from you what your pappy had."

And with that, he was gone, and my hand was ablaze. I soaked it in cool water, slathered it with butter, and wrapped it in a cloth. I kept another scar. Further, I had no idea what he was talking about.

I figured Alton compensated Ida well, because the days after his visits, she'd drive into Paramus and come back with new dresses and frilly underwear. Once a bottle of lavender cologne and two silver hair clips.

Meanwhile, at school, I studied ancient history. I learned that the Egyptians had cures for gout, leg cramps, and constipation. It was a shame Pap wasn't here to appreciate those things. Nights I cut cloth shapes that were Roman in design, or Greek, or Spanish, overlaying them onto darker shades for the illusion of shadow. Then I stuffed them and backed them and made twill bindings so the edges wouldn't fray. Before long I sold three finished ones to customers at Ruse's. After that, I had dollars in my pocket with which to buy thread, better scissors, and whole yards of pretty fabric.

The best thing of all was that Wing Harris had come to town. At first glance, there wasn't much to appreciate. He was taller than most boys and built like a two-by-four so that his trousers bagged, and he wore his pap's suspenders to hold them up. His face and hands were equally lean, and at thirteen, he had the longest feet in twelve counties. Teacher put him at a desk in the back of the room, but his knees would not fit, and after a while somebody brought him a decent table and chair.

Also in our class were three girls whose bosoms were rounding out. These girls gathered mornings by the maple tree, and rubbed rouge on their cheeks. They rolled up the waistbands of their skirts and licked their lips till I wondered what kept them from chapping. In the classroom they rolled their eyes at Wing and passed him notes. But his eyes shuttered down like he had other things to think about—which, after Miss Dovey's talk, surprised the heck out of me. I thought boys were driven to kiss pretty girls and do touchy things every chance they got. I wondered if Wing was part blind, or maimed in some way. But before a week had passed, he spoke to me kindly, and though I couldn't think why, one day he walked me home after school.

I began to speak, to answer his questions, and we went on to talk about Aurora and which creeks were best for swimming. How a body could buy cream puffs at the bakery, two for a nickel. Every day I left him standing at the bridge lest Ida see him. I wouldn't have set her on him for the world.

On Monday of the second week, I caught him trying to see my face better, so I told him straight out that if we were to be friends, he must never do that. He took my jaw in his hand, and I jerked away. But his hands were firm, and he turned me back, ran a thumb over my broken lip and the other ropy scars, and told me I was the prettiest girl he'd ever seen. I called him a lying dog.

Wing said he played the trumpet, and that his mama and pap had bought the old Kentuckian Hotel in town. A couple of days later, he took me to see them, and there they were, older versions of Wing, chiseling and painting, shaking out spanking white sheets like they were expecting the governor to spend the night.

"You both come to help?" Wing's pap grinned and handed me a paintbrush. I rolled up my sleeves and got to work. Then his ma made us flapjacks. When I got home, Ida was furious that I hadn't relieved her in the store, but I didn't care.

A few Saturdays later, the Harrises opened the Kentuckian's doors, and I put the Closed sign on ours because everybody had gone to town for the event. Wing stood on the sidewalk and played his trumpet. Inside the polished lobby with its velvet rug, Mrs. Harris served raisin cookies and cups of punch while her husband took folks up in the new elevator, a great wheezing thing that scared me to death. I, myself, was stationed on the second floor, with a ribbon in my hair, pointing out the bathroom with hot running water and the privy with its wooden seat and pull chain.

When all the guests were gone and his folks were sprawled limp as boiled greens, Wing came into the bathroom, closed the door, and kissed me from a distance so that he had to bend into it, his lips touching mine.

"Wing Harris!"

"Aw, Olivia," he said, and he put his arms around me and pulled me close. We kissed in a figuring-it-out way that made my lips sore. When he let me go, he said, "I'll be shaving soon."

I looked down at my body, wondering what I could contribute. I put a hand to my jaw.

"Don't," he said, kissing the welt.

I wanted to run away with him—or at least live forever with him and his folks at the hotel. Wing's kisses in the bathroom sealed my heart.

18

In the cloakroom at school, I heard the rouged girls lamenting. Wing probably had a crush on the teacher, or loved a girl back where he'd come from. I knew better.

The town took an instant shine to the Harrises. Wing played his trumpet for Christmas celebrations, New Year's, and track meets. He marched in the Fourth of July parade, and trumpeted for school graduations and weddings. He played at funerals. Nothing was anything without Wing's brass music. And he played for me.

Ida felt differently. "Get off of my porch with that thing!" she'd shout at us. "You're running off my customers."

"He doesn't run folks off, Ida. You do!" I said.

"Go on with you both!" She shook her fist, her yellow hair flying.

Wing and I fled to the woods, where I discovered that the space between his neck and shoulder was the perfect place to hide my face. He touched my ear and my hair and the tip of my nose as if they were beautiful, and he undressed me the way I'd seen little girls undress dolls. He never let me turn away or cover my private parts, but kissed them gently, and through all the times we laid each other down in those woods we grew closer in ways that stunned me. His body was long and smooth, and it gave off enough heat to ripen tomatoes. There was a sprouting of hair on his chest and fuzz on his cheeks. His privates lay comfortably against my hip, and although at first it embarrassed me, I loved what I did to him. I'd discovered a new dampness between my legs, and Wing seemed not to care that my bosoms weren't much. When he gathered them into his hands, they were more. I was nearly fourteen; he was one year older.

Timidly, I figured out ways to tangle our bodies, positions I was sure nobody had heard of. He laughed at my antics, kissed my eyelids, and touched me in places that set me on fire. Through it all, we talked.

"It was God that called me to play the horn, Olivia," he said one day when he'd buttoned his trousers.

I fingered the peeling mulberry root where I sat in my drawers and cotton undershirt, knees together. My bosoms had grown, although instead of being rounded like I'd hoped, they had dark red points that Wing said he liked. "You sound awful sure."

He gave me a smile that included his eyes. "I am sure," he said.

"God speak to you, did he?"

"Not in words." Wing leaned back against the tree trunk. "More like a feeling."

I knew in my heart that God wouldn't talk to me. I picked up a woolly worm and cradled it in my palm. "Like what, exactly?"

"Well," he said in a way that reminded me of him fiddling with the mouthpiece of his horn when he was ready to play. "Say you've got all these thoughts cluttering your head . . ."

"Uh-huh."

"You climb in there. And you root around till you find the highest, clearest one."

I pictured a kind of celestial billboard. "What if there isn't a clear one?"

"But there *is*," he said. "It's your grandest purpose. When you find it, you know it's right for you. Like with your quilts, Olivia."

"Sewing's not a grand idea."

"Something else then."

"Like what?"

"Well, what do you think about most?"

"You," I said. "I can feel you inside me every single minute."

"Oh-ho!" Wing reached for me. "All right. But besides that, isn't there anything—something that's stuck in your heart?"

I stood up and thought about that while he pulled down my drawers and I stepped out of them. He came out of his own britches, and laid down beside me on the dry leafy ground. Wing took my nipple between his thumb and finger. He groaned with my stillness.

"I think about Love Alice and Junk. And Miz Hanley and Miss Dovey—the way white folks treat 'em so bad."

"Well, there you go," he said. "What else?"

"I miss my pap."

Wing climbed astraddle of me.

"I never got to say good-bye. Or tell him I was sorry."

Wing's strokes were long and hard, and I never knew if he heard. Afterward, I rolled away. "I wish God would give me better instructions," I said.

He threw an arm across me. "I love you, Olivia Harker," he said. "And I'm gonna keep on loving you till the day I die."

Finally, I told him about Ida never wanting me. How she'd gone away after I was born—and about her coming home. I told him that on the icy road I'd killed Pap with my chatter, but Wing held me close and said it wasn't my fault. And that if Pap had to go, at least he carried with him to heaven the sound of my voice.

Wing and I loved for twenty-two months, four days, and three hours, and every minute was like the first. Ida knew. She said we should be dead of shame over what we were doing, and she prayed loudly and often for my salvation. But in my heart, I knew Wing had already saved me.

The following winter, Wing's pap died of influenza, and one night three weeks later, his ma went to sleep and never woke up. I had no doubt that she'd loved Mr. Harris the way I loved Wing, and she could not live without him. I was sick with grief for my beloved. The whole town went to both funerals. Each time, I stayed in the hotel kitchen, laying out spoons and peeling waxed paper from covered dishes. Wing himself was so broken that he could lift neither his head nor his trumpet, and if Pap had taken my voice to heaven, Wing's folks went without his music.

After that he seemed always to be busy somewhere in his head. He left school to run the hotel. I missed him desperately and went to visit him in town. I thought he'd take me up to one of the eight pretty rooms with the flowered quilts, but this was a new Wing, solemn and distant, standing crooked like his back hurt. I said I had come to see if he was all right. Then I told him the truth—I wanted to know if he still loved me. He looked away, and asked me the same. I couldn't get my breath, let alone answer. Our time together shut down that easy, both of us in so much pain that neither of us could see past it.

19

In the months that followed, the town grew silent, like all of Aurora had packed up and gone home. Around the Kentuckian the brick buildings emptied out and became sooty shells with rats and only a lodger or two. The newspaper office shut down, and even Williford the baker closed his doors. Wing's upstairs rooms were occupied by a couple of summer visitors or a hunter or two, and the honeymoon suite pretty much stayed rented to a man from Buelton who was cheating on his wife.

I missed Wing's arms and the sound of his breathing. I'd have died for five minutes alone with him. Suddenly I was fifteen and trapped in a house with Ida.

Christmas night, I put on my coat and wobbled on high-heeled shoes down the highway, to a honky-tonk that had opened up. I sat on a stool at Silty's Jamboree and admired the colored glass lamps that swayed over the pool table, and the way ladies sat in gents' laps. In a strip of purple light from the window I waited for someone to speak to me. It took all of five minutes. By midnight I'd struck up an acquaintance with a bottle of sloe gin and three boys from Buelton. When one of them took me out to the car, I dropped into his arms the way I'd fallen into Wing's. Afterward I cried. He left me blubbering in the parking lot, but soon the other two came out and kept me so busy I had no room to think. I saw then that this was how it would be. I gave the boys whatever they wanted, and I never stood by the road crying again.

Through spring and summer, I abandoned the store and school, and spent most of my time at Silty's. The light was always dim and thick with smoke from the ladies' cigarettes, so that everything seemed sad and blue. And then Silty hired Wing to play his trumpet on Saturday nights.

Wing and I never spoke, nor did we look at each other across the dance floor. If he was surprised to see me, he never said, and anyway there was always some gent to slip the bartender two bits for a half hour in the back room. I seldom declined. After a tussle on Silty's narrow cot, he'd pull up his trousers and light a cigar. While I cleaned myself up, he'd dig out a half dollar. Then I'd wobble out to the bar and climb back on my stool. Finally, I stopped my monthly bleeding. And my bosoms swelled—the gentlemen liked that. They wanted the silliest things—to snap my garters, tear off my drawers, and spank my bottom with the flats of their hands. They taught me to say things that at first sounded awful, but after several drinks became funny.

By fall, the fellow behind the bar was a new one—not the one that favored me and gave me drinks on the house. The windows were painted black, and the new neon sign that hung from the ceiling sizzled and blinked. In the back corner, Wing lifted his horn, and the room throbbed with its wailing.

One night, when I sat running a hand over my belly, a laugh ran down the bar, gents taking bets on which of them my baby would look like. Wing's trumpet whimpered, like all the air had gone out of it. That was the last night he worked there. My disappointment was bitter. I had relished him watching.

Just before Thanksgiving, the Reverend Timothy Culpepper came in, making right for the counter where I sat, my chin propped in my hand.

"Miss Olivia," he said before anyone could toss him out, "this ain't no place for a young lady."

"Lady?" I said. Most of the Reverend's hair was gone, and his whiskers were grizzled. "You callin' me a lady, Reverend?" It sounded like a line from a joke, and I laughed.

He took my elbow. "I'm goin' to get you home."

I shook him off. "You go on now, and save some other poor soul, 'cause I'm just fine."

"Miz Hanley don't think so, Olivia. Nor Love Alice or Junk—they sent me to fetch you. Said for me to bring you up to their place. You can stay with them till your youngun's born."

I could not bear the thought of Love Alice seeing me like this. And anyway, somebody had plugged in the Wurlitzer, and out on the floor the ladies picked up their heels.

"You wanna dance, Reverend?"

"Miss Olivia—"

I put a finger to my lips. "You buy me a drink, an' I'll tell you a secret—"

Above the white collar and tie, his face shone with sweat. "No, ma'am, I don't want to hear no secrets."

"Well, I'll tell you anyway. You know that fella Percy that comes by, sellin' stuff?"

"I seen him, yes."

"Well, I tol' him the baby is his."

"That be the truth?"

"I don't know." I shrugged my bare shoulders. "But I told him it was."

"Miss Olivia, this fella Percy—"

"You know what he's doing right now?"

"I do not."

"He's in the back room, peeling a cigar band and feeling sorry for himself. Now, go home, Reverend," I whined. My belly had begun to hurt, and I didn't want to talk anymore. I turned to the gent on the other side of me, a sweet-smelling fella who had just purchased a half bottle. I smiled at him, sleepy, and I wished for a glass, although I would have drunk straight from the bottle.

Percy, in a cloud of cigar smoke, came out of the office. He jerked me up. I crossed the floor with amazing ease, floated out into the night, and left the Reverend standing there with his hat in his hand.

"Get in the car."

He climbed in, too, and the Ford coughed. We moved onto the road and away from the place and its hazy lights.

After a while I pressed my legs together and said, "Percy, I gotta pee."

But he looked straight ahead, and his mouth was set. I sighed and leaned into the corner, my face to the door. I was in that swampy place where nothing mattered.

Pain roused me. "Let's go back, honey, and I'll do you 'round the floor." I giggled, but it came out a no-meaning sound. My belly hurt, and I was thinking it might just be my time. But that was too much to worry about. Whatever was going to happen would happen.

The mountain road was thick and black like even the moon was hiding. Inside the Ford, I didn't open my eyes. I knew the only thing to be seen was Percy all whip-starched and pissed, and the little white lights winking on the dashboard. I did not want him to take me home. I began to think of ways to make him pull me into his arms.

"Lover—" I said, but the word came out like I'd only dreamed it, and anyway, he was already stopping in the middle of the road. He opened the door and gave me a shove, and I rolled out, landing with the gravel sharp under my shoulder, the blue sequined dress ripping beneath me. He threw the bottle out, too. I heard it shatter, and when I opened my eyes, glass and blue sequins twinkled together like stars that had fallen on this side of the road.

"You're white trash, Olivia," Percy said, hunched over the wheel. "Just like your mama."

I heard the Ford putting away, rattling on the bridge below, and I laid my head on the sand and waited for Ida to come down the steps and find me.

Wolves howled, high up and far away, my grandpap's wolves. But my pap had said there was nothing to be afraid of. In fact, it seemed funny, me lying here like a wounded deer. Before long, Ida sure enough came down and laid a hand on my belly, while the gentleman she was entertaining stood off to one side blinking. Ida barked at him, and his thick hands took me up by the heels like I was a hog to be slaughtered. They hauled me in with Ida grunting and kicking open the door, and they carried me through the grocery and put me down in the middle of the big poster bed. Ida drew back her arm and slapped me good. Then again, without missing a beat.

She rolled me over to unfasten the blue frock and pulled it down past my underdrawers, but something like syrup was flowing from me, and the pain had gotten all wild and wrong.

"Go on and fetch Doc Pritchett," she said to the man. And again, "Goddamit, fetch the doc!"

He took up his hat and shuffled out, saying, "But I paid good money, Ida Mae—"

I opened my mouth, and a long thin scream came out, like the highest of high notes on Wing's golden horn. It shook the window glass and stuck like flypaper to the walls and ceiling. And I knew that what was supposed to be happening, was not happening at all.

20

My daughter was born before morning, and I named her Pauline because Love Alice had said I would. Maybe I just wanted Love Alice to be right.

I hadn't the slightest idea what to do with this whippet. For once, Ida let Miz Hanley come to our place. She showed up on a Thursday with her spine starchy and her mouth set. She clucked at how grown-up I was, and how sweet the baby, though I know she'd heard all about me from the Reverend. She showed me how to fasten the baby to my nipple, how to stroke her throat so she'd stop wailing and suck. I was miserable with Pauline in my arms and clamped to one breast. I suspected I should feel something warm, but it was all I could do to spoon oats in her mouth and change her stinking diaper while Ida reminded me where Pauline had come from. She called me Jezebel and Satan's daughter. I told her I was Jezebel's daughter, all right, and that brought such a barrage of shattered scripture that the baby woke screaming.

In the alcove by my bed, Pauline slept in an old dresser drawer. Against the cool nights, I'd nailed newspapers on the walls and folded quilts under her, but I had to creep in and out of bed so's not to wake her, and my corner was no longer mine.

When she was a few days old, Wing came to visit, leaning in

the kitchen doorway with his hands in his pockets. He was polite with Ida and played with Pauline, but said nothing to me. In the end, he laid Pauline in her drawer and bought canning wax and a box of salt. Finally, we stood on the front steps, him mumbling that he would marry me if I wanted Pauline to have a daddy, but stiffly I said no thank you, get on with your business. And he did.

At the end of winter, when my daughter had begun to crawl and every blessed thing was caught in her fist and directed to her mouth, Mr. Solomon Cross came to town—to our door. He was covered with road dust, and had a front tooth missing so that he whistled when he talked. He held his cap in his hand and said to Ida, "Excuse me, ma'am, we're paving the farm road, and you-all won't be able to travel west for a day or two."

She invited him in, saying, "I'm Ida Harker, wife of Tate Harker who's dead and gone." I thought she was setting him up for herself, but then she gave him a cup of coffee to warm him, and my wiggling baby, and said, "This here's Pauline. Healthy a child as there ever was—and look what a sturdy mama she has. My daughter's plain, but she makes fine bed-quilts and a tasty apple cobbler—takes after me in that way. Her name's Olivia."

He nodded and said yes, ma'am, what a nice family—and he came to call on me the next night.

This time he was cleaned up. Both his suit and his manners stood out like blinking lights in our sad little house. He told us to call him Saul. The only place for socializing was in the kitchen, so he sat at the table while I slouched in my chair, with a pair of Pap's old trousers pulled over my long johns, two flannel shirts, and my hat in my hand like I was fixing to run. Ida and I had fought bitterly over my presentation, me arguing that I was what I was. That seemed all right with Saul.

He was a squat and balding man, but his manners were fine

and his eyes the purest blue I'd ever seen. He told me he made fair money with the road crew, but he'd be willing to settle down and find something else in Pope County—if he could have me for his wife. Said he'd take Pauline, too, and locate a house. Ida called from the bedroom that this was a fine enough house, and there was plenty of room if the two of us didn't mind sleeping in the alcove until the undertaker moved her out of the front bedroom, which would surely be soon. Saul said he guessed that would be all right.

I consulted Love Alice. I should have been embarrassed to go up there after all that had happened, but Miz Hanley scooped Pauline right up, put her arm around me as I had known she would, and settled me in her rocking chair on the porch. She wagged Pauline off into the house and came back with a glass for me—lemon water and sugar. She didn't ask after Ida, but stood cooing at the baby. I closed my eyes and drank my sweet drink, and I tried hard to pretend I was nine again, but I could not get it straight with Miz Hanley's attention on Pauline's babbling. Time has a way of ripping things from us, and it's true what they say— a body can't go back.

Presently Love Alice came up the road. When she saw me, she dropped the bundles she was carrying, causing her mother-in-law to cluck her tongue, and she ran up on the porch and hugged me tight.

"O-livvy," she cried in her funny little voice. "It's so good to see you, and that's a truth!"

I had hungered for the sound of her, for the great dark eyes and the swoop of freckles like sparrow's wings. Miz Hanley took Pauline inside.

"I've missed you so much, Love Alice."

"Oh, ain't it been awful," she said.

"Please—will you come to see me sometimes?"

She sat down on the porch and crossed her legs, tucked her dress around her. "I do come, O-livvy. I shops there on Wednesdays when I got a nickel or two."

"I don't mean that," I said, putting down my glass. "I mean—in my kitchen. I'll make us tea like when we were girls."

"That a long time ago." Love Alice looked like she wanted to fly away. "Miss Ida be there."

"Never mind Ida. I'll take care of her. Please come. I've got a jar of sweet pickle that you like, and I'll cut up a peach. Love Alice?"

"Mm-hmm?"

"I got things to think through, like Saul Cross wanting to marry me and take Pauline, too."

"He seem a nice man."

"But it scares me, you know? Bein' with one man for all time. Especially one that Ida picked out."

"Not me. I don't want nobody 'cept Junk." Then she got up on her knees and looked hard in my eyes. "You go on and marry him, O-livvy. It goin' to be all right. An' I will come on Tuesday."

21

Saul and I were married in Ida's side yard. My hair was done up in ribboned braids, and I wore a long green dress to cover the boots that were all I owned. Most of the town turned out, I'm sure in deference to Pap's memory. They stood around drinking cold tea and cider. Others clustered by the barn. While Ida served wedding cake to the whites, the coloreds settled in the back lot, laying out fried chicken on squares of newspaper and wagging their heads over Pap's privy grave. Love Alice blew me kisses. I was edgy and near tears, jiggling Pauline on my hip, and maybe that's why Ida said nothing about Junk and Love Alice, about his mama or Miss Dovey and all their friends and relations eating their dinner out past the goat pen.

Later, Wing came to me in the kitchen where I sat in a straight-backed chair, and he asked me if I really loved Saul. I said how could I, not knowing him at all, and what did it matter to Wing anyway. He said he guessed he'd find him a wife, then, and see if they couldn't make a go of the hotel. I said why didn't he just do that.

22

Four years later Wing went off to a hotel convention in Paramus and brought home one Grace Marie Saunders, a wisp of a thing with eyes as big as bread and butter plates. I saw her only a few times—Wing could've put both hands around her middle—but everyone liked her. She seemed always to be cold, with a sweater wrapped about her, or sniffling into a hanky. She told Little Ruse, however, that she was right as rain and did, after all, have Wing's love to keep her warm.

I did not go to Wing and Grace's wedding, although Saul did because he thought it was the neighborly thing. He wore his now-thready suit, combed his hair over his bald spot, and drove Ida's truck to the white church on the highway. He said afterward folks went down to the hotel lobby, where they served sandwiches no bigger than his thumb and punch with lemon slices floating on the top. He said Miz Grace was a fairy princess, decked out in flowers and lace, and that Wing couldn't take his eyes off her.

Saul, himself, was a hard worker. He clerked for Mr. French in his hardware store because he knew wing nuts from lock washers, and could spot one flathead screw in a barrel of stove bolts. He knew something about everything. If a body needed indoor plumbing, or linoleum laid, Saul was right there. If nobody called on him for some time, he'd go off looking to see where he was needed.

On Saturdays, Saul obliged Pap's memory by firing up the still in the shed and turning out his own brand of Sunday morning brew. At one time, revenuers had plagued my pap mightily, once even bringing a federal marshal to our place, but the government's mind apparently had turned to other things, because they left Saul alone. Although money was at an all-time low, customers came to us, the gents sampling Saul's whiskey on the sly while their wives bought groceries. Ida no longer entertained gentlemen in the house, but took to wandering up and down the road, preaching pidgin gospel to neighbors who said it looked like the sickness was coming on her again. Ida called them backbiters, and told them to go to hell.

While Saul was both moonshining and selling hardware, I stitched my quilts and sold a few. The next summer, he built me a stall where Farm Road One ends at the highway to Paramus. On weekends, I sat up there with a hat on my head and a few bills for change. From time to time, folks stopped their cars, and for four or five dollars they took home a quilt.

Although we never talked about it, or about anything else that really mattered, Saul and I raised Pauline the best we knew how. When she was three, he drove over to the county seat and filled out papers that gave Pauline his name. And he was good with Ida. He asked nothing from me except to fix his supper, which was fine because a terrible ache occupied my head and my heart, and rendered me useless in any other way.

Finally I walked up to Doc Pritchett's and had him look me over, and much to my embarrassment, he pronounced me fine and said it was probably all in my head. I knew what he meant—

if my ma'am had been crazy, then I would be, too. I told Ida and Saul I'd had a case of the grippe, but was now right as rain. I never mentioned my hurting again—not even to myself. Instead, I planted twice as much squash in the mounds by the back porch, and cleared another patch for the sweet potatoes I'd drop in when the weather turned. I hoed till I couldn't stand up straight, and at night I snipped fabric, squared corners, and stitched till I fell asleep with my head on the table.

After a while, Saul and I addressed the problem of Ida, how crazy she made me—and how hateful she was to Pauline, who was already wild as a March wind. Ida could no longer tolerate Pauline sleeping in her room, so nights we carried Pauline's cot to the grocery and hauled it back to the bedroom in the mornings. Meanwhile, Pauline's nightmares kept us up. Finally, Saul drove Ida's pickup over to Buelton where he bought lumber enough to start work on a cabin across the yard. He built one room with a single window and a door on the south side. I dragged the cot out there, and paid Big Ruse fifty cents for a chair.

We moved Ida into the cabin on a fall morning. I think she was secretly pleased with the attention Saul had given her, and she came over for breakfast, lunch, and supper. She conversed with Saul and took her tea at our kitchen table. I served her in silence, but every night when supper was done, I sent her home. I reveled in the hours that I had without Ida underfoot. And in all those years, I never opened the cellar door.

Saul was covering up the tar paper on Ida's place when at four o'clock on a Saturday afternoon, he had a heart attack and died. I wasn't surprised, somehow, for he was too hard a worker, and he'd overly loved my brown sugar cakes. I buried him up in the foothills, right where the land starts to rise. I didn't cry. I was weary of tears, although I hadn't shed one in years.

Pauline, on the other hand, fell to pieces.

There was no handling her, and in my heart, I understood that, too. Without love, there is only a great empty space that we fill with whatever's handy. By the time she was fourteen, Pauline had taken up with a crowd that traveled in an old jalopy from one juke joint to another. One night in spring, she left home.

Rather than figuring out where life had gone wrong, it seemed easier to think that what happens to us happens. Saul was buried on the hill, Ida was living in her tar paper shack, and somewhere Pauline was awash in gin. I, on the other hand, was stitching with a frenzy, and hoeing, planting, reaping, and canning. I raised two crops of new potatoes, turnips and mustard greens, beets and red and yellow peppers to sell in the store. I built a chicken coop and bought four more laying hens and a rooster. Sold eggs for a penny apiece and purchased two more layers. When the mule died, I bought another—Ida called him Sanderson Two—and I hitched him to a plow. There wasn't a square foot of earth I did not turn up, except for Pap's grave.

Along about October, when I'd worn myself to the nub, I laid down my hoe and spread out on the earth as I had on so many nights of my childhood. I longed for a change, but I couldn't imagine what.

23

own at the Kentuckian, Miz Grace Harris apparently did not get on well—in fact, she got considerably sicker. Over the years, I heard through Love Alice that Wing drove her the length and width of the state in his Ford, looking for a doctor who might cure her. But it was some kind of double lung problem, they said, and there was no fixing it. Finally Wing sent her to the South of France to lie in the sun. He borrowed the money from Big Ruse to do it. But when she came home, the doctors recommended she be put in an iron lung. Miz Grace said that was no way to live out her days, with a machine to do her breathing. I could appreciate that. She stayed in the hotel. Wing fixed up two downstairs rooms for them and rented the rest.

I never went there to visit, but I listened when folks talked of her, and of him. And I begged Love Alice for news. He never played his trumpet, she said, nor left the hotel, for Miz Grace had taken to her bed. And she stayed there for a half dozen years.

Sometimes, in those days, Ida came out of her cabin and watched me hoe. To further irritate me, she stopped brushing her hair and never took a bath, wearing one flannel gown till it fell from her body. She said I was loony, lying there on the ground at the end of every day, but I laughed and told her I could hear its heartbeat.

Then one day, Pauline showed up on my doorstep, a dirty blue blanket in the crook of her arm. It was like time had backed up, and this was my own child being handed to me. But it wasn't. This was a brand-new life. I took that tiny thing, sat down on the floor of the grocery, and buried my face in it.

"He hasn't got no name," Pauline said. She wore shoes with high brittle heels, and her hair was oily. She looked tired beyond her years, and her no more than a child herself.

The baby smelled sour, like it hadn't had a bath in its life, its scalp flaky with cradle cap, and altogether not much bigger around than my wrist.

"We'll call him William Tate Harker," I said. "After my pap."

She shook her head. "Not Harker. He's a Cross, like you and me and Daddy Saul."

I nodded. "William Tate Cross, then."

Her face was stained with grit. Or tears. So was the baby's. I sat there rocking him. "He needs fattening up."

"I know."

"We'll mix honey in some milk. Put in an egg."

"You do it, Mama," she said. "I can't stay."

"What?"

"I need you to take him."

"Pauline—"

"I'm goin' to California. Gonna be in motion pictures. I'm pretty enough, don't you think? An' I can't be weighted down with a baby. He won't be much trouble for you, he's real good, don't hardly cry at all."

God love me—a small, wounded thing had come to my store. But I loved this one even before I unwrapped his blanket. I never felt so sad in my life as when Pauline left us sitting there, and went out the door and down to a car full of racketing young people that was waiting for her on the road.

24

At first I thought Ida was crazy as a loon. She stood outside her shack nights, even in the wind and rain, her hair blowing wildly about her head, an old horsehair blanket around her shoulders. Then I realized she was looking through the window, watching me and the boy with God knew what on her mind. Only once did I wonder if she was lonely, then decided on the spot that I had ached for my ma'am since the day I was born. It was her turn to hurt. Still, after that, when the weather was bad I bedded the baby down, went out, and led her into her shack and to her bed. From somewhere she'd gotten a corncob pipe. I brought her tobacco, and she smoked into the night.

In the house it was just me and Will'm, and it wasn't long before he was crawling about and then toddling, and begging for sugar teats and other syrupy things.

I manned the store, worked on my quilts, and taught Will'm at the kitchen table. When he was six, I walked with him daily to the schoolhouse. I told him the only rule we lived by was to love each other and ourselves—which I had to say over and over, because Will'm was old enough to see that I did not include Ida. He loved her anyway.

Ida lived her life in her bed, reading her Bible and railing at everything. She ate the food I brought her, and although she was allowed in our house at mealtime, she hardly ever came. As Will'm grew, I often sent him to take her tea, or a cup of coffee. Twice I eavesdropped and heard her conversation with him to be gentle and even wise. Will'm covered her when she fell asleep. More than once, he tamped out her pipe. At first it angered me that he could pull this from her while I could not. Truth was—Ida and I were a roller coaster of hurts, a runaway ride that would never stop.

Will'm grew tall, with a soul as straight and as right as any I'd seen. He had his mama's yellow hair and great round eyes. He didn't fear work, and in the absence of a gun, which I would not let him have, he devised clever traps in which he caught rabbits and possum, the latter being stringy and tough in the stewpot—but I was grateful for the meat. He didn't bring home a single thing we couldn't eat. He loved to read, and he read aloud nights until I had heard all of Mark Twain and William Faulkner, while I sat at the table embroidering squares.

Most of all, although I tried to steer him away from it, Will'm had an infinite capacity to care for hurt things. I suspect that, no matter how I worked at it, he could not separate them from himself. He was a quiet, generous child with a stubborn streak that I guess he got from me.

I was glad he never got a bee in his bonnet about the locked cellar door.

25

Now, however, Ida has gone and killed the wolf. While it's still early, Will'm and I bury the gray on the north side of a boulder—the only place on the hill with earth soft enough to take her. Then I fire up the stove in the corner of the kitchen, and we find a piece of old plywood to block the cold that pours in through the open window. We sit at the table and drink tea and eat bread with the jam I've put back. In the corner stands Pap's rifle that I ripped from Ida's hands. I took her no breakfast.

"I guess there's no use to go looking for the pups," Will'm says, looking into his cup.

"None at all."

I've never made bones about telling Will'm anything—about how poor we are, although he doesn't seem to get the idea. He walks around like he owns something fine and is the richest man in these parts.

"We're near down to our last dollar," I say, turning away from the cubs.

He licks jam from his top lip. "I could take another job," he says. "Work Dooby's fountain once in a while, more than just sweeping up—or hire on at Ruse's for Sunday dinner. Maybe Wing could use a hand at the hotel."

At the mention of Wing, my thoughts break like pearls and run all over the table. "You got school—by the time you get off the bus, it's near five o'clock, and you help out in the store. Then you got homework."

Will'm runs his finger inside the neck of the jam jar.

I slap his hand.

He grins. "If Wing's missus would go on and die, you and him could get married, and then we'd own half of the hotel."

"Will'm!" By now I have figured out how to keep from reddening when he talks this way, but it bothers me mightily.

"Then we could go down there and live."

"And do what with Ida? And what about the store?"

He rolls his eyes, drinks up the last of his tea, and wipes his mouth with the back of his hand. He studies his second piece of bread, folds it in half, and stuffs most of it in his mouth. Then he gets up, and puts on his coat and cap and winds the scarf about his neck. "It smells like wolf in here," he says, reaching for my tea to help get the bread down. "If we had those pups, I'd take care of them. I'd feed them, and be their regular ma'am."

And without waiting for an answer, he goes to stand out front with his lunch pail and his rucksack. I watch him from the window. In a few minutes, the school bus sluices up on the ice. Will'm goes down the long front steps, climbs aboard, and the bus pulls away, taking him over to Buelton, to the new school there. He's not happy; he'd rather be on the mountain, looking for cubs.

I'm not yet ready to put the Open sign on the grocery door. I wash up the few dishes, smooth my bed and the boy's, study my face in the kitchen looking glass, wondering whether it's the mirror or me that's mottled and rusty. I brush out my hair and re-braid it down my back, and with a sigh so loud I'm sure Ruse can hear it at the cafe, put on my cape and hat, and fold over my arm the blanket the gray slept on. Then without even a glance at Ida's cabin, I set out for the mountain and the place we found the wolf.

It's late in the morning, and the sun is high and weak. Both the silvers that'd been shot are gone, their carcasses dragged off by scavengers. Perhaps, I think, the meat has saved some other thing. In the daylight, the gray's den is not hard to uncover. She'd settled on a small cave, about a hundred feet from where she lay wounded, and birthed her babies there. I imagine her, yesterday, leaving her hiding place, maybe drawing the hunters away from her children—six of them.

Their mewling is weak, and they barely stir. When I sort out the small bodies, three are dead, and the others whimper like field mice. They're miserable and ribby with hunger. I dig a hole in the snow with my hands and bury the ones that are gone, for I can't bear to think about vultures and hawks. Then I fold the others into the wool blanket that smells like their ma. They each weigh less than a silver spoon.

26

Love Alice hikes over to our place because today is Tuesday, and while I make tea with ginger and cloves, she looks around. She does this every week, like she's never been in my kitchen before, and all the while, she's humming—"Amazing Grace," and "Come Down Lord." Then her eyes settle on some piece of bric-a-brac, or a book, or the quilt I'm working on, and she tells me its truth. That's what she's always called it. Truth.

And that's what she calls the wolf cubs. She loves them, each no bigger than her hand, and she sits on the floor and strokes them and says in her voice that sounds like birdsong, "Would you jus' looky at these sweetie thangs."

I stir milk in a pan and add a bit of corn syrup, twist a corner of a kitchen towel, and dip in the end. I lift a pup and pry open his mouth, but my fingers are big and coarse, and I feel awkward. The pup sucks. "I never in my life knew how to take care of a small thing," I say.

"O-livvy, you doin' fine, uh-huh. They love that sugar teat, and they love you, too."

I look at her.

Before he is full, the pup gives out, and I put him down and begin on the second.

"This will never work," I say. "I got to think of a way to force food into 'em."

"You will," she says. Then she sits at the table to wait for her tea.

The truth is I can't afford milk for the cubs and the boy and Ida, too. Ida will have to give hers up—I'll take her a cup of tea with her supper and add a drop of honey. The second pup won't suckle at all, and I wring the rag with my fingers and hold him every which way, trying to get the milk down his throat. But his eyes are closed, and his body works with the labor of breathing. The third one swallows some and goes to sleep. They're going to die, and I hope they hurry up before Will'm comes home. When the pups are tucked back in their box, I pour the tea, sit down, and take up my embroidery cotton.

Then the bell rings over the grocery door, and I go through the curtain and wait while Mr. Haversham chooses a couple of russets and a can of creamed corn. I ring him up on the clangy register we've had for eons, and put his things in a paper sack.

In the kitchen, Love Alice is fingering the quilt I've worked on so long my fingers bleed around the calluses. "Ain't this quiltie a prize thang," she coos.

I take up the thread, and my hands fly with the tying of knots.

She sits across from me in her stockinged feet. Her eyes are opaque. "You know—" she says.

A prediction is coming.

"—A fat ol' rich man gonna sleep under dis quiltie. He love his mama. Meaner'n a snake with his wife, but he do love his mama. He keep a dog—no, two dogs, an' he scared of the dark."

And on and on it goes until I raise my eyes. I've known Love Alice a long time. Before she tells me what she sees in my own eyes, she makes sure I want to know.

She gets up from her chair and wanders about the kitchen in her shapeless black dress, laying hands on things—cups on the drainboard, a pot holder, the cellar doorknob. "What in here, O-livvy, you don't mind me askin'."

"Stairs. To the basement."

She tips her head over like spring's first robin, listening for worms.

"Uh-huh," she says. "This door need to be unlocked."

"That's just my pap's old work room."

"It need to be," she says, shrugging.

I pour tea into cups. "I was down there yesterday."

"Go agin."

"Why?"

" 'Cause what you thinkin' ain't so. But it a place to start."

"Let's talk about something else. How's Junk?"

"He fine." She comes to the table and spoons sugar in her second cup of tea. "How Miss Ida? Actin' the fool, like always?"

She makes me laugh, Love Alice does, and I get up to fetch her a slice of dried apple turnover and a fork. "Just like always."

She reaches across, lays her hand on mine. "You take this quiltie down to Mistah Wing's place. He puttin' in a shop, buyin' brooms and candles and such. He can sell your quilties, too. An' anyway, Mistah Harris a sweet thang—his wife's gon' leave us real soon."

I look at her. "How do you know that, Love Alice? How can you be sure?"

She smiles. I've always marveled at how big her teeth are. "Don't matter how I know, she crossin' over. What you really askin' is—what happen then? He comin' after you in a fine white carriage, flower in his hand?"

I prick myself with the needle and swear and suck at the blood.

"It all right," she says, forking up apple. "It ain't no secret. You want to know, I tell you. He askin' Jesus to take her soul to heaven." Love Alice leans across. "O-livvy, what you an' Mistah Harris did weren't wrong."

"That was a long, long time ago."

"You love him like earth and water." She put a bit of crust in her mouth. "If I'm lyin', you take back this pastie—but I speak the truth."

I put down my needle and look at her. "I was through with all that twenty years ago. It wears a body out to go on day and night in that single-minded way. Never thinking about anything else."

"Don't it, though?" she says, nodding. "That's a truth."

We sit without speaking, and then she runs her finger over her plate to pick up the crumbs. "Well, I got to pull on my boots and git along. Thank you kindly for the tea."

I reach in my apron pocket and lay a nickel on the table. "Thank you for your company." It's the price of a reading, or maybe just a gift for a friend, and I always leave the taking to her. Every time, she opens her pocketbook and drops in the coin.

"Love Alice—" I say. "Sometimes, when you're in town, you go to the drugstore, the post office, the hotel—"

"Say what you want to, O-livvy."

"Do you—do you ever look in Wing Harris's eyes? Do you see—his truths?"

Her smile is like the sun coming up. "Oh, I do. I see thangs there. He drownin' in the hurt."

I want to ask if I'm a part of the pain, or if I can help somehow. But it seems like too much to ask, and way too much to know.

27

I listen for the tinkle of the grocery store bell. In between, I scatter feed for the chickens and milk the nanny goat, chop the ice on their pans, shovel snow, and heat water for washing, which I do on the back porch. Steam rises from the tub, burning my fingers and clouding the windows. I hang sheets and underwear on the line out back, and they freeze before I have the last pin in place. After that, it begins to snow, darkening the sky and coming down so hard that I put the stew on early, potatoes and onion and a joint of rabbit Junk left on the porch. I take Ida hers with bread crumbled in it, setting it on a box inside the door, and I back out before she can utter one Dutch-ugly word.

When the boy comes home, he makes over the cubs.

"I knew you'd get them," he says, grinning all over himself.

I go off to wait on customers, and at six o'clock I turn over the Closed sign on the door. "They're a lot of work," I say, putting stew in two bowls and setting them on the table.

I tell him how I've stirred up their milk and tried to feed them, that it's an endless job. "Don't set your heart on them living, Will'm. They're not meant to be without their ma'am." I slice bread and fetch butter from the bin on the porch.

"I'll be responsible for them, Gran. I'll do everything." He puts the cubs in the box and comes to the table.

I want to tell him responsibility's fine, but it doesn't guarantee. Things live, and they die. Instead, I scoop up the last of the turnover for him. Pour cups of hot tea with milk from the nanny. I sit down to my supper, and clear my throat. "Will'm, I hear Alton Phelps is lookin' for a donkey."

Will'm looks up from his bowl. His eyes grow round as platters. "You're not thinkin' about Sanderson Two! He's older'n earth, all sway-backed and broke down, and mean as a snake—"

"What I hear, he just wants something to keep the coyotes away from the lambs on the south quarter." Something about that picture makes me want to laugh. If he wasn't damned near dead, that donkey'd have those lambs for lunch. Still, I think I'll scrape the ice off the truck in the morning, and load ol' Sanderson Two up. It's a long time since I've been out to the Phelps' place. I try not to remember.

Will'm mops his bowl with the heel of the bread. Looks around to see if there's more.

"Go on then," I say. "Eat up the last."

"You're not even gonna ask Ida? He's her donkey." Will'm grins. He loves the old stories my pap told me—of Ida riding the preaching circuit. Says he can't picture her loping along on her donkey.

"Ida shot the wolf," I say. "And anyway, Sanderson One was hers. That old donkey'll bring a few dollars, and it'll give me a chance to confront Phelps about the wolves."

"Oh, Gran."

"I'll go in the morning. Then I'll stop at Dooby's and ask if there's anything to be done for the cubs. While I'm in town, I'm goin' to take a couple of quilts over to Wing's hotel—see if he'll sell them in his new gift shop."

Will'm clears his throat. "All right, then." He lowers his face to his bowl, thinking I won't see him smile.

28

The next morning, I put on my cape and my hat. With the flapjack turner I scrape the ice from the windows of the truck. Because no new snow fell in the shadow of the barn, the wolf's blood still colors the snow, and I kick and stomp till it's mostly gone. I start up the old truck, letting it rattle in idle. It reminds me of the one Pap had when I was a kid—the one he was driving the night he died. Except this one has two good door handles. The tailgate's been ripped off, and rust has spread where most of the paint used to be.

I drive it over into Ida's yard, lay some lumber down, and lead Sanderson Two into the bed of the truck. He's as bony as a chicken wing. I tie him tight to the four corners with the rope. Ida doesn't come out, and it's a damned good thing. We're a sight, that old donkey riding with his head up, braying like he needs the attention.

West of town, the roads are scraped clean by men who live to do Phelps' bidding. In summer they become his gardeners, gatekeepers, and private assistants. Will'm calls them his bodyguards.

The land, here, is bound by white slatted rails, and snow clings to a couple hundred magnificent Scotch pines. This private forest makes it hard to see the house. I recall that he fancies himself a master hunter, and have heard that he displays his trophies for the world to see. I wonder how his missus can stand to have all those dead things in her house.

I drive up the long curved drive, past the front door where a man is standing guard, and around to the back—with Sanderson Two braying and kicking in the back of the truck. I park in the same place my pap parked the wagon on that afternoon when I stowed away in back. I rap on the door.

Miz Phelps is in her kitchen, which surprises me, for her husband has money enough to hire three or four cooks. She's flushed and pretty in her yellow dress, taking peach pies from the oven—and I stand in the doorway with my hat in my hands, just like my pap must have.

"Baking. It's how I keep busy, Olivia," Miz Phelps says, and her smile is warm. She pours me coffee even though I say no thanks, pours another mug for herself, and we sit at the table in her big enamel kitchen. I wish I could do business with her and not have to see the mister at all.

"I'm sure he'll take the donkey," she says kindly and reaches across to touch my hand. "You tell him you want a pretty penny for it, Olivia. Not a dime less than twenty—no, thirty dollars."

I look at the dark coffee, the thick cream she's added, and say, "He's not worth that much."

"You're so like your daddy," she says, sitting back. "You even look like him."

I put a hand up, can't help it, though the scars have faded.

She shakes her head. "Once—when I was a very small girl—and I lived in that house above Rowe Street—you know it, Olivia, big green thing, falling down even then—your father came to our house."

She's telling me she didn't come from money, that we're alike, she and I.

"We had this old yellow dog. I guess he was a hunter in his younger days, and my father loved him. We all did. He'd go after squirrels in the fall—couldn't stop that in him. This one time he got ahold of something bad in the woods. Your daddy came to our house in his wagon. He took one look at that yellow dog and wrapped him in a blanket. You were there, Olivia, sitting up on that seat, proud as you please in your red overalls, and I envied you. Having a daddy who was so gentle-handed."

I swallow a mouthful of sweet coffee and say nothing.

"When women marry, they look for men who are like their fathers—did you know that, Olivia?"

"No, ma'am."

"I married a man just like mine." Lines appear between her eyes. "Anyway, we came to your place to see about the dog—I've forgotten his name—and your daddy took us down to his basement. And there was that old hound, dining on boiled chicken meat. He sat in the pen, and looked at us with his head cocked over and his tongue hanging out, looking healthy as you please. Your daddy said he'd bring him home in a day or two, and he did, and never charged us a penny. When we all ran out to welcome that yellow dog home, he was laid out comfy on the wagon seat with his head in your daddy's lap." She laughs, like it's a good memory she hasn't recalled in a very long time.

I smile with her. "His name was Governor."

"Oh, my land!" She puts her apron to her mouth and laughs some more, and the minutes there in her bright kitchen are so good I don't want them to end. But I stand up.

"Yes, of course," she says, wiping her eyes. "You've come about the donkey. I'll show you to my husband's study—I think he's alone this morning—and when you're done, come back through the kitchen, and I'll give you a peach pie to take home."

"Oh, I couldn't—"

"But you must—as a thank-you for Governor."

She takes me through a long hall, and a marble entryway, then under a great polished arch. She knocks lightly on a door and puts her head in. They talk in low voices, and finally she opens the door wide. Before I know it, I'm standing in front of Alton Phelps' desk, which is a monster of a thing that a man could see his face in. Sitting behind it, Phelps is a pale little man with a wrinkled face. His hair, too, is colorless, hanging long in the back and on the sides, maybe to make up for what's missing on top.

"Miz Cross," he says without looking up from the papers in his hand.

"Mr. Phelps." I hold my hat, and am hot in my cape.

He puts the papers in a drawer, closes it, and locks it with a key. Directly over him is a buck's head with ten—maybe twelve-point antlers. A woolly boar stands in the glass case on the far wall, and other small things are stuffed and mounted over the fireplace, on the coffee table, and in every corner. Guns are stored in racks around the room. Everything in the room is bigger than he is.

When Phelps stands, I see there's no flesh on his bones. Alone, he'd hardly make a dent in the snow, and I see now why he needs other people to do his work.

I say, "Word's out you're looking for a donkey to keep scavengers off the place. So I've brought our Sanderson Two. He's old, but he'll run off coyotes, vermin."

His cheeks and chin are pockmarked. He raises his brows and steeples his fingers like this is big business. Comes around and half sits on his desk, looking at me. Takes a cigar from a box, bites off the end, and spits in the wastebasket. He lights the thing with a silver lighter and puffs until the air turns blue. "How much you want for him?"

The cigar smoke chokes me, but I will not cough. "Twenty dollars."

His cheeks go in and his lips push out. He's looking somewhere over my head. "Done," he says, and moving back around, he opens a drawer, takes out four five-dollar bills.

"One more thing, Mr. Phelps. About our mountain—"

His brows shoot up. "What mountain would that be?"

"Big Foley, behind our house."

He draws out his words. "I wasn't aware that you owned the entire thing, Miz Cross."

"The south strip I do. Somebody shot two of our wolves up there. Cut off the ears."

Whole minutes go by. I look up at the buck, its soft dark nostrils, the great round eyes.

He looks up, too. "Beautiful animal, that one."

I want to hit him so badly, I sway on the soles of my boots. "What gall it must take for you to say that and then kill it. Maybe someday I'll mistake you for a wild thing up there and shoot you. Twice."

All things considered, he holds himself well. "You listen to me, Miz Cross. Today, I am all right with you driving your ugly truck up my driveway. And I'll buy your goddamn broken-down mule, but you will not speak to me that way. And you'll remember your place."

My place? Smoke cyclones around my head. "I posted signs. I can get the sheriff from Buelton—"

"You'll want to pay attention, Miz Cross. Sheriff Pink is a friend of mine."

His face is so close I could spit and blind him.

He laughs through his nose. "I'm sure whoever's kilt your wolves would like to see papers of ownership—and where old scores were settled."

He means James Arnold, the way he died. But he leans away and rearranges his face. "Miz Cross, I paid dearly for the right to hunt on that land. I'll remind you that I have left you alone for a very long time. But I see that you're getting uppity in your ways. Now, if you're goin' to cause trouble—"

"The mule is yours. What happened to James Arnold I cannot fix." I pick up the bills and turn away. But the doorknob sticks, and I can't turn it to save myself. I've never claimed to have one ounce of dignity.

I stand in the marble entryway, not wanting to go out through the front, but I don't want to encounter the missus again, either. It has to be one or the other. I keep my chin up and my eyes straight ahead—down through the hall and find the kitchen, where I slip out the back door. Miz Phelps is nowhere in sight. In the gravel curve behind the house, Phelps' men come running and tell me to follow them out to the pasture. I get in and start the truck, and there on the seat beside me is a pie wrapped in waxed paper, making the cab smell like warm fruit and pastry. I follow the two in their fancy pickup, along a narrow road to a stable, where they fix up a ramp, untie Sanderson Two, and walk him down. I figure that old mule is already the joke of the place, although they spend more time looking at my truck than anything.

When I ask if there's a back way off the property, they point, and I rattle away, skidding in the ruts. I'm relieved to be away from the big house, off his rail-fenced land, and for a while I swallow my anger, but after a time I pull over. I get out of that truck and walk around it twice, banging the fenders, kicking up snow, and swearing. Then I climb back in, my boots muddy on the floorboard, and slam the door. Goddamn Phelps, I'm sure he could tell by looking at me that I needed the money. My belly twists, and if I were so inclined, I'd cry. But what's done is done. There's enough money in my pocket to pay this month's bills and stock a couple of shelves.

29

In truth, I can't wait to show Will'm what I've got for our supper. Ida may not get a single bite, she who never gave me anything but grief. I think about Miz Phelps' yellow dog and the way my pap tucked it in the back of his wagon—the same way he wrapped up Ida when he took her away. I marvel that he could love all things and people, and wonder if he learned that in his doctoring books. Wouldn't hurt me to learn the same. Which leads me to think—if I could find those books, I might know more about saving the cubs.

I drive back to town with three wedding-ring quilts on the seat beside me. I stop first at Dooby's, and wait for him to finish filling a prescription.

"Do something for you, Olivia?" he asks from behind the glass partition. He counts tablets into a bottle.

I'm not sure how much I should say. If word gets out I have wolves on my place ... "I had a wild dog about the place, Dooby, and she's had babies. I've taken them in, but they're not doing well. Is there a way I can save 'em?"

"You've got no choice," he says. "You'll have to put 'em down."

"I can't do that."

"Well," he says. "She won't touch 'em now because they've got your smell on 'em."

"She's dead," I say. "And Will'm's got his heart set on keeping them."

Dooby sighs. Will'm has swept up and made deliveries for him these last two years. "Then I need to know about the bitch before I can do right by her pups."

"She—was part wolf," I say.

"What kind of dog would mix with a wolf?"

I'm a lot of things, but not a good liar. "They're wolf cubs, Dooby, but—"

"Shoot 'em, Olivia. They'll eat you and Will'm, and Ida, too."

"I don't plan on keeping them forever."

"But you'd have to," he says, looking up at me. "In for a penny, in for a pound. They'll depend on you. Won't know how to find so much as a blade of grass."

"If Pap was alive, he wouldn't turn them out just like that. Dooby, I had that she wolf in my kitchen all night, and if I'd known what to do for her, she'd be alive now."

Outside, cars shush by, and the clock over the fountain ticks away.

He clears his throat. "Your pap and I had an arrangement, Olivia."

"What kind of arrangement?"

He comes out from behind the counter, we sit on stools, and he opens two bottles of pop. The bell over the door jingles, and two ladies from up Mount Sumpter come in. "Help you, girls?" Dooby says, and he goes off to sell them things.

By the time he comes back, I have finished my drink.

"What arrangement?" I ask again.

"I used to trade supplies for your pap's home brew."

"Well, I'm sorry we're not making whiskey anymore, Dooby. But I can give you one of my best quilts in exchange. That's fair."

He thinks this over. "You promise me you aren't goin' to try to save every wounded thing, Olivia? I can't use more'n one quilt."

"I promise."

He shakes his head. "You're Tate Harker all over again. But—all right. My missus'd like a quilt fine."

I get down off my stool and go out to the truck and fetch him the red one with blue and white daisies, the one I like least.

Meanwhile, he gathers packets of things, marking each with his fountain pen. Chamomile to help the cubs sleep and ginger for the bellyache. Sulfur drops, tweezers, an eyedropper. A chest warmer of flannel that he cuts in pieces, jars of things to increase their appetites, strengthen their bones. He writes down how often and how much.

I tell him thank you. "Dooby, I recall my pap having doctoring books. You got any idea what might have happened to them?"

"Bet Ida could tell you, if she will. We all saw you goin' by this morning with that mule in your truck. A few of us thought Ida'd up and died, but Little Ruse said no, she'd just acted the fool again, and you'd got rid of it to teach her a lesson."

I say nothing. It's mostly true.

"Now you take this slip on over to the dairy, and Nels will give you a pint of sweetmilk for the pups and another next week. Good luck with all of this," he says. "And Olivia—bring home rabbits, possum if you got to—but no more wolves. They got mighty sharp teeth."

I leave the store with the parcels under my arms—and the certainty that the two doses of old chloroform I gave the gray probably sent her right out of her head. Maybe that's why she went through the window. If Ida hadn't shot her, some other thing would've got her.

I sit in my truck and contemplate the last two quilties. No matter how hard I try, I can't make myself go across to the hotel, and I drive back up the hill, irritated because I've kept the store closed and haven't done what I'd said. Anyway, I've got to feed those cubs that are costing me money in more ways than one. When Will'm gets home, he can clean out their straw.

Just now I can't afford to replace the broken window. And anyway, the view's nothing special. It looks out at the falling-down barn and the goat pen where the snow looks wallowed and dirty. I set the pie in the larder. Maybe in summer I'll sell an extra quilt and we'll have new glass in the kitchen window.

Ida, apparently, has taken her willow bark and gone off to sleep because there's not a peep from her side of the yard. And it's quiet in my kitchen, only a tiny mewling coming from the box on the table. In the farthest corner, one of the cubs is dead.

I sigh and feed the last two with the eyedropper Dooby gave me, and tuck them back in their box. I carry their brother and a big cooking spoon out to the rise, bury him next to his ma'am and say a prayer in Will'm's name. I mark the place with a stick. It's an extravagant funeral for so small a thing. But all living things do not feel about their ma'ams the way I do. In fact, maybe this one missed his so much, he went off to be with her.

That's what I'll tell Will'm when he comes home, that its dying was a loving thing.

30

Around noon, Levi the Box Man arrives, as he does regularly, and I go across to his supply truck and look through his stuff. I choose six tins of raisins and one of figs, a barrel of flour because it's what I can afford, another of sugar, three bolts of calico, for spring will be here if we live long enough, and four bottles of vanilla. I need coffee beans and brown sugar, cream of tartar, and rubbed sage. I choose a jar of licorice sticks, needles, pins, and tobacco, but I must turn down oranges and bananas, grated coconut and cheese. The store has a case for cooling things, and years ago I kept wedges of cheese, fresh-killed chickens, and smoked pork, but I unplugged it long ago.

I take eight bundles of batting—four for myself—and go into the kitchen and take out Phelps' twenty and another ten against my account. When Will'm comes home, he can restock the shelves. On Saturday, when he gets back from Dooby's, I'll send him to the barn to unwrap the batting and beat it with a stick to make it light. Then I'll put together the quiltie that's now just a shell. It's folded on the foot of my bed—a wedding-ring pattern in silver and gray. Tied in black it should bring a good price.

By three o'clock there's been no more business, and there's no reason not to put the quilts back in the truck and head for town. I'm fearfully nervous. A couple of cars are parked in front of the hotel, so I know Wing has guests. I marvel that anyone traveling through Kentucky knows this place is here, but I've heard the service is a wonder, and the beds so feather soft that folks keep coming back. They used to drink Wing's coffee by the gallon and gobble up hot cross buns, jelly rolls, and fruit turnovers. I wonder if he ever makes them anymore.

He's reworked the doorways to accommodate Miz Grace's wheelchair. I still love the smell in this old lobby—wood and wax, the only elegant place left around here. The carpet's as thick as when it was new. A round-faced girl, Molly, sits behind the counter, fingering her braids and reading a dime novel. Wing's bent over a glass case in the front window.

He sees me with the quilts on my arm, and, as if I'm Lazarus rising from the grave, he cries out, "Olivia! I'll be through here in half a minute—"

"No hurry." I'm grateful for a moment to settle myself. It's absurd, after all these years, but seeing him sucks the breath right out of me. "The place looks real nice."

"Thanks," he says. "I'm thinking of knocking out that side wall, adding a dining room. I'd only open it in summer, and maybe hunting season. Little Ruse says he'll come over and cook weekends if it doesn't offend his daddy."

I scare up a laugh. Little Ruse is forty-five. Big Ruse is crippled, and doesn't weigh eighty pounds. He still waits on customers, but has gotten so slow that the gravy's cold before it gets to the table.

Wing puts his hammer and screwdriver away in a toolbox. "Things all right up at your place? You haven't killed Ida yet?" he says, as if we've talked over coffee just yesterday.

While I look for my voice, I consider how much I should say. "We're fine."

"The boy's sure growing. I saw him at Dooby's last Saturday. Great kid—thoughtful. Takes after his gran."

I let that go by because Wing doesn't know me anymore. Like mine, his hair has gone partly gray. His glasses still sit on the end of his nose.

"Love Alice said you were puttin' in a shop."

"Just a case in this window. But it's something." He gives the glasses a push.

"Well. I was wondering . . ."

I'm an interruption in the flow of his life, an old woman in skirt and trousers and a heavy wool cape, thick hair wound around her head. For the life of me, I can't think why I'm here.

"You've brought quilts," Wing says, being helpful. He comes to look, runs his thumb over the stitching. "Good God, Olivia. In Louisville, these would bring a lot of money. I can't pay you much—"

"Don't expect you to pay me anything," I say, twitching and sweating under my clothes. "You sell them for five each, give me half."

Wing's face is still the most expressive I've seen—high flat cheekbones, only now the lines are so deep I could plant corn in them.

"Six," he says. "And I'll give you four."

"All right."

"I'm gonna wash up now. You got time for coffee?"

We've passed through the howdies. Is it possible that today we won't quarrel like we did all those years ago, won't hurt each other with words and hard looks?

I nod and leave the quilts on the counter—Molly smiles—and

I follow him down the hall to his kitchen. It's painfully familiar. He takes down the percolator and puts water in the bottom, grinds beans, and spoons in the powder. I remember where the cups used to be, but I stand by the table like a ghost of myself.

"Get the milk from the icebox, will you?" he says.

I pour it in a cream pitcher he's set on the table.

"I heard you sold that old mule," he says while we wait for the water to boil.

"I did. To Alton Phelps."

The coffee perks, a comfortable sound.

Wing nods. "His buddies take rooms here sometimes."

"They the ones that hunt up there on my land?"

"I wouldn't know about that, Olivia."

"It's been posted no trespassing for years. And it's not like they're killing for food."

"I'm sorry," he says, pouring coffee. "It's winter business for me, so don't be quick to pass judgment."

"Judgment?" I say.

Goddamn, I'm irritated now. Down the hall, I hear coughing, and a voice tiny as a child's calls out. Wing says, "Excuse me a minute. There're cinnamon buns in the box, there."

Wing's kitchen is purely his—white-painted wood and spoons and flapjack turners in a half dozen sizes hanging on hooks. Iron skillets and newfangled gadgets, a big enamel stove with six burners and a warming shelf. He always loved to cook, was a great hand with stirring and kneading and winding fancy braided pastry with jam in the center, or raisins and currants and walnuts. It surprises me that his breads and pecan tarts haven't fattened up his wife. I guess nothing can save her.

I haven't seen Miz Grace in a long time. Even when she was well, I avoided her. When I'd spot her in town, I'd nod and hurry by, and if she was at Dooby's counter, I'd pay eight cents for a tin of something that I didn't really need, and rush out the door. I'm sure she knows who I am—Saul knew her to speak to, and Ida did, too.

After a while, Wing comes back, and we sit looking at each other across the table. I have a hundred things to talk about, but nothing to say.

"Sugar?" he says.

I shake my head.

"You used to put sugar in your coffee."

"So I did." I don't remind him that sugar costs money, and I save it now for Will'm, and to soothe Ida when she raises holy hell. I sip my coffee. His shirtsleeves are rolled up, and there's white paint on his knuckles—and calluses, too. I wonder if Love Alice ever turns his hands over and reads the palms.

"I'm going to lose her soon," he says. "Love Alice told me. Even if she hadn't, I'd know."

I nod, because a truth is a truth. Also, I have never known Love Alice to be wrong. "You've taken care of her a long time. What are you going to do when she's gone?" It's a stupid question. I can't remember when I was this uncomfortable.

"Dress her in pink and put her in the ground, I guess."

"The earth'll be grateful to have her." As odd as that might sound, it's a fact, and I'm safe saying it.

He smiles. "I'd forgotten how you are about the earth," he says. "How you love spring. Don't think Grace is gonna make it till then. I hope the ground thaws."

I nod.

"And then," he says, "I'll probably cry awhile. And watch the grass grow back on top of her."

"Be nice if you played your trumpet over her."

He takes a swallow of coffee. "Hadn't thought of that."

"Wing—can I ask you something?"

He looks up at me.

"I know you don't remember my pap. He died before you came here, but—"

He puts his fingers together and his eyes focus on the wall. "Well, I heard of him, and you showed me a picture once. Tall, wasn't he? And thin as a pencil. Fine-looking man—that's where you get your eyes."

Wing saying that sets my face afire.

He sees, and laughs. "I heard he was good with four-legged things. Little Ruse told me once that your pap caught him hunting in the woods, asked him what he was shooting. Ruse told him he was out to drop a few bluejays, and right then and there your pap snatched the rifle away from him. Told him not to shoot anything unless he could eat it or it could shoot back. Then he drove off in his truck. When Ruse got home, his rifle was propped up on the front porch, waiting for him."

He looks into his cup.

"Wing, you could be boarding the people who are shooting my wolves." I hate that I'm spoiling for a fight.

"I can't take on every battle, Olivia. I'm too old."

I want to tell him about the wolf, about Ida, and the pups. Once, I told Wing everything, and I want to open my mouth and let the lost decades come out in a flood. But I can't. Instead, I say stupidly and without thinking, "Pap was the only person who ever truly loved me."

I busy myself breaking up a bun, and wish I could take the words back.

But he smiles his crooked smile and sets his empty cup down. "I expect he loves you still."

I let that tumble around in my head. "You don't think we stop feeling when we're gone from the earth?"

"I don't know. But I believe our souls go on, and if anything, I suspect they love more. You used to believe souls come again. Brand-new lives."

"I still do, but I haven't thought about what happens between times. Sometimes I think heaven and hell are here on earth."

"Maybe," he says.

"The body can get tired of loving," I say, and realize I've again been thoughtless with my words.

"Sometimes."

I get up because I fear where this conversation is going. I stack the dishes in the sink.

"Leave them," Wing says. "Sit here and talk to me."

But down the hall, Grace coughs again, and Wing rubs his eyes.

"I have to go," I say.

He nods. "I'll take care of the quilts."

I hurry down the hall and out the front door—into cold air that stings my eyes and burns my skin, and I stand on the sidewalk and try to get my bearings. It's been a week of firsts. I'm fighting to save wolf cubs in my kitchen. After thirty years, I've been down to the basement room. And most frightening of all— a cup of coffee in Wing's hotel kitchen is threatening to wake in me something I thought was dead.

I shake my head, and then lift it at a round of rifle shots from above my place. Another wolf is gone, I'm sure. I cross the street and open the truck door, my mittens freezing to the ice on the handle. My hands shake so badly I can hardly start the engine.

Blindly, I drive the road that runs around the foot of the mountain, and I park just beyond the bridge to Waynesboro. It's an easier climb from here to the Ridge. I cram my hat on and make my way up the wash, using the stones for climbing until they run out. I veer to the left a quarter mile where the going is less of an incline, listening. Another shot. Two. Three. The trees are thicker here, and from the middle of this grove, I can't see the sky.

I am too old and too fat for this, but my brain is fired up. It doesn't take long to find the wolves. I can't figure out why the hunter doesn't drag them away so I don't come upon them—then the answer is clear. He wants me to see their suffering. Does he somehow think his own suffering compares? Although I have always despised the Phelpses, if I could erase that terrible night and restore James Arnold's life, I would gladly do it. Then I'd have Pap here with me, whole and well and making moonshine.

The grays form a circle, their snouts striped and front paws stretched out like at the last minute they decided to run. One's pure gray, and two are darker about the chest and neck. All have been shot neatly in the head. Blood has trickled from the tiny round holes, and it glazes their eyes. All three have bloody gashes and clean white bone where their right ears once were. I drop to my knees and dry-heave tears while my body cramps as if I'm in the throes of some terrible illness.

Three more Alaskan silvers down. Before long, predators will find them, and only carcasses will be left. I wish, instead, it was the hunter lying here in the snow with his ear cut off. I'd leave him to the buzzards so they could sharpen their beaks on his scrawny bones. I can hardly make my way down to the truck. I'm fevered about the wolves, and sad for Wing, angry with Ida, and miserable for Will'm. The boy has no ma'am, he has only me. And I'm sure he sometimes feels just like one of the cubs.

31

There is no money anywhere in Pope County, nor in the rest of these United States, as far as I can see. There are government programs like the WPA, and the National Children's Fund that sends me one dollar and eighty cents a month for Will'm's care, but that doesn't begin to feed him. Not that I must have a dime—I'd give up my life for the boy anytime.

On the other hand, I'd give up anybody I saw hunting on the mountain. If an eye for an eye is a biblical thing, how can an ear for an ear be any different? Perhaps I'd just shoot off the hunter's ear, sending him bloody and howling, the way he's done the wolves. The more I think about it, the more I like the idea. I am aware, however, that left alive, he would have me arrested, and I'd be hauled over to Paramus where I'd sit in a cell, waiting for a trial that would put me away.

I'm sure it's Phelps, him and his odd sayings that give me the heebie-jeebies. I've seen his small boot prints, and studied the boots he was wearing. And I've heard his laughter high on the hill. It's a good thing it's raining this next morning, for neither of us can go up. Which gives me time to think—some good I'll be to the boy if I'm doing a lifetime of incarceration over at Kingston Penitentiary.

And thus my brain travels—twisting and spinning. I end up

thinking that on Sunday, I'll wring the neck of our scrawniest hen, the one that's given up laying, and cook it for supper. Maybe that'll satisfy my need for blood.

Rain's pouring down. I stomp out to the barn and locate a rubber slicker that I drop over my head, and I milk the goat, sitting on the stool with my feet apart and rain running off my hat because the lean-to roof is as bad off as the barn. Thunder shakes things up good. I cover the milk bucket with a big tin pie plate and set it on the step, hike back out to the chicken pen. The rooster struts around under the coop's overhang. Beneath the seven hens that need fattening, I find five eggs—I'll put two in the store and keep three for us.

I hang my slicker on the porch. In the dark kitchen, I feed the cubs while the storm crashes against the windows. I rub their bodies with a cloth warmed in the oven, and give them Dooby's tonic and oats thinned with milk. They settle down to sleep in a ball so tight I can't tell where one ends and the other begins. I stand over them, counting their tiny ribs while they breathe like each sucking-in is their last. They need true doctoring, and I need Pap's books.

When the rain slows up, I put on my hat and cape and go out to the barn where the truck is parked. I guess Ida has been watching because she flies out of her house, her nightgown trailing in the slushy snow. She has her boots on, untied and flapping.

"I'm hungry, Olivia. Where you goin'?"

"To fetch Junk Hanley," I tell her.

"Don't you bring that ugly man here," she says. "He scares the daylights outa me. He's got no business on white man's property."

"I'd move him and his in with me," I tell her. I scrape the ice off the driver's side window.

"Wouldn't hurt you to pay mind to what *I* want."

"Stop screeching, Ida. I can hear you all right."

She hugs her arms. "How come you don't take *me* out in this truck, Olivia?"

"Tomorrow morning," I say. "Put your clothes on, and your coat, and I'll drive you to Buelton."

"I ain't goin' to Buelton," she says, her eyes skidding. "You'd take me back to that asylum place."

The truck door is open, and my mouth's open, too. "You remember the hospital?"

But she's turned and gone, apparently forgetting breakfast, although there's hot water in the kettle and I've set cold biscuits and jam on the table. She waves her hands as if she's directing traffic, and her nightgown flaps. It's hard to know just how daft Ida is.

32

Rain has turned the snow sloppy, but the temperature is dropping and soon things will again freeze solid. In the mist, I drive past town and up Rowe Street, thinking about Ida's remembering. I wonder if I'll land in the asylum someday, too. I park in front of Junk's, get out, and knock on the door.

Miz Hanley comes to the door. "Why, it's our Livvy," she says, leaning on her cane.

I see she's gotten feeble, too, but I bet she's not one bit worried that Junk's going to put *her* away somewhere.

"If you aren't a sight for these eyes!"

I shake the damp from my hat and kiss her soft, wrinkled cheek. Her bosoms lay on her belly, and she seems smaller. Her kitchen, however, still smells of fried onions.

"I've come to see Junk. Is he home?"

"Sit a minute, and tell me how you are."

Bare as it is, I love this old house. Not one thing in it has ever been painted, and every inch is silvered from scrubbing.

"I'm all right."

"You and the boy gettin' on fine, then," she says.

I remember how easy it was to talk to her when I was small, how everything I said was something to be considered. "We are.

Will'm's gone and saved himself a pair of orphaned wolf cubs. I'll swear, I don't see how we're gonna keep them alive."

"You givin' 'em mo-lasses?" she says.

"I am. And sulfur, tinned milk. Things Dooby gave me."

"Well, ol' Mr. Dooby don't know ever'thang."

Junk comes in and stands listening. He's polite with his ma'am, not like I am with mine, sassing and saying what's on my mind. A thought comes to me, then—it's true that I tell Ida what I think, but I *never* say what I feel.

"First off," Miz Hanley says, "that she wolf kilt whatever rat or field mouse she could find, and ate 'em, and them being in her, her babies got the same. You got to get Will'm to catch a rabbit."

"If we had a rabbit, we'd eat it ourselves."

She laughs. " 'Pends on how bad you want 'em to live. 'Course, they also miss they mama's lovin'. Will'm don't know how to be a mama unless you show him."

"Miz Hanley, I'll tell you right now, I wasn't a good hand at being a ma'am."

"You took care of your girl the best you could. When she ran off, it weren't 'cause you didn't love her. And you done a pure wonder with that boy."

I don't want this wound opened, and I hate that what's under the skin is so raw. "I wouldn't count on that."

Miz Hanley pinches her lips together. "Well, I'm goin' to tell you now, like I shoulda tol' you then."

"I wasn't your responsibility," I say.

"I loved you like you was my own," she says. "You an' your pappy was good people all your lives. Someday before I die, I gon' tell you more truths than your head can hold. Right now, you need to know how to do for them pups."

"Yes, ma'am," I say.

She fiddles with the top two buttons on her dress, and Junk and I both draw back, but she laughs. Her neck is wattly and her chest is sunken. "You take one a them cubs," she says, "and you lay it belly down on your chest. *Here.* Put a blanket 'round both of you. They feel your heartbeat. Yo' breathin'. They think you're their mammy, they might stay on this earth."

I nod and change the subject. "Junk, it's time I cleaned out my cellar. I'd be pleased if you'd help."

"I wouldn't mind at all, Miz Livvy," he says.

Miz Hanley is buttoning her dress.

"Well, then," I say. "We'll start as soon as you're free."

"I'll come on up when I've finished choppin' for Aunt Pinny Albert."

His mama reaches up and pats his hand.

I thank her again and drive home to make lunch for Ida and the cubs. But Ida's asleep on her cot, her pipe having burned out in a saucer. Her soup is cold, but the buttered bread will be all right in its cloth. In the house, I put away the jam and throw crumbs to the chickens.

Junk comes in the middle of the afternoon. He's got a wide broom, a mop, and a gallon bucket of some kind of cleaner. For the mildew, he says. I unlock the cellar door and light a lamp.

"Everything goes," I say, following him down. "But there's one thing, Junk—my pap had a couple of big black books, and we need 'em badly if Will'm's to keep the cubs alive."

"Yes, ma'am."

"This cellar'll make a fine storeroom," I say bravely, but the farther we descend the less certain I feel.

I pull on the light chain, and the shadows retreat, but I'm glad Junk leaves the extra lamp burning. Love Alice looks down from the doorway.

"I'll make us tea in a while," I call up. "And there's a bit of sip-pin' whiskey for Junk when we're done. Lord knows he'll need it."

The whiskey is a new turn of events for me. It riles Ida, who says it's another rung on my ladder to hell, but a drop of it puts me to sleep when nothing else will. Right now, the important thing is to clear out this place. I lift a pair of cages from their pegs.

"Go on and take down those old shelves," I tell Junk.

They fall apart in his hands.

I use wire cutters on the dog runs and then leave him to scrub the four high windows that will let in light when the snow thaws. I tuck up my skirt, and take a hammer to the wall that separates the room that once was my pap's. After an hour, we're down to the center beam. We leave it, because, as Junk says, it holds the place up. He remarks that there's hardly any water seepage, and I ought to think about putting in a coal furnace as it would keep us warmer, but I say I've no way to pay for furnace nor coal. Junk says ain't that the truth.

There are boxes of powder that have turned to solid, and bot-tles of crystallized liquid. Rolls of tubing and tins of syringes, dried and rusty. He piles it all at the foot of the steps, says he'll bury it later. In the end, I'd be more help if I got out of his way, and I hand him the hammer so he can get on with the work.

Upstairs, Love Alice and I drink our tea with a drop of whiskey and a lot of sugar.

She says, "Spirits is good for our throats in this kind of weather."

Presently the door bell jingles, and I get up to see, but it's Will'm coming through. He pecks my cheek and puts his books on the table, seems surprised that the cellar door's open. I tell him he can go down, see what the hammering's about. He comes back up with a look on his face that says I should have waited till he was home, or at least told him my plan. He never gave me trouble about the locked door. I forget that when a body goes and leaps off his own private cliff, he leaves behind the people who knew him, and all they can do is stand there and mourn.

At least the cubs are familiar to him, and he goes to their box and lifts out one and then the other. He doesn't say much, but sits and strokes the fuzz that now covers their hindquarters. Junk lumbers up the stairs, puffing, carrying great armloads of stuff. He's already made several trips to the barn, where he's stacking the reusable wood.

Will'm rocks the cubs and croons to them.

Love Alice sips her tea. She's saying something—that she hitches a ride over to Buelton once a week, telling her truths to the Ladies Club there, and she and Junk hope to make enough money to pay rent on a house of their own soon.

Presently Ida comes across, carrying the empty soup bowl and her Bible.

"I could hear the racket clear to my place," she says, "and I knew you was up to something bad."

She stands at the top of the stairs in her slippers and shawl, clucking her tongue and wanting to know what's going on down there that's woke a righteous woman from her sleep. She shouts passages from the Book of Job while Junk hauls the dog runs and smaller cages up and out into the yard and scrubs them down with soap and water. He thinks they can be traded or sold. Ida scurries into the grocery every time he comes through the kitchen, then rushes back to peer down the stairs.

"You-all are goin' to hell!" she hollers.

"How's that, Miss Ida?" Love Alice chirps.

Ida sniffs. "This is all very upsettin'."

"It's my house," I tell her. "And it needed cleaning."

"Olivia, you are like the rich man, and the past is the eye of the needle."

Be that as it may. Junk has ripped out the mildewed wood. The one great disappointment is that I have not found Pap's doctoring books. I realize now that those books have become my personal crusade. I recall watching him make notes on the pages. Maybe it's his handwriting I need most—something to tell me he was really here.

There's only one other place the books might be—maybe Ida packed them up with her things when she moved to the cabin.

When Junk and Love Alice are gone, I go downstairs one more time. It's not a bad place, this cleaned-out room. Right now, it's colder than a well rope, but in summer it might be a fine spot for me and the boy to set a table, pull up our chairs, and eat a cool supper.

Will'm, at the top of the stairs, says nothing.

Ida, on the other hand, hasn't stopped talking. "God will look in your heart and see how cruel you have been, Olivia," she says. "Now fix me my supper—'fore a God-fearing woman starves to death."

I lock the cellar door. I can't help it.

That night, just before dark, I hear a volley of shots from the hill. Will'm covers the cubs, and, across the table, he looks at me. I'll bet money, marbles, and chalk that at least one more wolf is dead.

33

It's been twenty-four hours since Junk and I were in the cellar. Will'm's gone off to school, riding the bus beneath a threatening sky, and Ida sits at the table, eyeing the cubs' box and spooning up her breakfast. I'm tacking a quilt, a pale pink one with great dark roses. I've embroidered stems in a satin stitch, with leaves and thorns and curlicues. Although I've got two hanging in the grocery window, it's been a while since I sold a quilt.

I think out loud. "I've given them sulfur and molasses. I've tried every damn thing I can think of—all that Dooby's given me."

"Well, they're not getting my oats," says Ida. Thunder rolls, shaking the house like a tin cookie sheet. The rain beats hard against the window. Such a storm is almost unheard of this time of year, and it'll either melt the snow or freeze a new layer of ice over top of it all. Now that I've begun cleaning, I don't seem able to stop. I put down my work and take my cape from its hook.

"Where are you going?" Ida twists in her chair.

"To your house."

"What for?"

Ida's eyes are wild, but I am pulling on my boots. I go out the back door, into the rain. She leaves her breakfast and follows me.

"I want to find Pap's books!" I shout over the rain. "I think you may have them."

I open the door and stand in the musty room, dropping my cape and shaking out my hair, still in its night braid. Boxes are stacked everywhere, sour and sagging with dampness, and splitting at the corners.

"You can't touch my things without me saying so!"

"Then you'd better give me permission," I tell her, " 'cause that's exactly what I'm going to do."

I pull the first box to the middle of the room, on a colorless rag rug that butts up against the iron footboard of Ida's bed. The box has gathered years of moisture, and inside, wrapped in newspaper, are a half dozen chipped porcelain figures, a dictionary, and seven cups with no saucers. The next is a box of dresses I've never seen her wear. Hairpins, tins of buttons, dried roots wrapped in waxed paper, empty snuff jars, an old nightgown.

"Why do you keep all this stuff?" I ask her.

In her filthy gown, Ida sits primly on the edge of her bed. "My things are none of your business."

She's right, of course. This is her property. It's so sinfully little to show for a lifetime—three blue dinner plates, a faded evening gown, worn-out boots, a tarnished silver pitcher. Two of the boxes hold nothing but crumpled paper. I stack them outside the door.

"That pitcher was a wedding present," she says.

I can't imagine Ida as a bride. I sit back and put my hands in my lap. "Why did you ever marry Pap?"

"To get away from my own, if you got to know," she said. "He was a preacher man, like some kind of joke. Tate—" She paused. "Tate promised he'd take care of me for all his life. You see how he lied?"

I wrap everything and put it back, stack the boxes against the walls. "He didn't lie to you, Ida. He couldn't see his own death."

"His death was your fault, Olivia!" she shouts after me. "And you owe me an apology."

I turn in the rain and the muddy snow. "I apologize for not first getting your permission to look through your things," I call back to her. "But I'm mad as hell at you for throwing away Pap's things!"

"Why? What good were they?"

"They were his! And now they should be mine!" I shield my face with my hand. The rain has turned cold and it stings my cheeks. "There's nothing left to tell me what he was like! Or—or who I am."

"I can tell you who you are."

"You never *stop* telling me!"

She comes in the house behind me, sits down to her cold porridge. "Make us a fresh pot of tea, Olivia."

"Go home, Ida," I say. "Put on a dry nightgown. I'll bring you coffee later."

I take off my wet cape and go through the hall to the bathroom, pause at the same mirror Saul looked into while he shaved every morning, all the years he was with me. Here, in the glass, is the woman I've become. Great dark blue eyes, a set chin, a once-pretty curve of jaw, a mouth that has not worn lipstick since the night at the juke joint when I told a man named Percy that Pauline was his. It's no wonder that, sixteen years later, my Pauline did damn near the same. I never warned her, never said, *Pauline, here's what happens if you go down to the juke joint and come home with a baby. It'll change your life, and you can't ever go back.*

I come out of the bathroom. Ida is still sitting, wrapped in her blanket that's dripping on the floor.

"I told you to go home," I say.

"I can't. That ugly nigra is banging on the back door."

"What?"

"That man from Rowe Street."

I open the back door. Junk Hanley stands on the porch. His shoulders are hunched, and he holds his hat in his hands so that rain splashes on his head and runs down his face.

"Junk, come in here and get warm, have coffee—"

He looks past me at Ida and shakes his head. "No, ma'am, not just now. I come to tell you sumpin'."

"What is it? Is Love Alice all right?"

His eyes are full of sorrow. "Miss Livvy—Mr. Harris's wife—she's comin' to the end. She was scarcely breathin' around sunrise. And now he's askin' for you."

34

I scribble a note for Will'm on the back of a paper bag—fry an egg, and another for Ida. An orange apiece, a cup of tea. Brown bread, but not too much jam.

I squeeze the remains of the milk and honey into the pups' mouths, impatient to be away. Then Junk and I pile in the truck and set out in the rain that's turned to sleet. We slide partway, and it's a wonder we don't end up in the ditch or the river, for my heart's in my mouth and I drive like a mad person. On Main Street I run up on the curb, and we get out and go into the hotel.

There's no one at the desk. Junk says, "I'm gon' make sure them Ruses get home in this weather. I'll check on you-all later."

I hoped Wing would be in the kitchen, but he's not. I take the front stairs, but he's not on the second floor. Nor is he on the top floor, either, nor in the public bathrooms. Fool, I tell myself—his wife's on her deathbed, where else would he be? It's the one thing I've dreaded, seeing Miz Grace Harris, but it cannot be helped.

The side hall that leads to their parlor and bedroom is dark. I dare not call out, for I don't want to wake anything, nor send up so much as a particle of dust. I feel as if I'm trespassing on a carpet of eggs. I peek around the parlor door, but the room is empty.

Across the hall, he's sitting in a cane-back rocker by Miz Grace's bed, and his back is to me.

The room is papered in faded rosebuds and decorated with creamy curtains and embroidered pillow slips—likely done at the hand of the woman who seems lost, now, in the big bed. Her face is mostly bone, and her cornsilk hair is spun in ringlets. An odd sound comes from her throat when she breathes, the same way Will'm sounded when he took the whooping cough. I step in, feeling large and clumsy. My hat is in my hands.

Wing hears me, turns, and comes out of his chair like a very old man. "Olivia—"

I step back into the hall, but not before Miz Grace's eyes open, enormous green eyes with lids like butterfly wings.

"Come in," Wing says.

I know I must pay my respects, but I feel like I've stepped in quicksand.

Miz Grace turns her head, her eyes on my face. Her lips part slightly, and my name flutters out.

"Wing. Miz Grace," I say with a nod.

Her fingers move, a command to sit. I unbutton my cape. Wing takes it, and I ease into the rocker.

"Well," she says. " 'Livia. Tell me—about yourself."

I look to Wing, but he's busy hanging my things in the wardrobe, like I'm going to stay. I have no idea what to say. Her eyes flutter down, and I think that when she opens them maybe she'll have forgotten. Then I can talk about something else.

"Little Ruse has baked a chocolate cake," I say. "We smelled it out in the street, Junk and I. Ruse buys his bars of cooking chocolate at our place."

She nods, as if that was important information.

I look to the window. "It's stopped raining, it's ice that's coming down now. Sleet. And—it's near four o'clock. My grandbaby—Will'm—will be getting off the school bus. He'll find the note I left him. He'll be heaping jam on bread—two, three slices. Then he'll eat it right off the spoon."

Again, her eyes have closed, but she opens them when I stop. It seems a great effort for her, lifting those transparent lids, so I keep on. "I put up jam in summer—sandplum, apricot—he loves apricot. Not many strawberries around here, but plenty of blackberries. Love Alice Hanley and I go berry picking in summer. We take mustard sandwiches and—"

I don't know whether she's sleeping or not. I keep talking, mostly to cover the sound of her dying. "I've two wolf cubs in a paper box by my stove. Tucked into an old wool robe. They're hungry all the time. They've lost their ma, and Will'm, he's feeding them molasses and milk with a dropper. Thinks he can keep them alive—"

What an awful thing I have said.

She watches me through shuttered eyes.

"You should sleep now," I say.

"No…"

I search my brain. "Love Alice Hanley. If you don't know Love Alice, she's a sight. Freckles on her nose, never hurt a soul. She's got this gift—she can look at you and see your truth, that's what she calls it. She had a baby once—"

"I know—who you are," she says.

"Ma'am?"

"Wing—talks about you."

I don't know why this strikes terror in me. I look around, but Wing's gone, and I wonder if she's waited for this moment to accuse me of something. I'm guilty of so many things. I wonder if she's privy to Love Alice's gift, and maybe I'm the only one in the world that can't see the future. Or the past.

"I can't imagine why," I say.

She tries to cough. I want to clear my throat for her, cover her mouth with mine, breathe air into her. Her lips stretch out, a smile almost. It's a moment when truth is all that's left, and it passes between us with such force that I hang my head and close my eyes. I rock softly, and when her fingers flutter on the coverlet, I hitch the rocker forward and reach for them. Her hands are as cold as last month. I get up and go to the lobby, to the rack Wing's set up in the window, and bring her my best pink quiltie, cover her gently, slide one pale hand underneath. Then I sit by her bed, and the rocker makes its cricket sounds while I hold her other hand.

She sleeps for a long time, long enough for me to think that when she's gone into death, and rested sufficiently, she'll come again. After all, if it's intended for us to strive toward perfection, God wouldn't expect us to get it right in just one try. And I wonder other things—like, standing at the gates of life, whether a soul chooses its own body, or if it knows what's ahead. And, if *that's* the case, why would I choose to be born to Ida? Lord knows, I'm no hero.

After a while I feel Miz Grace looking at me. "Livia—"

"Yes'm," I say, leaning close.

"I want to go out in the snow," she says.

"Oh no." I tuck the quiltie tighter. "It's fearfully cold."

"Please."

There's a bowl of water on her bedside table, and a linen towel. I wring it out and wipe her forehead. There's lavender, too, for dabbing her wrists, and I fix her hair.

She reaches for my hand. "Livia—please."

My back is aching, and my heart is heavy. This is more than I can bear. As I pass through the lobby, Junk comes in, wrapped in a whirl of wet wind and stamping his feet. There's snow on his coat, and I can see by the outside light that it's coming down hard.

"Miz Livvy?" he says. "You-all need anything here?"

"My truck—"

"It's done buried out here. You ain't goin' no place this night."

"But Will'm's alone at the house—and Ida."

Junk rubs his hands together. Blows on them. "Doc Pritchett's boy brung his sleigh down. I'll catch a ride up with him, an' say you're still here."

"Thank you, and—would you mind staying on at the house tonight?"

"Don't mind at all. I'll send word to Love Alice."

"And, Junk, there are eggs and bread in the larder. And you sleep in the four-poster."

"All right, then," he says, although I know he won't. He'll have brown bread and coffee, and spend the night on the kitchen floor, but Will'm will see to blankets and a pillow. Junk hunches his shoulders and goes out in the storm. I close the front doors and slide the bolt.

Wing is in the kitchen, his chair drawn up to the dark window, elbows on the sill. The glass is frosted over, and snow has piled up, outside and in. I put the kettle on, and set out cups, rummage in the icebox for supper things. There's ham for slicing, and bread and butter, and some cold potatoes that I chop with butter in a skillet. It's odd, cooking in this kitchen.

"Wing?" I say after a while, and he comes to the table, sits with his shoulders slumped, staring at his plate. I slide his tea across. "Please eat something."

"She won't last the night," he says.

"Probably not."

"Twenty-two years."

"Yes."

"Life is hellaciously strange," he says.

I pick up my fork, but Wing hunches over, and his hands fold over his face. A terrible sound rises out of him, so that I stumble from my chair to stand helplessly behind him, then wrap my arms around him. We rock a little, him shaking and me holding on.

"You shouldn't be here," he says. "I shouldn't have—"

"Hush."

" 'Livia—"

"Wing. She wants to go outside."

He looks at me as if I'm speaking Chinese.

"She wants to see the snow."

"What for?"

I shrug. "I think we ought to take her. We could wrap her up, just for a few minutes."

"Olivia—"

"Wing—how many things has she asked for?"

From the attic, Wing brings down her wheeled wicker chair, and I dust it and line it with a woolen blanket. We wheel it in, and she sees, and smiles, and Wing turns back the covers. She reminds me of one of Will'm's cubs. Wing lifts her as easily as if she were a baby. He puts her in the chair, and I wrap a towel around her feet and add the quiltie, folded into six, she's that small. Then we trundle her into the lobby, and Wing stops while I lift the blanket around her ears and over her head. She looks like the Mother Mary from the Christmas pageant at the Methodist church. I open the door, and a great swoop of snow rushes in. Wing wheels her out backward, shielding her from the wind.

Every light in town is on—Ruse's Cafe lit up inside and out even though it's closed, colored lights over the old newspaper office, the general store, and another row on the barber pole. Left from the holidays, I guess. A lamppost burns at the end of the block, and lights shine from a few windows on the northern slope. Headlights move slow out on the highway. The whiteness of the snow multiplies all that by a hundred, and Miz Grace Harris frees her hands to clap them like a child.

She pushes back the woolen hood, and lifts her face. Snow settles on her pale brows and lashes, and she licks a flake from her lip, and a sigh escapes, sailing up past the top floors of the hotel and into the inky sky.

Easy as that, Miz Grace Harris passes, on Main Street, with every light winking and blinking, and Wing trembling at her feet, his face buried in her lap.

35

There comes a thaw over the next day and a half that surpasses record, and I am able to trek down and bring home the truck. The sun is brilliant, and it warms the kitchen, even though we've still only one window because I've not fixed the other. In the box by the stove, the cubs are fading. Will'm's anxiety is enormous. Something has shifted in me, too, maybe from watching Grace Harris leave this earth. I believe she wanted to go on and be done with it—for herself and so's Wing could get on with his life. Maybe she contrived the whole thing, and if that's the case, I admire her more than I've admired another soul.

All this coming after so many years of don't-utter-his-name, when I'd have fallen to the floor in a lovesick heap if Wing had so much as walked through my door.

We are quiet, the two of us, Will'm with a bit of a cold—and me ladling up oats. I've kept him home from school today, lest he take the croup, the possibility of which he's not yet outgrown.

I give him blackstrap molasses on a spoon, and there'll be a poultice around his neck at bedtime. Come right down to it, I'm terrified of losing him. He says nothing when I set his bowl in front of him, and I put on my cape and carry Ida's dollop of oats and a bit of bread. A cup of weak coffee. I cross the yard. It's dark in her cabin, the single window covered with an old sheet. Inside, I pull it back to let in some light. But Ida's not in her bed, nor in the chair, nor rooting around in her moldy boxes. She's not in the cabin at all—and she wasn't in the outhouse, which I've just passed. I set down the breakfast things and go back out, calling her name.

"Ida?" I stump off to the barn. "For God's sake, Ida, where've you gotten yourself off to?"

But she is not there, nor in the toolshed, or sitting in the truck—places I've sometimes found her when she was mad at me. I study my own boot tracks, winding 'round and messing up the snow, which is rapidly turning to water in the sun. There are no clear prints that match Ida's tiny feet, and that turns my stomach cold. It's still early. She may have been gone for a while—but where? Up the mountain?

"Ida!"

Along the road? Maybe she's taken off across some pasture, forgotten where she lives, gotten into a car.

"I'm going to look for her," I tell the boy.

He sniffles and runs his hand under his nose.

"Use your handkerchief, Will'm. She's wandered off, I guess. Can't imagine anyone taking her."

He's done with his oats, and pushes back his chair. "I'll help."

"No you won't," I say. I can feel the pulse hammering in my neck. "I'll take the truck, ask if anyone's seen her. Get dressed, Will'm, and mind the store. Weather's broken, there ought to be customers today."

He nods.

I back the truck out and head into town. There are cars everywhere, women taking covered dishes into the hotel. Doc, who doubles as undertaker, came early yesterday and filled out a death certificate. I'm sure a half dozen ladies have already arranged Miz Grace Harris for viewing. I wonder if all this puts a damper on Wing's business, and if he'll ever sleep in the rosebud room again.

I stop in at the drugstore, but Dooby shakes his head. "Ain't seen her, Olivia. But I'll put out the word."

"Dooby, Will'm's got a cold, don't know if he'll be worth anything tomorrow—"

"With the funeral and all, there won't be much business. I'll send a powder up for him. It'll ease his throat."

I take my coin purse from my pocket and open it.

"No, no," Dooby says, handing me the paper. "I take care of my employees."

If Ida has walked the highway, I cannot tell. There are no boot tracks along the side of the road. No one at the gas station has seen her, nor at any of the other places where I stop. I head back, this time taking the county road, stopping three or four times to shade my eyes and study the fields. I pull into our driveway, imagining her tucked in her smelly bed, complaining of cold coffee and sucking on her pipe—but she has not come home.

Will'm has two customers, and is doing well behind the register, even with his red nose and watery eyes. He sees my question and shakes his head. I take off in the other direction.

No one on Rowe Street has seen her. She has not been to Doc's, nor the schoolhouse where the teacher looks up at me but goes on reading aloud. Nor is she at Meltons' Garage, nor the pawn shop, nor Ashy Rosie's, which is a juke joint for coloreds. She's not wandering in the graveyard or along the creek bed. There are no holes in the ice so she hasn't fallen through and drowned. I pass Phelps' place, its driveways all cleared and looking like a postcard, and on out the winding road. About a half mile east, on the steps of the First Baptist Church, I see Ida hunkered down with her nightgown tucked around her ankles. I pull in and park next to the porch.

"About time you got here," she says when I get out and come around. "My feet are cold."

"For God's sake, what are you doing here? And where are your boots?"

She looks at her feet. They're dirty and bleeding and purpled up, great gashes crusted with mud and grime, the nails broken off. "I've lost my boots—"

I take off my cape, wrap it around her twice. "You can't go wandering off like this. You scared the bejesus out of us. What were you thinking?"

"You never take me anywhere, Olivia. God knows what a disappointing daughter you turned out to be."

"For the love of God—"

How ragged she is, so sad and lost that I can't even look at her. How has it come to this—Ida with her accusations and me hating her so much I can't be anything other than what she says I am. "Let's get you in the truck—"

"I can't walk in bare feet!"

"You got this far, didn't you?"

But I lift her in. Her nightgown is muddy, her hair matted. She weighs almost nothing, her legs so thin I could snap them like twigs. When did this happen, all this thinness, this loss? And how am I to keep this from happening again? I imagine tying Ida to her bed, putting her on a tether like the goats, running chicken wire around her place. She huddles on the other side of the seat, and I drive carefully so as not to jolt her, or break her.

"I know what you did, Olivia," she says.

I'm suddenly so tired I could slump over the steering wheel and go to sleep.

"What have I done?"

"You wanted me to leave." At first her voice is thin and wavering, but it strengthens, fueled by a new accusation. "You followed me. You made sure I lost my boots."

I work at keeping my eyes on the road.

"I didn't lose them at all!" she says. "You stole them!"

There's nothing for me to do but keep driving, although I want to leap from the truck and watch it carry Ida across the field and into the creek. What possible debt are we laboring under that makes us think we must care for old people?

I stop at Dooby's to say that I've found her, and I'm grateful that he asks no questions. Although my breath turns to ice on the inside of the windows, I'm not cold at all. There's a burning in my stomach, and in back of my eyes. I take her home. There's no point in talking to her—she's concerned only about her boots, and not much about them.

In five minutes, I'm taking off the cape, setting the tub in my bedroom, heating water for her bath. Outside the door, Will'm is weighing out two pounds of peanuts, from time to time blowing his nose and talking with a customer. Ida steps into the tub and sits, and I take a washcloth and soap to her, scrubbing as if she's a great stubborn stain, until she winces. I lather her hair, and pour from a pitcher, telling her, for God's sake, to hold still.

"You have no right to do this," I say when I'm toweling her off and she's gotten lost inside one of my flannel gowns. "It's not right, after all the misery you've dealt me, to be this needy."

Ida looks at me, her hair white and flying off in seven

directions. At least it's clean. She smells better than she has in a long time.

"Olivia," she says darkly, "I am not just a beggar off the street. God will punish you for the way you treat me."

Although I'd cut out my tongue before I'd say it out loud, she might be right.

36

It is almost five o'clock by the time Ida's had supper and is tucked in her bed. I turn up the electric heater in the corner, and set Will'm's old boots inside her door in case she needs to go to the outhouse. I don't know what else to do. The basement's too cold, the alcove belongs to Will'm—and if the four-poster were a half mile wide, it wouldn't hold both Ida and me.

Still, I stand looking around at her sagging paper boxes, the unpainted walls, the rag rug. Perhaps we should have done more, Saul and I, built shelves and cupboards, unpacked her things. Back then I could not. I had needed to remove her from the house, and that much I had done. I turn out the light.

Will'm's worked hard in the store today, and I imagine he's worn out from his cold. I'll bring from the bin two of the biggest potatoes I can find, light the oven, and bake them for supper. But he's standing on the back porch. I wave him inside.

But he's not seeing me, and I can't make out what he's looking at, for the sun's going down. I stomp on through the snow. When I come upon the thing that lies in the snow, I cannot focus, can't draw a breath. Here at the foot of my back steps is a small silver-face, shot in the forehead, its snout still lathered with red foam. The right ear has been cut off, and there's a long smear of blood to show for its dragging. Couldn't have been more than six months old. I am sickened in my heart and soul.

"Will'm!" I shout, as if he isn't ten feet away. "Hand me down a goddamn shovel!"

"Gran—"

"I've got to bury it, don't want things comin' in our yard to get at it."

"Somebody already came in our yard," he says, handing me the spade. "Gran—how many do you think are left?"

I search the hills. "Don't know. If they're smart, they've gone farther up. Anyway, it's late. I'm gonna take him a ways and bury him deep, so you go on and light the oven, put in two potatoes, then get into bed."

"I've got to feed the cubs," he says, shivering.

"All right, but I'll take the night feeding. Now get in out of this weather."

I set out, dragging the wolf by a hind leg. One of the hunters has taken home a fine silken ear and my anger could fill all of Pope County. A terrible truth comes to me then: I'm sliding into a place as bitter as the one in which Ida lives.

37

A new morning. I milk the nanny, feed the goats, scatter corn. Chop the ice on the water pans. Four more eggs. Last fall I had Will'm tack a horsehair blanket to the walls and floor of the coop, just in case. I'm glad I did.

When I come in, he's rummaging the larder. He finds an apple and while I boil water for the oats, we talk about Ida, and Miz Grace Harris, and the funeral being at eleven o'clock.

It was not until the middle of the night that I remembered the poultice for his throat, and, in my boots, by the light of the stove I mixed dry mustard and water, slathering it between layers of flannel to lay on his chest. It seems to have done the trick, and my worry over him settles.

"Put the apple back, Will'm," I tell him. "Breakfast is coming."

He looks into the box where the cubs are sleeping, their bellies still full of the vegetable broth I fed them before daylight. "I'm sorry I said what I did, Gran."

"What's that, boy?"

"That if Miz Grace would go on and die—you know. You and Wing."

"It's all right."

"After the funeral, I'll go on over to Dooby's and get in my hours."

"You feel up to it?"

He nods, and doesn't say another word, not even later when we sit at the table over our breakfast, pretending the wolf's blood has not stained our window frame and the wall underneath.

There are no shots in the hills today. The cubs are moving around in their box. Will'm picks them up and holds the soft things, stroking them, forcing oats in their mouths with his little finger. I tell him what Miz Hanley said about broth. For a minute he looks hopeful, so I hurry and remind him that there isn't any meat, not so much as a chicken beak.

"I could kill a rabbit if I had a gun," he says. "I bet I could keep us in meat all winter. I know I could." But he's half pouting because he knows the answer.

"We've got a while before the funeral. Go on out and check your traps if you're feeling like to it. You might've caught something, and when I've put it in the pot, you can have some of the gravy."

He nods, and I know what he's thinking—the cubs could also have his share of the meat. I lace up my boots and fetch my cape. "I'll take Ida's tray across to her now."

"What if she's not there?" he says. "What if she's gone off again?"

It's a fear I have, too. But I can't tie her up.

Fortunately, Ida's sleeping. When I wake her, she turns away. She's still mad at me for ransacking her place, although I've put everything back and done up the boxes.

She says, "Where's my glass of milk?"

I let in some daylight and sit on the edge of her cot. "There's no milk, Ida. I've put honey in your tea."

"Well," she says crossly, "Doc Pritchett says I should have my milk."

"So should Will'm." I tell her about Miz Grace Harris, and that I'll be in town awhile.

"It's time that Wing Harris was punished," she says, folding her arms across her nightgown. "Don't think I didn't see what the two of you were doing."

She'll drag up every sin I've committed. No point in being embarrassed about it, all these years later. Still. "You followed us?"

"As any decent ma'am would. I knew when he stuck his business in you and made you bleed."

"I'm starting a new quilt," I say, to change tracks. "Another wedding ring, in blues and violet. Love Alice tells me—"

"Alice Hanley is an addlepated half-wit," Ida says. "She talks like a screech owl." She flaps her arms for effect, and frowns at her bowl, but does not eat. I wonder why I hold out hope for Ida, thinking someday she might fall down and hit her head the way Junk once did, and it will change her forever. I hate that I do that, that I keep coming back to her, whining like a child, wanting my mother. "Ida—"

She smooths her flannel gown. "Don't say anything that will give me a headache, Olivia. You're so mindless about that."

It's a long time since I've looked directly in her face, into her eyes, and what I see is dreadful—dried cheeks and chin, like grapes left hanging too long. She's bone thin, and her eyes are dark, not blue like Pap's or mine, but sunk into bottomless sockets.

I want to ask her if she's sorry, if she ever feels pain at what went before—not wanting me, the accident that put me in the hospital, Pap's death, his unmarked grave.

"These oats are cold," she says. "I really wanted coddled egg."

"Ida, please."

She sighs. "What?"

"You must remember something good about Pap."

"Lord love us," she says. "Not this again. There at the end, you spent more time with him than I did."

"He's been gone thirty years—"

"Well, you went and kilt him," she says, reminding me.

"What was he like when you married him?"

She looks away to the frosted window, but she's seeing something farther out. "William Tate Harker was a handsome man. A fine dancer, and all the girls made eyes at him. They threw elegant parties, and we were invited to them all. Tate would twirl me out on the floor. Oh, I was a picture in fluted organdy and pink ribbon bows."

I can't imagine anyone having money to put on elegant parties. Nor can I picture Ida, who came from a dirt-poor family, dressed in such. "Tell about *him*," I say.

She lifts her chin. "He was so taken with me, at first I was blinded to his faults."

"He had no more faults than anyone else," I say, although being taken with Ida is fault enough.

"He kept you poor, and he dressed you in ugly clothes."

"We weren't poor. He worked at two jobs. People paid what they could for his doctoring."

"He'd come dragging home those flea-bitten beasts. Or he'd go to them. Sometimes he'd be gone for days, come home bloody to the elbow, wantin' me to scrub the blood from his clothes. And all he'd have to show for it was a handful of carrots and rutabaga. He thought himself to be a fine, fancy doctor."

"How did he know what to do for hurt things?"

She shrugs. "That first year, he asked if he could take a few things from the cupboards. So I gave him needles and thread, a scissor, spoons. But it was never enough. He'd call up to me— 'Ida Mae, bring me a saucer, fetch me an egg yolk, throw down a blanket.' Thought if he snapped his fingers, there'd I be. I bet he's sorry now."

If Ida were any more wicked, she'd burst into flame. "Tell about when I was born."

"Oh, that," she says. "I don't see how those primitive women had babies in the field and then went back to hoeing corn. You had a big head—and arms and legs like a monkey. The whole thing was a shock to my nervous system. And your father did nothing but hide out in his still and play in the basement with those filthy creatures. Later, he dressed you in trousers and left you to run. You hadn't the slightest idea how to be a lady. When I came home, I had my work cut out for me."

I gather the things for the tray. Someday, when she tells me what an ugly, wild child I was, I will slap her silly, maybe even throw her down on the floor and put a pillow over her face. But today I asked for this. I get up.

From the door, I say, "One more thing. Tell me, again, about when Pap died."

Her sigh is enormous. "That night, they carried him home."

"Who did?"

"I don't remember, Olivia. Whoever came along and found the two of you. He was all busted up. They laid him out on the bed, and I washed him proper and put his best suit of clothes on him."

"Was there a service? Did anyone come to say a prayer over him?"

"They did not. Nobody cared. The next morning I sent for a coffin, and I dug a hole and buried him."

"And that was that."

She draws her blanket up around her face.

I take myself off up the hill behind Ida's cabin, and find a shady spot with little snow. It's not as easy to fling myself facedown on the earth these days, but I do it with a cracking of knee joints, and grunting like an old hog. It's good to have my arms and legs spread out on the ground. But it's winter, and a slow freeze comes to the left side of my face while I take stock of things.

Wherever this bitterness in Ida is coming from, it's driving her clean out of her head. Wing's wife is dead. The boy has cottoned to creatures we can't save, and wolves are dying almost every day. Further, if I freeze to death here, the world will go on without me. Ida will, one day, wander from her cabin, drop into the creek, and be swept off to a better place. Wing might even marry again. But what would the boy do? And what would become of the wolves?

"Gran?" says Will'm, whose boots I now see, and who was, at one time, accustomed to finding me like this. "You all right, down there?"

I raise up on my knees, brush off the snow. "I am fine, boy."

He's still in his nightshirt and coat and hat. Perhaps he is more like me than I think. "Well, I've caught us a squirrel and two rats."

I reach for his hand. "Good. Give the rats to the goats, we're not ready to eat them yet. Go on and skin the squirrel, put it in the pot, and bury it by the back step. I'll cook it this evening."

He grins and nods and treks off to the house. I am not far behind. I'm not looking forward to the funeral, and just thinking about it sours my mood.

38

Will'm has taken care of the squirrel, lopping off its head and feet, gutting and skinning it. In my kitchen, I wash dishes. He comes in and dries them without a word, pours a little honey and milk in a pan, and feeds the cubs with the dropper. The pups' ribs heave when they swallow. I've thought every day that another one would surely give up. But their tummies are growing rounder. Their eyes close, and Will'm tucks them back in their box while I put the dishes away.

In the alcove, he pulls his nightshirt off over his head, and when he's standing shivering and leggy in his underdrawers, I realize he's not a little boy anymore. He buttons on the freshly pressed shirt I've laid out.

I have a plain black dress with white collar and cuffs. I made it ten years ago. It's got a row of white glass buttons down the front, and it still fits around my middle. In the piece of mirror, I don't look too bad, brushing my hair, twisting it this way and that to see what's best. Finally I pile it on top of my head and pin it with two silver clips. In my bureau drawer is a box of powder, and I apply some to my face, pinching in color. I'm glad my dress is long enough to hide my boots, and I vow that when there's money enough, I will buy a pair of real shoes.

With Will'm beside me, I drive the pickup six miles to the graveyard. There'll be a crowd, and Miz Grace Harris will go into the earth knowing she's loved. She knew who she was. I, on the other hand, know who I am when I'm selling vanilla and cardamom, or baking a brown sugar cake with Will'm. When I'm with Love Alice, I'm sure and strong. But something happens when I'm alone. When there are no other eyes to reflect my own, a great doubt blindsides me, and in those moments I wonder if I'm here at all.

Maybe it's Wing. As hard as I tried to rid myself of them, and as weary as I became, my feelings have never quite gone away. Or maybe it's not Wing at all, but something else that's left me wounded. Like missing Pap, or the lukewarm way I felt about Saul. On the other hand, could be I'm only getting an ingrown toenail, or waddling into the change of life. Perhaps I need a man to lay me down in the leaves on Cooper's Ridge. Or maybe it's all in my head.

I'm always amazed when grave diggers crack through ice to bury a body. Sometimes, though, a funeral has to wait for a thaw, with the winter dead piling up like cordwood.

Today, a path has been cleared through the snow, and Will'm and I make our way through mourners that huddle in overcoats and scarves, their hands in their pockets. The coloreds are off to one side. Will'm and I stand with Junk and Love Alice and take our share of looks from the Anatoles and the Standishes, Misters French and Andrews. Little Ruse waves. Miz Phelps sees us, and she lifts a hand, too, till her husband takes her by the arm.

I can't hear the service, but I can see the Reverend—the pastor of the Presbyterian church in Paramus. Wing's head is bowed. It was the biggest surprise of my life, him calling on me when Miz

Grace was dying. But he looks up and sees me, and although I could be wrong, it seems his shoulders ease some.

The pastor declares an amen. Two men in suits and tight overcoats lower the casket. Folks file by in silent tribute, there being no flowers to drop in the hole. Then they drift off to their cars and snake back along the road to town, where they drive up every which way in front of Wing's hotel. I park in the alley, and while the rest cluster on the sidewalk, I'm the first one in.

In the lobby, it's dark and quiet. I pull off my cape and shake out my hat. In a few minutes, Wing comes, too. I hear a *Hey, Wing* from the doorway, and there's Big Ruse and his family, and behind him is Darvis Butler, who owns the butcher shop in Buelton. Before long, the lobby, the halls, and the kitchen fill up. People overflow into the private front room where it looks like Wing spent last night. I fold his blankets and carry them to the bedroom, tuck them away in the wardrobe. The bedding in the rosebud room has been changed, the sick-room things removed, but my pink quiltie is folded across the foot of the bed.

In the kitchen, Wing stands by the window, looking out at the verandah he built over his garden so that his guests might sit there in summer. Snow covers it, now. Behind him, a half dozen ladies are already setting out cobblers and pies, casseroles and sliced beef. The table, the sideboard, every kitchen inch is filling with food. They nod at me. Although I'm usually the first to arrive with scalloped potatoes or beans and bread, today it never occurred to me. I touch Wing's shoulder, and when he turns, I put my arms around him. We rock back and forth, back and forth, and deep in his throat he makes a soft, frail sound that weakens my knees.

When we were children, I knew Wing's body, his heart, and his soul. But in all the years since then, the only time we've spoken was politely when someone wed, or grew ill, or died. Dismal decades of *Best Regards*. Now his body feels strange to me, this man grown old instead of the boy. I let him go.

He says, "I knew you'd come back. I knew it."

I figure all things come full circle. We are born, then we live and die, and so it goes. A tree buds, its leaves are green, and then yellow. They drop and turn to earth through winter. Then spring comes, and the whole thing begins again. Of course I came back, but with all new feelings. Somehow, I'm irritated, but this is not the time to tell him that.

There are so many people in the kitchen, I don't think anyone sees us. Wing fishes for his handkerchief. "It's such a relief," he says. "I should feel bad saying that, but—"

"No, you shouldn't."

He wipes his face and blows his nose. His eyes are dark gray and his face pulled tight. "I did what I could, Olivia. All that I had was hers."

His words cramp my belly and wrench my heart, but I know them to be the truth. They add to whatever's turned sour inside me.

"You did your best," I say. "Every minute, day and night."

He blows his nose again, reminding me of Will'm, who has two kerchiefs in his own pocket. I wonder where he is, and if he knows there's cake.

"Shall I make us some coffee?"

He draws in a shuddery breath that makes me want to forget what I feel and wrap him up in my very best quilt. "Tea, please. I guess I should go and speak to some folks."

He goes into the hall. I see now that there is an enormous pot of coffee perking—Ruse's urn from across the street—but I fill the kettle and put the strainer over the pot and add tea leaves.

Folks are picking up plates. I cut angel food cakes and ladle up steaming greens with pink ham hock, and hand out slices of brown bread with a dollop of butter. For a few minutes, I'm glad I have something to do.

Will'm is nowhere in sight—not in the kitchen nor the lobby, nor Wing's parlor. He isn't outside, neither front nor back. I take the stairs to the first floor—hoping he has not begun to feel worse and gone to lie down. But there he is, in the first room I happen upon, lounging in a rocker while the hired girl, Molly, makes a bed and runs the carpet sweeper. She's a pretty thing with peachy skin, her yellow hair tied back in a scarf, and she's talking ninety to nothing.

When I come in, Will'm flushes around the ears, but Molly goes right on.

"Morning, Miz Cross," she says, pushing the sweeper under the bed and around the bureau.

"Molly. Will'm. There's chocolate layer cake downstairs."

"Yes'm," Will'm says. "I was kind of waiting on Molly, here. It's all right if she has dinner, too?"

This is a new wrinkle to which I must adjust.

I tell him, "Both of you go on down when you're finished, and get whatever you want."

"Oh, Miz Cross," Molly says. "I'd be big as two barrels if I did that. 'Course, I work it off up here, these ol' men not knowin' how to leave a room. Sheets all in a knot, don't never put the lid down on the commode—"

Will'm blushes again and sniffles.

"Wing has guests?" I say.

"Oh, yes'm. They set up here nights, drinking and talking. Some of 'em's probably downstairs right now, grabbin' a free meal. I guess they know Mr. Wing—and Miz Grace, she was nice to everybody."

"How many hunters are there?"

"Oh, goodness, quite a few."

I wonder what the price of membership is. "Molly, do you ever see Alton Phelps here? I mean, does he come to visit with them?"

"No, ma'am. 'Course I only work three days after school, and Saturday mornings."

"How long do these hunters stay?"

"Two, three weeks. Not always the same. Funny, though, if they bag anything, I don't ever see it. I think they're up to something."

Of course there's no game, I think, but I must ask: "Why do you say that?"

"It's like they're playing," she says, "and telling secrets. They whisper and point and laugh and whisper some more."

"You ever hear what they're saying?"

"No, ma'am. They hush up when somebody comes around. They give me the willies. Mr. Wing's nice to them, but I don't think he trusts them, either."

Food for thought. "Well, come down soon and eat," I say.

Downstairs, folks are chatting and less somber now. It's almost an hour before Wing comes again to the kitchen. I pour tea that's kept warm on the stove and ask if he's eaten today. He has not. I butter him a slice of bread. He folds it in half and takes a bite.

"Was it like this when Saul died?" he asks.

"A few came."

"No, I meant—his passing."

I shake my head. It's been a long time, but I remember it well.

"One day when he was covering the tar paper on Ida's place, he just fell over dead."

People are still coming. Angus Sampson and his wife, and Elizabeth Phelps, a half dozen others.

"Olivia." Dooby nods. "You doing all right?"

"I am."

"Afternoon, Olivia." Elizabeth Phelps comes into the kitchen. "It's nice that you're here. I'm sure you're a comfort to Wing. You have that gift."

I tuck up hair that has come loose. I look at her pink wool dress, and at my own black twill.

"Miz Phelps—"

"Elizabeth," she says.

"The other day, you told me about my pap caring for your Governor, and I was wondering—do you remember anything else about Pap?"

Her smile is gone. "Why do you want to know?"

Her question confuses me. I look at my ringless fingers. At her pretty hands, her silver bracelet with square pink stones.

"Olivia." She puts her hand on my cheek. "I've said too much. You let sleeping dogs lie. Is there coffee made?"

"Yes, ma'am, right there on the drainboard."

"Thank you," she says. But she goes out instead.

I run soapy water, wash cups and saucers, slice a cake that's just arrived. And I try to sort out what little I know. Will'm and Molly come down, and while they spoon from the platters and bowls, Molly talks enough for us all.

By the time the party, if it can be called such, thins, I am worn to the knees, and Wing looks the same. I figure he needs to be alone. I drag Will'm away from Molly, and he goes on over to Dooby's while I drive back to the house, change into trousers and shirt, and dig up the squirrel. I cut it in pieces and set it to boil. The cubs are in their box, mewling in their sleep. I should wake them and force thinned mush into them, but I've something more important on my mind—how to defend our property from these hunters. Clearly it's going to take some kind of action on my part. It would be useless to threaten them and then not follow through. My brain is tired, but it's like a dog with a bone.

I take up a knife and chop fiercely at an onion. I add salt to the pot and when I feed the cubs, they don't care that my hands are shaking. It's growing dark. Will'm should be coming soon, and he'll be hungry. I slice bread and lay it on a sheet for the oven, mix cinnamon with a pinch of sugar.

There's knocking on the front door now, not Will'm, for he never uses the front entry. Likely somebody needing soda for a bellyache or something they've forgotten for tomorrow's dinner. Again comes the rapping. I go through without lighting a lamp, and turn the knob. A woman stands there, her hair fuzzy against a halo of gray light. She says nothing.

"Yes?" I squint my eyes, the better to see.

"Mama," says Pauline, standing on the doorstep. "It's me. I've come for the boy."

39

Stepping aside to let my daughter in is maybe the most confused thing I have ever done. Part of me wants to throw my arms around her, forgive her for everything and ask for the same. I could peel potatoes, kill us a hen—I've been planning to anyway—and make a feast with fried bread and cream gravy. But I heard what she said, and my heart bangs in my chest like a wild bird in a cage. "You can't have him."

She looks at me. "Can I come in?"

Yes.

She walks slow, looking at the floor, like with each step her feet are remembering the boards. How pretty she is, coming through to the light—so pretty I can't take my eyes off her. Short yellow curls, but not the same nose, and she puts her hand to it.

"I had it fixed," she says. Then I see the lines, hundreds of them, like she's lived hard and run a long way. Her coat is thin and worn at the elbows. She stands in the middle of my kitchen, her hands clasped tight.

"You doin' all right, Mama?" she says.

"I'm fine." I don't want to ask how she is, afraid to hear that she's gotten so rich in the films—which was what she left here to do—that she can now buy Will'm the moon.

She pulls out a chair and sits down. "You got coffee in that pot, there?" She speaks softer than I remember, but she's an actress, and maybe that voice is put on.

I shake the pot. Pour a cup. "Where you living, now?"

"In Hollywood, California," she says. "Is he here?"

"He's out. He'll be home directly."

"I can't wait to see him," she says and takes off her coat. The lines of her body are long and lean, and she's got a pretty shape under that sweater. She's wearing a long, tight skirt and high-heeled shoes. But in the dead of winter she's got no stockings on.

"How'd you get here?"

"Bus," she says. "Five days, I had to change three times. Cost me near thirty dollars. I got another thirty for going back—and half the price, for William."

"Bus drop you in Buelton?"

"Yes'm. I caught a ride and walked from the highway."

"You could use some boots."

She turns in her chair. "I rented me a room, Mama, upstairs from a liquor store. It's got a sofa for William to sleep on."

It irritates me, the way she says his name. "He's got a proper bed here." I nod at the alcove and its curtain made from an old bedsheet.

"He won't mind the sofa. I got an icebox and an electric burner so I can cook for him. And he can come and watch me work on the set sometimes," she says.

"You been in some films, then?"

She looks at her fingernails, bitten to the quick. "Some. Mostly I'm a stand-in, but that way I learn all the parts."

There's a picture show in Buelton. "You been in any movies that come out this way?"

"I guess not, but the directors think I have promise."

"Promise," I say, unable to decide whether that's a blessing or a curse. A couple of times my life held promise. I take things from the larder to start our supper. "They pay you all right?"

"I knew you'd ask that. I make a few dollars on the set. I work in the liquor store coupla nights a week. And I dance at the Starlight Ballroom, start at three o'clock, keep a nickel out of every dime the gents pay after midnight. They're good about let-tin' me off for auditions."

"You working nights wouldn't be good for the boy," I say.

"He'll be safe."

"You've got no right to decide that, Pauline. You don't know one thing about him!"

"I can learn. I'm his mama."

This can't be happening. I've fallen asleep waiting for the boy to come home, and I'm having a dream. But when I strike a match to light the stove, the sulfur will sting my nose and wake me. I warm the coffee while she walks around looking at things, her heels tap-tapping on the broken linoleum.

"This is his home, and it would be cruel to take him. And any-way, he's got a cold."

"It never snows in California," she says. "It's warm all winter long."

How can it be that I'm already in one mess with Ida, and sud-denly find myself in another with Pauline? Half an hour ago, Pauline was just a memory. I wish she had never come to the door. Right now I need peace. It's not like I'm asking anyone else to take on my burdens, but a little time with no worries about money or family sure would be nice. But for now—what will I say to Will'm? How will I explain Pauline?

She sighs. "I had to leave here, Mama. I'm sorry for puttin' him on you like that, but I had to do it, you know?"

I know. The sad part is that I do know. My stomach has sunk so low it's making my knees weak. I hold on to the stove. Still, her going off then doesn't mean she can waltz in here now and pick up like nothing's happened.

I want to be cruel, to ease my own hurt. "When the boy was small, I tried to explain about you. We haven't spoken of you since."

"That's fine, then. At least he doesn't think I just up and left him."

"But you did. And he's a smart boy."

"Well, I'm back now," she says. "And that's what counts."

It's not what counts, and when I get my breathing slowed, I say, "He's not yet twelve. What do you know about eleven-year-old boys?"

"I'll learn. I'm making a good place for us. I got a radio, and he can go outside without passing through the liquor store. There's this yellow dog comes around, I guess he'll like that."

"Will'm's not a stray dog," I say, things getting mixed up in my head, which makes me sound like Ida. "You can't move him from pillar to post."

"He'll get used to the change. Kids do that all right."

"No, he won't!" I'm yellin' now, and to no good. Besides, I hear the bus stopping in front. "I want to be the one to tell him."

"All right," she says, smoothing her skirt and her hair like the King of England's about to walk in. "But if you make me out to be somethin' terrible, Mama, so help me—"

Will'm comes up the drive, stumps on the back porch, and opens the door. He looks at Pauline and at me, puts his things on the table, and leans over the box, lifting out a cub like we're not even here. If it were another day and anyone else was sitting in our kitchen, I'd have cuffed him for his bad manners, and that makes me wonder if he's been expecting this. I watch him stroke the pup's head and tickle its ears, put a bit of milk on the burner to warm. And I wonder how long he's been waiting.

There's no easy way to say it. "Will'm, I regret not telling you sooner, so you'd be ready. This here is Pauline."

Will'm stands there, looking down at the cub cradled on his arm.

"Hello, William," Pauline says. "I'm your mama."

He never lifts his eyes, and I'm glad. I remember when Ida came home, how I'd looked into her face hoping for happiness at seeing me, longing for something that never came, and just now I could give him some tips. Most of all, boy, don't trust what betrays you.

Pauline clears her throat. "Before you were born, I was waitin' tables in Paramus, hoping you'd hurry up and come so's I could try out for a part in this play. The director was a real nice lady. She took me in, helped birth you. You had that same yellow hair, those big eyes. Now look, you've gone and grown into a handsome man."

Will'm is quiet, like he's swallowed his tongue. I wonder if he'll ever speak again.

Everything in my kitchen looks foreign and out of place. "Take your coat off, boy. I'll make you some cocoa."

"William," Pauline says, standing. "You come on now and give your mama a hug."

But he does not move.

"Well, that's all right," she says. "You take your time. That's one fine-looking puppy you got there."

"There's two of them," he says then. "And they're not puppies, they're wolves."

"Is that right? I got me a big yellow dog. An' there's a soda fountain right next door to my place. In Hollywood, California, you heard of that?"

Will'm nods.

"Sometimes on Saturdays, I go to the movies for a nickel," she says.

He looks over at her. "Why'd you come here?"

"Well." Pauline fusses with her dress. "I come to fetch you."

"Gran?" Will'm says, like he's hoping I'll not only answer the questions, but ask them, too.

Truth is, I don't know what to say. I think about those two women in the Bible, both laying claim to the baby, so King Solomon takes out his sword to cut him in half. At the last minute, the mama who loves him lets go of his hand, and Solomon says, "Then it's you that shall have him."

Only I can't let go, and that makes me the wicked one. Ida would say that was so, and just now I can't argue. After all, I've thought of murdering hunters for killing the wolves—what, then, might I do to this woman who sits in my kitchen and cuts out my heart? If I speak up now, while Will'm fetches the broth and the eyedropper—if I shout he can't go, that he's mine because I've raised him—he'll be like a piece of old cloth we're ripping in half. Pauline's talking a good story with her soda fountains and picture shows. Still, if I let her walk out the door with him, I might as well take Pap's gun and blow my head off.

Will'm tucks the cubs' box under his arm, takes the pan of broth in the other hand, and elbows back the curtain to his alcove. Then he turns and looks at me with enough fire in his eyes to devour Kentucky. It knocks the breath clean out of me.

40

I send Will'm to fetch Ida in her nightgown and a woolen shawl. A dark look is spread across her face, so I expect he has told her. He pulls out her chair for her, then digs in the drawer for a length of string. Pats her hair and ties the string around it. It hurts me to watch.

I recall my conversation with Saul on the hill, and wonder how my loving got to be so messed up. I ladle beans and salt pork into a bowl, take corn bread from the oven, and give them each a spoonful of fried potato. It's Will'm's favorite, but tonight he doesn't lift his fork until I tell him to.

"Ida," I say. "You remember Pauline. She's all grown-up now, and pretty as a picture." And she is, but I say it because I want to keep Ida from making some nasty remark.

"Who?" she says.

"Our Pauline. She's come home."

"How you doing, Grandma?" Pauline says across the table that I've had to pull out from the wall for the first time in years.

Ida looks at her. Then at me. She says, "Tell that woman to pass the corn bread, Olivia."

If we were friends, Pauline and I would look at each other and shake our heads. I'd like that, another woman to share this trouble. But I can't make it happen. I feel myself sinking lower and lower. Maybe I should ask Pauline to take me over to the home in Buelton, and have me put away.

"Will'm," I say, "how're the cubs doing?"

"All right," he says.

"I saved back a bit of pork fat. You can give 'em that."

He nods once.

I get up and go to the grocery, bring back a jar of honey, and open it. Will'm's eyes grow round at this extravagance, but I stick a spoon in it and hand it to him. He puts honey on his corn bread and some on Ida's. I guess he's given himself over to Ida, and doing for her is bringing him comfort.

"I meant to tell you," I say, "that I'm moving Pap's grave."

Will'm puts down his fork.

"He's going up on the hill by Saul. It's long overdue."

Ida cuts her eyes toward me, and then fades away, picking at her corn bread, putting crumbs in the palm of her other hand.

Nobody says anything. I don't know what I expected. I mean to do this quickly, and it would be nice, lowering Pap into his new spot, if we had some kind of ceremony, but nobody seems interested. I guess I'll do what I need to, and that'll be that. At least Junk will be there, and Love Alice, too.

I bring what's left of the beans and set the pan on the table. "Ida? You want some more?"

But Ida looks at Pauline. And then at Will'm. "You read to me tonight, boy?" she says.

"I will. From the Letters of Paul?"

"Anything," she says, "but Revelation. It scares the bejesus out of me, all them devils on horseback."

"Well," says Pauline brightly. She takes another slice of corn bread from the pan. "I been thinking that I might stay on a few days. Maybe a week."

She's telling me how long I have with the boy.

41

Will'm takes Ida back directly after supper, the last of the corn bread wrapped in a towel. His hovering over her irritates me, although everything bothers me just now, and God knows she needs someone. I look in on the cubs while he's gone, and they're sleeping but not one whit bigger, and I wonder how much longer they'll hold on. If I can't keep Will'm, and he leaves with Pauline, what will I do with them?

Sometime later, Pauline falls asleep on the bed beside me. Her beat-up suitcase lays open on the floor. I can't help looking at the few things she's brought, and wondering if she doesn't own much, or if she's put her money back for Will'm's comfort. Or maybe people in California wear the same clothes over and over, and if that's the case they must do a lot of wash.

Sometime before dawn, I wake feeling suffocated by my own daughter's breath, and I get up and light a lantern, turning the wick low. I put my coat and mittens on, wrap a scarf around my head, and go down the back steps. I can still see the shallow snow where the wolf laid two days ago, and the track I left when I pulled it up the hill.

Because ours is a sliver of land, and unfenced, it's easy to see how the wolves have wandered, and there's nothing I can do about the shooting of them past our boundaries. But slaughter on our land is something else.

The whole thing is a sloping foothill actually, because once a body reaches the crest, there's greater hills to the north and east. On the pointy southern tip of our land is the house, what's left of the barn and shed, a boarded-up outhouse, a goat pen, a chicken house, and Ida's cabin. Because the ground is so rocky, there are paths and washes carved into the hillside, all of which make going up easier. In the last few days, Will'm and I have tromped down the snow as far as Cooper's Ridge, which is the next near-level ground, although it's thick with brushy copses and caves. Beyond that the boulders are slick-faced clear to the top, where they're smaller until it's like walking on finely crushed gravel, as if all the heavy pieces have rolled downhill.

Near the western edge of our land, on the Ridge, I buried Saul. Junk and his uncles dug a grave there, under a pair of weeping willows. In spring, violets the color of sunset push through, and three-pointed trilliums and dogwood, and bushes with yellow blossoms. Just now, the willows are bare, and the grave is covered with snow. But it's shady here, and I suspect the earth is soft.

I look down at Saul's thin upright stone with snow drifted smoothly against it, and feel the need to do something I haven't since his last day on earth.

"They put Miz Grace Harris in the ground," I say. I like the sound of me talking to Saul. He was so responsible, I half expect him to answer. "Made me think of how kind you were. The way you took on Pauline and me. You didn't have to do that, Saul— you surely were a good man."

I remember how his shoulders stooped, those last years, making him even shorter than before, and how he liked beef stewed with rice, gravy spooned over bread. He loved anything made with apples, and boiling hot coffee at dawn. Nights, when he came last to the bed, I'd curl against his back, which was probably the only closeness I showed him.

He took everything in stride. Days, he worked in old man French's hardware store, knowing all the sizes of nuts and washers, and he could sharpen a saw blade so a man could shave with it. Once a week he ran the still, although he seldom drank, but he kept two or three customers. I believe he did it for the perverseness of it, and was just waiting for a revenuer to show up.

I remember him bouncing Pauline on his knee. He loved her like his own, and I'm glad he died before she took off, so he didn't have to watch. Like Will'm, he had a way with Ida, teasing her and twirling her around the floor. She'd bat at his hand, call him a fool, and give me the evil eye. I'd stomped around in one Ida-snit or another until Saul began to build her cabin. I wonder, now, if he was ever happy.

"I could have loved you more," I say. "Or maybe I loved you all along, and was just too stubborn to see."

The sun's coming up. I lie down beside him. My knees crack, and my back gives me fits. I meant it when I said Pap should be buried here, instead of by that stinking outhouse. I'm not sure what it'll entail, for there can't be much of him left in the ground. If I can get Junk's help, we'll dig anyway and move whatever there is—wood or bone. Then, in spring, I'll haul rocks up here and make a little graveyard for the two of them.

I never talked to Saul about the Phelpses. I wish now that I had.

After our noon meal, eaten in silence, I take the truck and without a word to Pauline, or Will'm, who's holed up in his alcove with the cubs, I drive to Junk's place. They're eating their after-church dinner, and I wait on the porch with my hat in my hand until Junk comes to the door. This is the second time in a week that I've dragged him away from his family because I've got a bee in my bonnet.

"Junk." I lay my hand on his arm. "I need your help with something. In exchange, I'll give Love Alice a quarter's worth of store credit."

"Twenty fi' cents," he says, wiping chicken grease from his chin. "That'd be a help."

"Well, what I want might sound strange, so don't be surprised, all right?"

"All right, Miz Livvy," he says.

"Up at our place, I want to move the box with my pap in it."

He stands there like I haven't made good sense. His eyes are on the porch post or something. "Ma'am?"

"I want to take him up there by Saul. Day after tomorrow," I say.

"Miss Livvy, I know once you make up your mind, it's a sealed thing, but I just don't believe this is the best idea."

"He deserves a decent burial patch, don't you think?"

"Yes'm. But it's winter. And disturbin' the dead is—flat wrong."

"How is it wrong? I've got to do away with that outhouse, come spring, and the toolshed, too. Fill in the tunnel to the cellar, finish fixing things up."

He shakes his head, looks around like he's worried someone's listening. "It don't seem right."

"We aren't going to open the coffin, nothing like that."

"Miss Livvy, by now that box is turned to rot."

"We'll have it tightly wrapped. I'll do that myself in one of my quilts, if you'll just help me dig."

He wipes sweat from his forehead like it's a whole lot more than ten degrees.

"Junk, please don't go talking about haints and things. No ghosts are goin' to visit your house for doing this."

"I don't know—"

"If you won't help me, I'll do it myself."

"Hard work for a woman," he says.

"I'll make it a half dollar's worth of credit."

"My mammy won't like this," he says.

"Then we won't tell her."

"I ain't ever lied to her—"

"We won't lie. We won't say anything."

"You know Love Alice'll come with me. She'll want to be takin' tea with you."

"Then we'll swear her to secrecy."

He sighs.

"Seventy-five cents, Junk." If I go on paying to have my life put in order, it'll cost me a pure fortune. "And what's left in the whiskey bottle."

"I don't feel good about this," he says.

"But you'll do it. I'll come for you in a day or two—a morning when Will'm's in school." I go down the steps and out to my truck before he can argue more.

It's another long afternoon. I wonder if the hunters are out today. Last night they probably tied one on in one of the rooms and slept late, with Molly or Wing cleaning up after them this morning. I bet they ate ham and eggs at Ruse's Cafe, and any time now, they'll be taking their rifles and heading for my hill. I can't think of a single reason why I shouldn't do the same.

Sure enough, before an hour passes, there are shots above the Ridge.

I ought to be in the kitchen, working on my quilts for spring, figuring new patterns. I've been thinking about pine trees—cutting patches of snowy-white branches with deep brown trunks, backing them with puffed cotton, and stitching them onto a field of blue.

When the thaw comes and the days warm, I'll fold the quilts over my porch rails and have Will'm string a line between the sycamores. Maybe he and I will drive over with a hammer and nails and see if we can't resurrect that old stall by the highway. He wouldn't mind peddling one or two on a Sunday afternoon, him getting coins for each one he sells.

But here I go again, making plans as if Will'm will be with me in spring. The truth of it is, if I raised a ruckus and took Pauline to court, any judge would give him to her because she's his ma'am. I've had a lot of years to think about this. Trouble has come to me backward and forward, like too much gravy running off my plate.

42

My mind is not on quilting, but on hunters. I was never one to sit still for anything, so I might as well give this a push and see what lands on its feet. Once more, I hike up the hill with Saul's rifle. The snow has crusted over, and my legs ache something fierce. This steep-angled land has sometimes not been a blessing at all—or maybe I'm just getting old.

I keep climbing. The afternoon has warmed some, but not enough to make the icicles melt—which reminds me of when I was a kid, and how I used to break one from Ruse's overhang and suck it down on my way to school. That was a long time ago, and I sure as the devil wouldn't go back. I've heard folks talk about the fountain of youth, but if I had a tubful of its water, I wouldn't drink. Whatever's ahead is going to come.

I pull one foot out of the snow and put the other in—until the crack of a rifle shot near snaps my neck. I look up toward the Ridge, but can't see anything from here. I wonder if Will'm's sitting in the kitchen with the cubs in his arms, listening.

There are sharp-edged tracks on the Ridge, recent ones. Looks like two or three men. I follow them around gorsebush thickets and jack pines through which I cannot see the sky. They run off into the dark woods, and among the stunted evergreens, which seems fitting, I come upon Alton Phelps down on one knee. In front of him is a she wolf, a neat round hole in her side. She's barely breathing.

With one hand he lifts her right ear, and in his other is a fishing knife that he uses to make a quick downstroke, as if he is slicing butter. Another slices the ear away clean. I raise the rifle and pull the trigger. Smoke erupts, and the wolf jerks as the bullet enters between her eyes. The boom is so loud I wonder if I'm in danger of starting a slide. Phelps falls over backward. I have purposely not hit him. I could have, though, with an ease that amazes me. I'm so close I can smell the blood on his gloves.

"Jesus Christ, Miz Cross!" he says, slapping his ear with his hand like the ringing might fall out. "I thought you'd shot me."

"You're not takin' me serious, Alton," I tell him. "These wolves are my kin. Now you leave that ear lay and stand your sorry ass up."

He rises slow, palms turned out. "Hold on, now—"

"I've got every right to shoot you. Signs been posted here for twenty years. That's fair enough warning. You can shoot all the game you want, a quarter mile either side. But you've taken a liking to our hill. You tell me why on God's earth that is."

"You know perfectly well why," he says, pulling his lips back so I can see his teeth. "It's an eye for an eye, the Good Book says that."

I take a breath so deep the cold hurts my lungs. "I'm sorry about your brother, if that's it—the way James Arnold died. It was an accident. It was dark, the road was icy."

His small eyes narrow. "I'm not talkin' about that night, Miz Cross. Now you got things in your head that I assumed you'd forget. But as long as you're goin' on doggedly, askin' questions and digging up things, I've no choice but to close in on you and yours."

Things in my head?

Because I can't fathom his meaning, I say, "I oughta cut off your ear. Or at least put a hole in your kneecap."

At that, he pales a little.

"Or I could plug you in the foot with your own gun, and we'll call it even."

"You can't—"

In truth, I have no idea what I'm going to do. I won't know till it comes down to it. I wonder if I've seen or heard something regarding the Phelpses, and clean forgotten. Clearly, he thinks I remember.

I say: "Oh, yes I can. Nobody likes you much, Phelps. You and your brothers caused hurt around here as long as I can remember. I can find twelve people before dark who'll swear I was with them when you were shot."

His grin widens. "You make me laugh, Miz Cross. Olivia—" He runs his tongue over his bottom lip like he's testing a fever blister.

But then hands come around me and lift the gun, my grip still so tight that it goes off in the branches. The shot brings down snow on our heads, and Phelps hollers, "Well, shit, Buford!"

The man called Buford, and another in a red stocking cap, give me a shove, and I go down on my hip bone. I struggle to get on my feet, and I lunge, but they step out of reach, sorry bastards.

Phelps pockets the ear and retrieves his rifle from the rock where he's laid it. "I can play that game, too, Miz Cross. Let Buford shoot you, and we'll swear we thought you was a bear. Or a crazed bobcat, that's nearer the truth. Or we could just bury you deep and let 'em look."

I knot my fists. "You sonofabitch."

"Well now, that don't help things at all. You realize, do you, which one of us is holdin' the gun?"

Buford laughs, a long windy sound, and spits tobacco on the snow.

"You have to admit," Phelps says, "I got double reason to hang you."

Hang me?

"For what?" I've turned cold in my bones, and wish someone would come. But nobody will.

"You Harkers caused me more misery than one man ought to have—"

The man in the red cap nods and says, "You got a fine way with words, Alton."

Phelps ignores him.

I say, "I told you, my pap would never hurt a living thing on purpose."

Phelps' face darkens, and he comes toward me with his lips pulled back and his teeth together, yellow-stained and reminding me of a rabid dog. Even Buford steps away. Phelps has gone over the edge like Ida, only quicker and with a Winchester in his hands.

"First Tate Harker, and now his kin," he says. "Looks like I got to do somethin' about you and that boy, Olivia."

His words clutch at my heart. "What the hell are you talking about?"

"Don't play the fool, woman. You tell me what you know, or I'm comin' after the boy. I got no worries with that crazy bitch Ida—she don't make sense twice in one day." And he laughs.

Snow drifts down from the evergreens. Soon it's going to be too dark to see.

If Phelps kills me now, at least Pauline is here to take Will'm. The state can have Ida.

I say through my teeth, "James Arnold died, and you shot my wolves. I call that even."

He shakes his head and puts out a hand for my rifle. Buford gives it to him. "I'll tell you this—one word to anybody about our little talk here, and not only will I kill him, I'll do it slow." He empties the chamber, puts the shell in his pocket, and throws the gun down the hill. He gives the wolf one last kick. Then the three of them move off into the trees.

I stand there for a bit. Then I take up the gun and stumble toward home. Because I've been holding my breath, I suck wind till I think my ribs will crack.

By the time I can see the house, and Will'm on his stool, milking the goats late and blowing on his hands, I know one thing for sure. I must get him clear of Phelps, clear of here, till I can figure this out. And the only way I know to do that is to pack him off with Pauline when she goes.

Ida's in the kitchen, when I come through the door, and she and Pauline are going at each other over bread slices that Pauline's toasting in the oven.

"I'm trying to make us a celebration, Mama!" Pauline waves a sheet of paper at me. "A boy brought this telegram. I got an audition next week."

"An audition," I say.

"Yes. Aren't you excited for me?"

"I been telling her," says Ida, "that I can't eat cinnamon, so don't put any on my toast. It upsets my digestion."

Pauline throws up her hands, while smoke curls out from

around the oven door. With a cup towel I yank open the door and pull out the pan, open the back door, and fling the toast in the yard.

"I got to leave tomorrow, Mama," says Pauline. "This could be my big break. Be happy for me, please."

Happy? The wolves are done for, Will'm and I are on Phelps' list, the house smells like a fire sale. And my boy is leaving. Worse, Will'm stands in the doorway of the alcove, looking like we've taken turns whipping him. I can see the veins pulsing in his temples. His hair's gone every which way, and his eyes look like he's moved out of his head.

"You-all?" he says, tripping over his voice. "One of the cubs is dead."

43

There aren't enough ways to comfort Will'm. I'm so sorry for the state of things that I can't bear to look at him. I bring paper from the store and wrap the pup.

"While I have my boots on, I'll take the shovel and bury it out past Ida's," I tell them. "You-all sit in your chairs like civilized people. When I come back, I'll put supper on. Till then, nobody moves."

Will'm puts on his coat and follows me. He's still sniffling, but I can't tell if it's sadness or smoke from the toast. I must remember to tell Pauline he has a cold. We cross the property and find a spot.

"I'll do it," he says, taking the shovel.

"Lord, Will'm, there's been too much burying lately."

He lays the cub in the hole and covers it over. We walk back to the house, neither of us giving up another word.

"It was just cinnamon toast," Pauline says to no one.

I pull off my boots, hang up my cape and my hat. "I thank you for trying, but there's no use making Ida something special."

"Well, honestly," Pauline says, still miffed. Her hair is pin-curled flat against her head with a hairnet pulled over.

"Indecent way to come to the table," Ida says. "You can tell she ain't kin of ours."

"She is, Ida." I bang the skillet on the burner. "She's your granddaughter."

Any other night, I'd have put them to helping, or Will'm at least would've offered, but tonight I need quiet because that, at least, is some kind of order. In no time, I've set on the table a stack of corn cakes and slices of fried mush. I've warmed butter beans from another night's meal, and a cupful of bitter greens, though I'm the only one who will eat them.

Ida forks a corn cake on her plate and slathers it up. I wish there were signs that might tell me when Ida's really gone off somewhere in her head, and when it's only put on. I might try pretending to be crazy, sometime, just to see if it's a comfort.

Pauline pats her hairpins. "I thought I'd go on down to the juke joint tonight, Mama, and don't look at me like that. It's just for an hour."

Will'm stares at his plate.

I hold my coffee cup so tight it's in danger of shattering. "There's no good comes of the juke joint," I tell her. "You know that."

"Don't be silly," she says. "In the morning we'll pack Will'm up, and he and I'll head out."

"Will'm," I say, "you sure can't haul that cub to California with you. Not on a bus, day and night. It'll be all right here. I can look after it."

I don't think he's eaten a thing. Pauline can hardly sit still; I've just given her permission to take the boy.

I must keep moving, too. I clear the table before Ida's done and when I send Will'm to take her home, he folds the last corn cake and tucks it in his pocket. He'll slip it under Ida's pillow, for when she wakes hungry in the night. I wash up the dishes while Pauline combs out her yellow hair, and rouges her cheeks and lips.

"Don't I look pretty in this dress, Mama?" she says, twirling. "Isn't this a lovely shade of lipstick? I bought it at a drugstore on Hollywood Boulevard."

I'm reminded of the night Ida and I wrestled around on the bedroom floor. "Looks like your rouge could be softened some."

Pauline's hands flutter like sparrows with no place to land. "Oh, you don't know anything, being stuck back here in these hills. You ought to get out more."

I can't think why on earth I'd want to get out more. What could there possibly be for me anywhere else? But then, of course, there's Will'm, and it would behoove me to visit them in California. The thought of life without him is more than I can stand.

Pauline fishes her high-heeled shoes out from under the table and wiggles her feet into them. Then she puts on her cotton coat. "I reckon Pete's place is still there and open on a Sunday night?" she says, referring to the smoky little beer joint around the corner and up the hill from Ruse's Cafe. It is indeed. I won't let Will'm anywhere near the place with its insides as dark as a whale's behind and smelling of week-old ale. Silty's, where I used to go before Pauline was born, was torn down a long time ago.

She pats her hair and goes out the door.

After that, it's just me and the boy and the beating of our hearts, while he sits at the table cradling the pup. Will'm loved the other one so much, I wonder if he didn't flat stroke it to death. It gets late, but neither of us goes to bed. I'm in danger of dying right here in my kitchen—Love Alice would say that's a truth. But more than anything I need Will'm to be safe.

44

At midnight, Pauline still isn't home. I should have known it would be so. Will'm will grow up loosening his ma'am's fingers from the neck of a bottle. But dead is far worse.

It is nearly two o'clock when Will'm, in his longhandles, wakes me. Pauline's snoring in the bed beside me, although I never heard her come in.

"The last one's dying, Gran. I think it's lonesome for its brothers—"

I get out of bed, my toes curling on the cold wooden floor, and wrap a thick shawl around me. He's right, the cub's breath is a death rattle. I am amazed that anything that small can make a sound so enormous when it's leaving this world. I have always believed when the soul makes up its mind to go home, there's not much a body can do, and I'm fairly certain these cubs have souls, same as every living thing and some things that aren't.

But this is my boy, my Will'm, who shouldn't have to take on more pain, and in my kitchen the stove has gone out. The bulb burning over the box is not enough, and the cub's shivering miserably. Will'm lifts it out while I bring kindling and wood from the porch, and make a fire. I leave the oven door open.

I pull out a chair. "Bring him here."

He sits in the chair, and I unfasten the top three buttons of his long johns.

"What are you doing?"

I slap away his hand and put the pup's belly to his chest. "Hold him—so." Then I button the long johns around them both. I hitch up my own chair and wrap the shawl around the three of us. Will'm's eyes are wide, as if we're waiting for some miracle.

Before long I hear the pup sigh, and Will'm says, "Gran?"

"Well," I tell him, "I believe he's gone to sleep."

Not for anything would he let go of the cub, nor I of him, and inside my shawl I hold us together, as if one of the three might fly away. "He can hear your heartbeat, Will'm, your breathing. He hears your tummy rumble. He remembers those things—they remind him of his ma."

Will'm leans into me. I reach up and turn off the light. A lovely orange glow spills from the oven and warms the floor and our bare feet.

"When I was little," he says, "did you hold me like this?"

I stroke his hair. "Well, you were never this little, but I rocked you, yes."

"Even though I wasn't your boy."

I wonder how much it cost him to say that. How blunt he is, and how brave!

"You *are* my boy. You have my bones, and my blood. It took your ma to put us together. We ought to be grateful. You and I, Will'm, are peas in a pod."

"Peas in a pod."

"Yes."

"But why did Pauline leave me here?"

So he's going to call her by her first name. I admire this child, the way he figures out what he can take on and what he can't. He's going to be one of those purely good men.

"Women hand things down," I tell him. "Generation to generation. When I was born, Ida was out of her head. She wasn't any ma'am at all. So, when I had Pauline, I didn't know how to take care of her. Then, without me to show her, she didn't know what to do with you."

"But you took care of me."

"A body learns over the years."

"If you could go back and do things again, Gran, would you do them different?"

I put my cheek to his ear. "Well, that's the thing. We can't back up. Even if we could, I imagine we'd make the same mistakes."

"But . . ." He rubs his chin on the pup's soft head. "If you could change one thing, what would it be?"

That's almost too much to think about. There's Pap, of course—I'd not have run my mouth so much that night when we went into the ditch. Or Wing. Maybe I'd have been more understanding when he lost his ma'am and pap. Then there's Pauline, and Ida—or any one of a million other things.

"If I could do it over," I tell him, "I'd have us sit like this, together, every night of our lives."

"Then why," he says, in a voice I can barely hear, "do you want me to go?"

One question shouldn't carry so much weight. The only sound is the wind howling around the eaves. "Because it's best."

After a moment he asks, "Why is it best?"

"Will'm—"

He pulls away from me. "I do for you. I help out all the time."

"You do, yes."

"I don't give you trouble. I finish my schoolwork. Bring home A's."

"It has nothing to do with—"

Pauline stands in the doorway, in her nightgown. Even with sleep in her eyes, she's pouting. "I heard you-all talking."

"Go back to bed," I tell her. "Or at least put something on your feet. There's a pair of old house shoes under the bed."

"You-all were talkin' about me, weren't you? Mama, you can't tell me what to do with my boy."

I want so to smack her, I can hardly stand it. Or maybe it's that she's interrupted this moment.

Will'm talks like she's not there. "I want to know why I got to go."

He's stubborn, and I don't blame him.

"You're trying to get him over to your side," Pauline says.

Neither of them understands. There are no sides. I settle things in my usual way. "Since we're all up, I'll start breakfast."

"Gran," Will'm says before I can move, "are we like the Bible story with King Solomon and the baby with two mothers? And the one that loves him most says, 'You take him'?"

Lord, Lord, he can read my thoughts.

"Stop that talk right now," Pauline says, stamping her bare foot. "I birthed you!"

"Oh, for God's sake, Pauline," I tell her. "How is it, in all these years, you never grew up?"

She hugs her elbows. "You got no right to say that to me, Mama. Don't you ever think I'm sad and lonesome, too?"

"You could have come for a visit anytime."

"No, I couldn't. You didn't want me. After Daddy Saul died, nobody wanted me."

"That's foolish talk." I'm throwing words at her now, without thinking. I tamp the fire, add a few sticks, pour water in the pot.

"That's it?" she says. "That's the only thing you've got to say to me after all these years?"

"What is it you want to hear?"

"Some mamas tell their daughters they love 'em."

I take out a box of Farina and open the lid. Pour. Stir. Feel it coming—in another minute, Pauline's going to walk out of here, and it will be years before we see her again. Ida has taught me one thing—ma'ams don't necessarily love that which they squeeze out of their bellies and into this world. And Pauline appears only when she wants something.

"If I knew you, Pauline, I might come to love you."

She turns away. I stir in the cereal and feel sick to my stomach.

"Well, it should matter what I think," Will'm says. "And I don't want to go to California."

"Hollywood's real nice, Will'm," Pauline says, changing her tone. I see how scared she suddenly is. "Movie stars, just standin' on the corner."

There's a long silence while the Farina cooks. I put the pan on the table and ladle it up. Pauline sits down and stirs hers with a spoon.

How torn I am! If Will'm stays here, heaven knows what will happen. I have no right to put him in harm's way. Still, Pauline's going to be no better a ma'am than I was. She'll tuck him away over that liquor store and leave him alone days and nights, and there's no telling whether he'll finish school or have enough to eat. One other thing's itching me. "Pauline, after all these years, why do you want him now?"

"Look what a good-looking boy he is, Mama."

"You want him because he's got a sweet face?"

"Child stars are the rage," she says. "If producers give him even bit parts, he can help pay our rent. If he makes it big in the films, we can move to our own place, and I can drive around in a fancy car. I'll get a maid and—"

I'm both glad to hear it, and outraged. I plunk myself down in a chair. "Well, that does it. He's not going with you if hell freezes over."

Will'm's eyes widen, and his mouth opens up. "You mean it?"

"Don't talk with your mouth full. Of course I mean it."

"You can't do that," Pauline says. "You can't just change your mind."

"I can do more than that. Soon as you're done eating, Pauline, pack up your things and get out of my house. No judge in the country will give you the boy to use in that way."

Her eyes fill with tears, and air jerks around in her throat while I look at a spot on the tabletop. With what sounds like a sob, she gets up and flounces off into the bedroom. I hear her throwing things around, and in a few minutes she comes back wearing the same dress and cloth coat, the same high-heeled shoes, that she came in. I wonder if she's going to apologize to her son, but she simply takes her handbag from the drainboard and walks out through the grocery, slamming the door.

Will'm's eyes are round as quart jars.

"Eat your breakfast," I tell him.

"Yes, ma'am," he says, but we are both on fire with the need to grin. In another instant he's gotten up from his chair and come to put his arms around me, bury his face in my neck.

"Well!" Breath explodes from my chest. "Peas in a pod shouldn't be separated. Besides, I can't care for that cub near as good as you can."

"I love you, Gran."

"I love you, too, Will'm. But now that you're staying, there's things you've got to know. Bad things."

"What things?"

"There's going to be trouble—though I'll be damned if I know why."

He sits down in what was, a few minutes ago, Pauline's chair. "Tell me," he says. "I want to know."

"Will'm, I came upon Alton Phelps on Cooper's Ridge yesterday. Most of what he said didn't make a lick of sense, but he threatened us both."

"Threatened us how?"

"Said—first it was the wolves, and then us. That he didn't have to worry about Ida."

"What'd he mean?"

I shake my head, put down my spoon. I don't tell him what Phelps said about killing him slow. "I thought he was talking about the night James Arnold died—I told you that story—and was still holding Pap and me responsible. I said over and over how sorry I was, but I don't think that's it."

"What, then?"

I shake my head. "Maybe he believes Pap ran over James Arnold on purpose."

"And did he?" Will'm says.

"I can't think why."

"What do you think he'll do now?"

"I have no idea. But he means us harm."

"And that's why you were sending me away."

I let a few seconds pass, and then I nod.

"Well—now that I'm staying," he says, rubbing his hands together in a way that would make me smile if this wasn't so serious, "we'll figure this out."

"Will'm, this is not a game. We've got to put the pieces together, all right, but I can't have you in danger's way while we're doing it."

"We'll have to watch each other's backs, Gran. You could have been in a mess all alone, while I was off in California, starin' at palm trees."

"If anything happened to you—"

"Same goes double," he says.

"Well, here's the thing. I'm keeping the rifle loaded. If I think there's trouble coming, if I see it ahead, you go down to Wing's and stay till I fetch you."

"But—"

"Will'm, it wouldn't take me five minutes to catch up with Pauline. Is it a deal?"

Will'm sighs. "It's a deal."

45

Before noon I'm up and dressed. In fact, I've just finished feeding the goats and the chickens and gathering four eggs when Wing drives up in his station wagon.

"Olivia!" he calls, getting out.

"Wing," I say, clumping up the steps, banging snow from my boots. I feel myself tightening, closing up.

He comes around to the yard. "I see lumber stacked out in your barn. You renovating?"

"Something like that." What business is it of his what I do? But the illogic of that stymies me and forces me to put it away. "I've cleaned out the cellar and—things."

Even though we're on the porch and out of the wind, Wing shivers with cold. I'm so irritated with him I could shove him down the steps. A realization comes—the opposite of love is not anger, it's indifference. But which is it I feel?

"Any chance you've got coffee on the stove?" he says.

Under my cape, I wipe my cracked hands on my apron. "Come in. I'll make us some."

"Warm in here," he says, rubbing his hands over the stove that has not quite gone out.

I hang my cape on its nail, set the eggs in a basket with the two

I collected yesterday, throw into the stove a medium thickness of wood, bit of kindling, damn waste. Run water in the pot and add two spoons of coffee. Set it on the burner. Rub a bit of melted tallow on my hands.

"Place still looks the same," he says, pulling out a chair and sitting.

"You didn't have to wait thirty years to come out."

All the time I've spent in this kitchen, I don't know when I last looked at these chairs. Ladder-backed, bare wood worn to a blade. Table's the same. How shabby we must look.

"...I recall being here a lot," he's saying. "I'd come get you, and we'd walk the highway, down toward the river. I think everybody in town knew about us. Remember how Ida used to give us hell—"

"Wing."

He looks at me, but I turn and adjust the pot on the burner. "That was a lifetime ago."

I try not to think about the peeling linoleum, pitted wood showing through. I cannot help it if he's done well while I... I bring his coffee and pour myself a cup. Two weeks ago, I'd have wanted him to stay; today I ache for him to go.

"You been all right out here, Olivia? I mean, since Saul died and everything."

"Saul's been gone twelve years, Wing." I feel as if I've swallowed a head of cabbage, and it's lodged in my chest.

"The grocery going OK?"

"Yes."

"Remember the Fourth of July picnics we'd have down on the river?" he says, picking at a loose thread of memory.

I nod.

"Dooby's wife made the best peach ice cream. His old

freezer—we bigger boys took turns cranking. That pretty Olivia Harker would come flouncing along and sit on the lid while I turned the handle. Then I'd take your hand and we'd run off—"

"Wing."

He looks up.

I look off out the window, remembering Phelps' angry face and swallowing my secrets.

"Olivia?"

"What?"

"Would you like to ride over to Buelton, see a picture show with me next Saturday night?"

Saturday night. Something passes across me like a shadow. "Will'm—"

"He can come, too. Or stay at the hotel, if you feel right about it. He might like to listen to the radio—"

I see a possibility, the very thing I talked to Will'm about. I'm going to have to be pleasant, change tracks. "No movie, thanks, but while I'm renovating around here, you think Will'm could spend a night or two with you?"

Wing drains his cup, looks around for the pot. "Of course he can. I'd be happy to have him. When I'm away, Molly's ma comes up, runs the place fine. So, Olivia, how about dinner?"

Something important has come and gone, but I can't think what. For a moment I thought I heard Pap's voice. And Phelps saying, "I know what you're doing, and—"

What was it he'd said?

"—and I want it stopped."

Of course. It was the day I asked Love Alice and Mavis Brown to ride out there with me, hidden in Pap's wagon. The Phelpses had talked to Pap in words as mysterious as what Alton had said to me on the Ridge.

I get up from my chair and stand at the stove, looking at nothing. Press both hands to my belly. "Wing, why are you here?"

For a moment he's silent. "To see if you'd like to take in a show. Coffee, a piece of pie after."

I turn and look in his tired face, lines deeper than any man ought to have.

"I have missed you, Olivia," he says. "The way a man misses an arm or a leg."

"That's not fair."

He drains his cup, stands up.

"There is nothing," he says, "fair in this life. Things are what they are. I have loved you all these years, sometimes so much I could hardly stand it."

I am clamped in the jaws of an anvil. A while ago I wanted to shove him down the porch steps. Now I want to beat him with my fists. "You married Grace—"

"Why wouldn't I? You'd found someone, had a baby. I asked you, I said did you want me to give it my name."

"*Give it a name?* What kind of love is that? And anyway, it's not fair of you to tell me all that now. It's belittling of you, Wing, to mention Pauline."

"Don't talk to me about belittling, Olivia. You can't imagine how I felt, all those Saturday nights, playing at Silty's, watching the woman I loved make a fool of herself. I'm sorry, but it's God's own truth."

I should say nothing. Instead: "I was angry and lonely without you, and I couldn't stand living with Ida—"

"Watching you lay down with one man after another—"

I wanted to take up the skillet and beat him senseless.

"—after all we'd meant to each other."

"We were children! How can you be so unkind?"

"I'm hurting, Olivia. Did it make love any less, because we were young?"

My knees are so weak I can hardly stand. "God, Wing, I don't know what was real. My heart was breaking. I put you away."

"I don't believe that."

"Only a fool would grieve for a lifetime!"

Wing nods slowly.

"That's a lie," I say sadly. "I never stopped loving you."

"You don't much sound like it."

"Neither do you."

Wing sets his mouth, reaches for his coat, shrugs into it. I'm sending him packing one more time. But there's no other way. All I've felt for him amounts to nothing.

"Wing—"

"Send Will'm down. Anytime." He pulls the door shut behind him.

46

I have not told Will'm about my quarrel with Wing. I do, however, tell him that I've seen Wing and that he's invited Will'm to stay at the hotel now and then. The boy is delighted. In the event of trouble, I've covered all my bases.

We sit, after supper, when Will'm's taken Ida home and read to her. We're at the kitchen table, sorting out what we know. Not that anything gets in any way sorted. After a while, Will'm brings his notebook and writes things down, hoping that will make it clearer.

"We know this," I say while he writes. "Alton's taken a strong liking—or disliking—to our wolves. He's cutting off as many right ears as he can." I look up from the muslin square I'm embroidering. "Molly said the club comes three or four times a year." I knot an intricate stitch. "Funny I don't remember ever seeing them on the hill on a Saturday."

The word *Saturday*, clearly, has stuck in my mind.

I look up, past Will'm to the boarded window.

"Gran? What're you lookin' at?"

"Saturdays."

"Why?"

"When I think of them, I see the back of Pap's head."

"Gran—"

"Pap said something about Saturdays. Then I asked him what happened at the Phelpses' on Saturdays."

Will'm says nothing.

I'm thinking out loud. "He told me to forget we'd been there. Huh. Not likely the boys were makin' whiskey; they bought their liquor from Pap. When Pap cut them off, it was the start of all the trouble...."

"What trouble?" Will'm says.

Has all this been about running whiskey? Or gambling, maybe. Did Pap owe them money, somehow? Still, what difference does it make what Alton Phelps did at his place all those years ago? Unless, of course, he's still doing it. On Saturdays.

I can't imagine Pap involved with the likes of the Phelpses. Still, bootlegging wasn't exactly legal. Did any of that tie in with James Arnold's death night on the road? Had James Arnold come looking for Pap that night? Had Pap seen him climb up out of the ditch and made a quick choice to be rid of him? But Pap would never have deliberately put me in danger.

Phelps said, on the Ridge, that I *had information*. What is it, exactly, that he thinks I know?

I mix mustard paste for Will'm's poultice. He has no option but to pull on his nightshirt and climb into bed. I smooth the smelly flannel on his chest, kiss his forehead, and go off to my room where I change into my gown and huddle under the blankets. I want so badly to figure this out.

47

Tuesday night, after Will'm's breathing better with his cold, I realize that Phelps believes Pap let me in on a secret—whatever that was. He did not. Along those lines, I wonder if Pap ever told Ida. I've always suspected she knows more than she's saying.

On Wednesday, while Will'm is in school, I sit quilting and waiting on the coloreds.

Across the room, Aunt Pinny Albert is picking out canned goods. Her sisters Iva and Wellette are haggling over thread and lengths of elastic. Lengths of yardgoods.

"I got a nice bolt of red in," I tell them. I count four running stitches and draw the thread through. "Would look real good on you, Miss Iva."

The sisters look stunned.

I look up. "Something wrong?" I say.

"This a nice yeller," Miss Wellette says, quick. "Jus' right for spring."

"Sisters, that's two months off," says Aunt Pinny Albert, batting their hands. "You-all forget, we shoppin' light today."

"Just saying, you'd look real fine in the scarlet, Miss Iva. Done up pretty with a belt or a big white bow."

Miss Iva's face freezes, and she's barely breathing. Her mouth pinches up, like I've maybe spat on a grave, or suddenly cussed a blue streak.

I get up and come around, looking over at the bolts of new cloth.

"Not a thing, baby girl," Aunt Pinny Albert says, slapping Miss Iva a good one.

I ring up their purchases. There's a great deal of haggling over what they'll pay for and what will have to go on account, but they're distressed, and I'm saddened to think I caused it.

For now, however, I've got enough to brood on. I take up my needle and replay the day Pap drove the wagon to the Phelpses', how I stood up in Alton's face. By nightfall, my eyes burn from tiredness—or from looking so far into the past.

Will'm and I agree to sit tonight, and try to figure things out, but he's equally tired, and by eight o'clock we're ready for sleep. I've taken to tucking him into bed, the way I did when he was small. I drop a kiss on his forehead, and give the cub a pat before they both close their eyes. It's a ritual that keeps us sane and safe and remembering who we are.

On Thursday, there's almost no business. I make myself tea and sit at the table, listening for the bell over the front door. I work on the silver-blue quilt, and I remember more. After I came home from the hospital, Alton came often with presents and money—I'd always thought they were thanks for Ida's services. But maybe Ida knew something, and Alton brought her gifts to keep her quiet.

Another thing I don't understand—if he feels so threatened, it seems like over the years he'd have just killed us all.

I can't think anymore. Sometimes I've shared thoughts with Will'm, but he's busy—getting off the school bus in town afternoons, stopping by Wing's for a cup of chocolate. Then he goes

on to Dooby's or French's for a quarter's worth of shelf-stocking
and to sweep up at closing.

On Friday I realize I have not fetched Junk, not given one
more thought to the moving of Pap's grave. Some memory in my
mind won't show itself clearly. Whatever it is, I've dragged
through the week with the sheer weight of it.

One night, Will'm comes late from French's store where he's
been uncrating nails. While he eats his supper, I ask, "Stop by
Wing's, did you?"

With his mouth full, he nods.

"He doing all right?"

Will'm forks another potato. "Says he is, but—were you mean
to him, Gran?"

I put down the scissors and hug my elbows. "Why do you
ask?"

"When I talked about you, he got real quiet. There was this
look on his face—"

I need to change the subject. "Phelps' club still there?"

"Molly was running on about them tracking in mud, but I
didn't see any of 'em. You hear any shots?"

"Couple," I say. It is then that I see clearly what's to be done.
Like a pool of water, the notion finds its own level—so logical, I
never question it.

Thus far, I have shared most of my thoughts with Will'm, but
I'm terrified something will happen to him. First thing in the
morning, I'll see Wing. If things fall into place it'll be a sign that
I'm on the right track. Wing and Will'm have become fast
friends, and if Will'm's well enough with his cold, their closeness
will serve my purpose just fine.

By the next afternoon I'm a full case of nerves. Will'm's

delighted to be staying at the hotel, and although we've never been apart one night, I can't get him out of here fast enough. I end up sending him down an hour before Wing's expecting him. That way, I say, he can see Molly before she leaves for the day. He's sweet on her, and that gives me a new set of worries, but none that I can think about right now.

I fold his nightshirt into a bag, add an apple and a cold biscuit, hope he doesn't tell Wing. Clean drawers for morning, and a laundered shirt. At the last minute I give him a hug that he stoically endures and returns.

When he's gone, I close the grocery and pass another hour walking the floor—around the creaking boards of the front room, through the kitchen to the porch where the cold slaps me sharply. Then I head for the front door and begin again. Through the one kitchen window, I watch the sun go down as if its bottom's on fire, and I swear twilight's brighter than midday was.

I must wait for full dark, for it's Saturday, and tonight I'm going to see what goes on in Phelps' barn.

But an icy fog has begun to roll in.

48

If I catch Phelps running prostitutes or gambling, I'll call the sheriff, clear my mind, and get back to the business of moving Pap's grave. I've seen Junk twice this week, but I'm sure he's hoping I've forgotten or given up. Or that I've gone and done the job myself.

Still, something about this just doesn't lie flat. And Phelps has said Sheriff Pink is a friend of his.

Even full dark, this night is not black. The fog is lit by particles of ice and the snow on the ground, making everything a sort of silvery white in which, from the back door, I can see only the porch steps. Still, it's a perfect cover for snooping.

I back the truck out on the road and head east. Headlamps are no help at all. In fact, they make the going harder. Normally, it's a twenty-minute drive, but tonight it takes at least forty-five. I haven't made a plan, but I tell myself that's all right—there's no way to predict what I'll find, if anything. I'll decide on the spot—I've had plenty of practice at that.

To my considerable surprise, there are two cars ahead of me on this highway that usually carries so little traffic. Both lanes have been cleared so that the road's almost dry. I'm mildly grateful for it wouldn't do to have Phelps to find me in a ditch in his neighborhood come morning. I am taking this whole thing too much as a lark. Of course the road hasn't been cleared for me, but for his club—which probably accounts for the cars in front. They turn into his driveway and shut off their lights. This last thing, in fact, raises my curiosity several notches. Perhaps they are guests, and merely being considerate. I doubt it. I drive past.

A quarter of a mile on, with no traffic in sight, I make a U-turn and approach again. By now my eyes have adjusted to shapes, and between whorls of fog, I see that cars are parked behind his barn and the hedge, and along the road to the stables. I consider dousing my headlights, turning into the drive, and following the others. But no. Nor would it do to park on the side of the road— a Johnny-come-lately might recognize my truck. All the light, of course, spills from the barn.

I drive another quarter of a mile, step hard on the brake, and fishtail some—then grind into reverse and locate the narrow back road. It's rutted solid with ice, but seems my only means of getting close. Still, I've made no commitment. I could let this be the end—but Alton Phelps wouldn't see it that way. He's unwilling to forgive me for something I've either forgotten or never known, while, in fact, it should be he who is begging forgiveness from me.

I ease up on the clutch and down on the gas pedal, then turn in with my lights off. To stay on the road, I open my door, lean out, and follow the ditch. Pray no one comes from the opposite direction. It's maybe two miles before I find a place wide enough to turn around, and my eyes ache from straining in this light.

This must be it. No gate, just a break in the rails and tire tracks in the snow. I sit contemplating. Wish I'd remembered to put a shovel in the back of the truck, and a couple of feed sacks. And

that I'd been smart enough to leave a note, for if I get stuck between here and the barn, I'm as good as dead. Neither Will'm nor
Wing will ever know what's happened to me.

With every foot, the tires break through new crust and sink
until the snow is almost up to the running board. I'm not sure
what I'm doing, don't know where I am, and there's no pulling
over. I turn off the ignition, get out.

On foot, the going's no easier, and now there's no light at all. If
I cross the field, there's no telling what I might stumble into. I
plow ahead until I hear shouting. Liquor talk. Whatever Phelps is
up to, why here? How can he afford to be so obvious, so blatantly
breaking the law—unless he isn't. I am almighty tired of this cir-
cular thinking. But if this is just some damn barn dance, at least
I'll know.

But no—something is greatly wrong when a family I never see
nor speak to harbors such hate for me. And with Phelps, it appears to be more than harboring—he savors it. He rolls anger in
his mouth like an almighty gumball.

I come to the hedgerow. My boots are full of snow, and my
toes ache like bad teeth. I hunker down while two more cars arrive, five men I do not recognize. A woman is with them. They
pull dark handkerchiefs from their back pockets and shake them
out. Then they open the big barn door and disappear inside.

With as little noise as possible, I move around the hedge, and
into the space between bushes and the south wall. Almost no
snow has collected here.

When I press my face to the planks I see maybe twenty men
having a fine time. Light glints off the bottles and glasses they
hold in their hands. Off to one side are several bales of hay—
other than that, this barn is not a barn at all. Under the lights,

three young women in tight, shimmering dresses dance with el-bows locked and hips bumping. I have never in my life seen shoes with such high heels.

Phelps steps onto a platform. They all turn to him. The only other one I can make out, through the crack, is Doyle Pink, who's sure enough the county sheriff. The music scratches to a stop, but the women keep dancing. Phelps is talking, and although I hear words, I don't catch them. In unison they slide handker-chiefs over their heads, and then I see that they're not squares of cloth at all, because every man's head is anointed with a peak, and all the peaks are the reddest of reds. Blood rackets through my arms and legs as my heart turns loose of my breastbone and thuds into my boots. And there in the barn, above the bales of hay, hangs a loop of hemp, knotted into a noose.

Then an arm comes around me, and a hand covers my mouth so that I bite down and kick with my feet.

"Shh!" Elizabeth Phelps says. "Come away from here!"

In her eyes I see tremendous fear. I look back once, then let her lead me to the house, to the pretty kitchen now full of shadows. There's not one light on. She slips out of her coat.

She keeps her voice low. "In another half hour they'll be drunk as lords and urinating in the snow. You'd have been caught as sure as a rat in a trap."

"I'm caught now."

For a moment she says nothing, then sighs and sits down heavily in a kitchen chair. "Oh, Olivia. Why do you have to do this now?"

"Because your husband is killing my wolves."

"Well, it's certain you didn't come to be inducted. Your pap wouldn't hold with it, and I expect you won't, either."

"Inducted?" My eyes are adjusting, and I can see the white of hers. "Into what?"

"You don't know what I'm talking about, do you?"

"I'm getting almighty tired of hearing that," I say.

"Whatever's made you come here, Olivia, you could have forgotten. Saved yourself sorrow."

"I've already got sorrow, Miz Phelps. So why don't you tell me."

"There's no one to help you, Olivia. You saw the sheriff, tonight, out there in the barn. French, Andrews. The Detwieler brothers. They're all part of it just like their fathers were."

"Part of what?" I pull out a chair and sit facing her. Our knees touch. "Who are they? *What* are they? You talk to me now, or I'll drive into Paramus and bring back a federal marshal."

She laughs, a sound like something breaking. "By the time he got here, there wouldn't be one red robe left."

"Red robe?"

"That's what they wear when they hold the cotton trials."

Cotton trials. The words leave no taste on my tongue.

"I made every one of those robes myself," she said flatly. "Tonight they're taking in new members, so they'll only wear hoods."

The handkerchiefs I thought I'd seen hanging from their pockets....

"They think you're onto them," she says. "You can't just go home now, and run your store and sew your quilts. There's no going back. Olivia, Cott'ners were the dregs of the Klan. Men so cruel that even the Klan wouldn't condone what they did."

My stomach turns over. "Tell me about my pap."

Her voice has gone flat. "He came spying just like you. Only it was Booger that went out and hid him in the bushes."

"Booger!"

"Yes. That very night, James Arnold shot Booger in the back of the neck."

"Why?"

She shrugs. "Maybe they saw him with your pap. Maybe he was going to tell on them, who knows? Olivia, I used to work for Alton's mama. One morning they found Booger in his bed, staring at the ceiling with what was left of his eyes. They told everyone he did it himself. But I knew."

She looks away.

Booger saved my pap's life.

"Please, Olivia, forget what you saw tonight."

"They're coming after me and my boy."

"They won't—because you're not colored."

A flash of guilt lights the backs of my eyes. The pain is as deep as the night when I begged God to change the color of my skin. "He threatened me—"

"He's hurt a lot of people to get where he is. It's extortion, Olivia, plain and simple. Like taking a child's milk money. He collects payment from families—or he hurts them bad. His pa did it, before him." Her voice grows vague, and she looks away. "Maybe that's what he's planning to do with you."

I know she is lying. "Elizabeth—"

"No more, Olivia! Get in your truck and drive away from here! *Hurry!*"

49

I can't close my eyes, let alone sleep. Even awake, I dream of men in long robes, invading my house. In a way I wish I'd gone on looking through the crack in the barn wall. Maybe I'd have witnessed a man admitted into this Cotton Club. I wonder who the new man is.

So Pap hit upon something whether he knew it or not. Or maybe he had already seen them, or guessed, and that day, when we delivered the brown jugs, he was letting them know that he knew the truth. And the Pope County sheriff is stupid Doyle Pink, a Cott'ner himself.

Who else, I wonder.

Before daylight I'm up—having never undressed. It's Sunday, and there's nothing to be done today. Around noon, Will'm walks up from town with Wing's copy of the *Buelton Sunday News*. The paper reports that half the school is out with colds and influenza, so they've closed the place down. Will'm's not disappointed, and wants to know if he can stay at the hotel for one more night. Wing's going to show him how to make his famous sticky buns. Will'm asks, too, if we can sell the buns in the store.

"For a percent of the profits," I tell him. "Wing could have come and asked me himself."

I pour coffee. All morning I've worked on a red and white striped quilt top, my needle dipping and pulling, fingers tying dozens of red knots. Still, the work doesn't keep me from trying to fathom men so cruel they've been turned away by the most malicious tribunal in human history. And I know who they are.

"He says you're mad at him, Gran."

"I'm not mad at him. I'm not *anything*."

"Yes, you are."

I give Will'm a look. At Wing's he'll be safe for another night....

"Tell him—fresh every morning. The second day I'll mark them down. After that they're fodder for the goats."

Will'm grins.

I sleep that night because I'm exhausted. The next morning I'm up before dawn, and driving toward Buelton. I considered Paramus, but I don't want to be away from the grocery any longer than I have to. I cannot think of a single pay phone in Aurora that's guaranteed safe. There's no one I trust. Wing has a telephone, but he must be kept clear of all this. A sudden thought threads itself down my spine—might Wing be a Cott'ner?

I arrive in Buelton an hour and a half before the place opens, so I find a cafe and sit drinking cups of black coffee. Finally I drive back, park out front, and go in. I tell a woman at a desk that I need a telephone number. She sends me to another woman behind a counter.

This one asks me if it's long distance, and I tell her I think so. I'm woefully stupid on the subject of telephones. I'm sent to a back room, to a spectacled young man behind a desk. I can barely see him over stacks of directories.

"What city?" he says.

"I don't know."

"Well, is the number you're looking for in this state, in Kentucky?"

I don't know that, either. Perhaps marshals keep offices only in Washington, D.C. Pap talked about revenuers from the Treasury office. *G-men,* he called them. But I'm not calling to report moonshining.

"I need to talk to a federal marshal."

"United States ... federal ... marshals," he says, pulling out a book and thumbing through. He runs a finger down one page. "Twelve cents for three minutes, and you can use that phone, there. Put on the headpiece. I'll connect you."

I nod, open my purse, and give him the change that he drops in a drawer. I sit at the other desk and fit the set over my head. Adjust the ears. Hear clicks and humming and dialing, and then a woman says, "United States Marshals Service."

"I beg your pardon," I say. "My name is Olivia Cross, and I need to know where you're located."

"Wheeling, West Virginia. How may I help you?"

The only thing I can say about help coming from West Virginia is that at least it's on the right side of the country.

"Is that the only office you have?"

"Oh no, ma'am," she says in her perfect voice. "We're stationed in every state. Where are you calling from?"

I tell her.

"We have offices in Lexington and Bowling Green. What city are you calling from?"

"Aurora."

"I'm sorry, I don't know that area. Can you be more specific?"

"Just north of the Tennessee line—about fifty miles east of Route sixty-five."

"I'm looking at my map," she says. Then, "Yes. Our nearest office is in Nashville. Would you like that number?"

Nashville. Nearly sixty miles away.

"Yes, please. Just a minute." I look around for the young man, but he's gone. I reach for a notepad and tear off a corner, open a desk drawer, find a pencil. I write it down.

"If you'll hold a moment, I'll connect you—"

Behind me, a voice. "Why, hello, Miz Cross. What a nice surprise."

I jerk off the headset, and it clatters to the floor. "Mr. French! What are you doing here?"

He followed me, of course.

"Trouble with my telephone bill. You?"

"Thinking of putting one in," I say, glad Will'm and I once talked about this. "It'd be good for taking orders—making deliveries."

"I thought," he says, looking around, "that this was the long distance room. My mistake. Well—" He reaches for my hand.

I bend to pick up the headgear and tuck the scrap of paper in my boot. Grip his cold thin bones. Murmur, "Good to see you."

I think, *Better to have seen you Saturday night.*

I never liked Henry French. Now I know he's no more than pond scum.

I scurry outside. Climb into my truck, so nervous that at first I can't start it. Drive away. The man behind the books will be easily bribed to tell French everything. In the end, these are hard times for us all.

50

I wonder if I've beat Henry French back to town. I open the grocery, set change in the till, and glance around to see if there's any straightening to be done. But I'm accustomed to doing this at the end of each day, and things are in order. And then they aren't.

I have to look twice, and then again, walk over to the counter, lifting and lining up, and then looking again.

The bolt of red cloth is gone.

I'm growing accustomed to being afraid, to glancing into the dark corners of the store, under counters and my bed and in the kitchen alcove, although I'm not sure what I'm looking for. In the end, the bolt of cloth is still gone.

I keep the grocery open for the rest of the day, then run some errands and pick up the boy at Dooby's. Will'm balances the cub's box on his knees. Carrying it with him is the only way he can work and keep the pup constantly fed. The cub has taken an intense liking to curling up behind the boy's ear.

"I'm fixing to name him," Will'm says. "I didn't before because I wasn't sure . . ."

"Wasn't sure what?"

"That he'd stay."

Words well put. We head home. But when I turn in the driveway I can tell more things are wrong than just missing cloth. A body can't live forty years under one roof without knowing when the house has been changed. I get out of the truck. Whoever was here has left the back door open, and from the porch we see the mess of broken dishes, poured-out salt and bacon fat, the knives and forks slung around, and I know French called Phelps from the telephone office. It's a wonder Phelps waited until I was gone. It will take me days to clean up what probably took him ten minutes to do. And when I step through the rubbish to the grocery where sacks of flour and sugar are slashed and every bin has been emptied on the floor, I know it's time to tell the boy some things.

First, though, I check the cash box in the drawer—six ones, a five, eighty cents in change, exactly what should be. With a razor blade I set Will'm to scraping syrup from the oven door, inside and out, so we can at least build a fire. Then I sit on the floor, still in cape and hat, pinching spilled salt into one cup and ground coffee into another.

"That's the best I can do," he says after a while. His hands are a globby mess. "I'll wash up and then throw in some kindling. It's freezing in here, and I reckon we're just going to smell like a candy factory for a while."

I nod. "Put in a small log, boy, we're going to be warm." On the porch are sacks I've made from unbleached muslin. I'll measure flour and sugar into them, see what all I can save.

But first I must tell Will'm what's happened. I also tell him about how I hid in Pap's wagon, all those years back, and what I heard.

"You say Mr. French was nice to you today?"

"Right there in the office he shook my hand."

"Maybe Mrs. Phelps was mixed up. Maybe all these Cott'ners do is hunt rabbits."

"And wolves. Will'm, with all the losses you've suffered, the things I've denied you, the hundreds of bowls of thin oats you've eaten—how is it you can still think the best of folks?"

He turns away and begins sweeping up glass.

"Look around you, Will'm! There's bad in this world! Now give me the broom, and I'll do this while you get into your nightshirt. In the morning we'll start on the store. See what we can salvage."

51

And, before sunup, we do. I heap the worst-dented cans in a crate—three for a nickel. The sacked-up flour and sugar look festive in bags tied with string. Customers will wonder what Harker's Grocery is coming to. I have scrubbed most of the grocery floor, and I'm ready to pour myself a cup of coffee when I look out and see Junk coming up the road, carrying a pair of shovels. The bedroom's still a mess, and we haven't done much with the kitchen larder. I pull on my cape, wrap a scarf around my head, and meet Junk in the driveway.

"I guess I'm ready, Miss Livvy," he says, looking anything but ready to dig up the dead. "You want to show me first where we're goin' to put him?"

I lead the way up the hill, the day bitter cold but no different from any other. The sky is gunmetal gray, and our breath freezes on the air. I up the pace because there's already pain where my face is exposed. I adjust the scarf. Junk's clearly wearing two pairs of trousers, and a thick Army coat with holes in the elbows. Ear flaps hang down from his knitted cap, and his lips are dry and cracked.

I choose a spot not far from Saul's, and Junk stabs it with the spade.

"You don't think we oughta wait till spring, when the ground ain't froze?"

I've got to admit, when I saw him coming up the drive, back there, I considered it. But no, I want it done and over, and we might as well. I don't think Phelps' men will come again right away. The boy should be safe in the store, today.

"I don't believe it'll be bad, Junk. Not under the snow—it's shady here, even in winter. These cedars—"

He nods, and we begin to dig. It's damned hard work. Finally, when the sun is high and he drops into the hole and measures it with six of his big steps, we declare it done. We take our shovels and go down to the house. I'm grateful for the chance to look in on Will'm, and one glance tells me he's cleaned up the larder.

Now he's happy to sit at the table and spoon up soup with Junk and me. I put a whole loaf of bread out and watch Junk break several thick slices into his bowl. Then Love Alice looks in at the back door, and I fetch another bowl. We're good company, the four of us. I wish I'd made a custard from yesterday's eggs because I know how Junk loves them. But Love Alice has brought a tin of baking powder biscuits, and I send Will'm to the grocery to fetch jam. I make a note in my head that I owe the register another eight cents.

When we are done, Will'm goes back to the store. I tell him, if he sees Phelps drive up, or anyone he doesn't know, he's to lock the front door and yell out the back.

"Any of those Phelpses ever have kids?" Will'm asks.

"No. But Alton and James Arnold had a little brother— Booger."

"*Booger?*" Will'm says.

"He was one sad little boy. Four steps behind on the day he was born."

"Booger," Will'm says again. "What happened to him?"

"He died a long time ago. They buried him in the hard ground."

"Why'd you say it like that?"

"Like what?"

"The hard ground. You said it funny."

I don't need him to tell me. That's how Alton said it—or maybe James Arnold, when Pap asked if he could help with the burying.

"Let's get back to work," I tell Will'm.

Out in the yard, Junk says we need a pickax for this job. He and Love Alice and I troop to the shed. Love Alice, with her thin bones and lack of fat, shivers under her thick layers of wool. Junk digs around for an ax. "Miss Livvy?"

There's a knot in my stomach, and I wonder, now, if I should have waited, and what is this need for so much housekeeping. This strange business with the Phelpses is what I want to erase. On the other hand, if I hold off, Junk might have had to dig two graves, or three, instead of one. He might yet dig more. The whites of Junk's eyes are uncommonly large, thick lips puffing circles of anxious breath.

"What time of year Miss Ida bury him?" Junk asks.

"Winter."

"Then he gon' be on the south side, all right. Which way you think she laid him, crosswise or long?"

I have no idea.

Junk looks at Ida, wrapped in her blanket. "I reckon she won't tell us, neither."

"Probably not." Beneath the blanket, I hope Ida's wearing boots. In the last week or so, she's lost most of her hair. Great hanks of it lay on her pillow in the mornings, and what's left is thread-limp and in need of washing. Her pipe's clamped in her teeth, and a curl of smoke rises from it.

"We'll just dig, and see what we find," I say.

Junk nods, sets the edge of the shovel on the crusty snow, and applies his foot. I dig, too. For more than an hour, we turn up dirt, and before long there are two great earthen piles. Junk and I are in a hole to our waists. Love Alice makes tea in my kitchen and brings us a cup. We drink it fast because our feet are freezing, but the warmth feels good in our bellies. Ida, refusing hers, produces a match, relights her pipe, and sets the tobacco blazing. She draws on it mightily, and a blue wreath circles her head.

We begin again. My back has long since passed merely aching, and my arms refuse to lift one more shovelful. Junk, heaving dirt up and over the edge of the hole, makes the noise of a great bull elephant while Love Alice, in her woolly layers, squats on the rim.

I survey the breadth and width that we've dug. "Junk?"

"Yes'm?"

"She said nobody came to his burying."

"Yes'm," he says softly.

"So she must have dug the grave by herself. But it was winter—she couldn't have dug any deeper than this."

"No'm."

"He—isn't here."

"Seems that's true."

"She didn't dig here at all. Then where is he?" I look at Love Alice, and on past her to Ida. In that instant, sparks fly from her pipe, and the bottom of her blanket is wrapped in smoke. Flames race around the binding, find the hem of her nightgown, make a quick neat circle above her boots. Before I can climb out of the hole, the fire's rushed up her gown and ignited her hair. Ida never even opens her mouth.

Then Junk's beside me—Love Alice is screaming. I knock Ida to the ground. Junk scoops handfuls of snow on her. I rip away what's left of the gown, and we roll her, naked as the day she was born, along the thin crust of snow. She's so light, she doesn't even break through.

I struggle out of my cape and wrap her in it, Junk lifting her as if she weighs nothing, and we run, me shouting for Will'm to bring the truck keys. It takes forever for the engine to turn over. Against the far door, Love Alice cradles Ida who seems to be sleeping. Junk climbs in back. My belly wrenches as I back down the driveway—leaving Will'm alone. He stands by the barn. Our eyes meet, and then he turns and hurries inside. I pray to God he locks himself in.

It's only a mile to Doc Pritchett's. I pull right up to the porch steps, and by the time I get out and come around, Love Alice has run inside to fetch Doc, and Junk is lifting Ida from the truck.

No one says a word, me holding the door, Junk carrying Ida past a few curious folks who are waiting. In Doc's examining room, he lays her on the table. Doc peels back the wool cape, studies the burns, lifts Ida's eyelids, looks in her mouth, puts his stethoscope to her chest.

"Well," he says at last. "How'd this happen?"

"Her pipe—" I tell him.

"Poor old Ida."

"Yessir," says Junk. "She went up like kindling."

Love Alice stands with her hands over her mouth.

Doc fetches a wash basin and soap. "I'll clean these up while she's out," he says. "Olivia, you-all go sit in my front room. I'll call you when I see how bad she is and get these burns dressed. Go on, now."

Junk and Love Alice go, but I can't. I drop onto a stool, as numb as if I'd frozen in that hole. When Doc has pulled off her boots and is cleaning the black patches on her legs, I say, "I should've known it would happen, her smoking that pipe. It's a wonder she didn't burn up in her bed."

"It was one of her last pleasures, Olivia. She would've raised holy hell if you'd taken it away from her. You-all wouldn't have been able to live with her."

"Couldn't hardly live with her anyway."

"Well, this is probably going to send her 'round the bend. She won't be able to fend for herself."

"What am I going to do? I can't watch her every minute."

With tweezers Doc works at the bits of cotton that have stuck to her knees. He applies salve. "Well, somebody's got to."

I close my eyes.

"Leave her here tonight, Olivia. I'll keep her on laudanum, watch her close. By tomorrow we'll know what's what. I heard you and Junk were digging up there by the outhouse."

"Word sure travels fast."

"When did it not?" he says. "You and the boy get some rest tonight." He applies ointment to Ida's forehead in a way that reminds me of myself, back in the hospital, my face rearranged.

But Doc is saying, "Her hair's gone, and her eyelashes, too."

"Doc?" I know I am talking, but my voice sounds far away. I wonder if the cold has done something to my ears. Or my tongue. "We were moving Pap today. I was putting him on the hill next to Saul, but when we dug down—there wasn't anything there. Not a box nor a shard of bone. Do you—do you know where she put him?"

He sighs heavily. "I reckon that's something you'd have to ask Ida."

"But you said—even if she wakes up, she won't have her wits about her."

"Might not," he says. "This has been a long time coming."

"But—if she doesn't come around, how will I ever know?"

"Maybe you won't," he says. "Come by in the morning, and see how she's doing."

52

Will'm washes two plates, two forks, and his milk glass. Neither of us felt like eating, and although he drank the precious milk, I wound up throwing supper to the goats.

"We didn't accomplish one thing today," I say, "except for digging a couple of big holes out there—and Ida setting herself on fire."

Will'm shakes his head. "Know what?"

"What?"

"I didn't hear any shots today."

A shudder passes through me. Clearly, Phelps has had other things on his mind.

"If we told Wing about Phelps," Will'm says, hanging up the dish towel, "he'd help us."

"Phelps and his buddies are paying customers of Wing's. I can't fault him for renting them rooms."

"But Wing's pretty smart about stuff like that, and he wouldn't tell anybody—"

I shake my head. "Wish I'd asked Miz Phelps what all those Cott'ners do, what those trials mean. But telling Wing anything would put him in harm's way, too."

As if he has heard us, Wing's station wagon pulls in the driveway. Will'm lets him in. I'm surprised that he's come. His glasses fog over with sudden warmth. "Will'm," he says. He nods in my direction. "Junk told me about Ida. How is she?"

"Not good," I say.

Wing watches Will'm take up the cub. Will'm unbuttons his shirt and tucks the cub in. The purring is loud enough to be heard in the next room.

"I'll be damned," Wing says, grinning at Will'm. He hasn't yet looked at me. "So what's Doc saying?"

"The burns aren't as bad as they might have been," I tell him. "The worst is—"

Then he turns to me. His glasses have slid to the end of his nose and he studies me over the top of them. When I don't answer, he says, "Of all the damn accidents."

An accident. This is something I have not wanted to think about. Whether it was or not, the timing was extraordinary, for my next words to Ida would have been, *Where the hell have you put my pap?*

Wing puts out a hand and strokes the cub. "Olivia—I'd be glad to help. If there's something I can do."

I shake my head. The man has gumption.

"Listen, you and the boy ought to come down to the hotel tonight. You'd be closer to Doc's place, each have your own room. There's the telephone, and I could drive you up to Doc's quick if the need arose."

Will'm's eyes grow round.

"We couldn't—" I say.

"Double shocks today, of course you could. Besides, you can use the rest."

So Junk has told him about the empty grave.

Wing pulls out a chair and sits down, splays his legs—seems at home, and I wonder how, after our last conversation.

Rest. At some point, I got past needing relief from Ida, and my body just kept on. Eventually, I forgot how hard it all was. But other things have worn me down, too. "Pauline was here."

After a minute, Wing says, "I'd like to have seen her."

I fetch the broom from the porch and sweep around his feet like I've just given him a haircut or something. "She came for the boy. I wouldn't let her take him."

"Well, good for you." I think he wants to say more, I can feel it hanging in the air. "Please come to the hotel, Olivia."

"Gran—"

"You've got to catch the bus in the morning—if your cold is better. Which reminds me, I've got to make you a mustard plaster. You can't leave the cub, and tomorrow's Colored Day. Will'm, don't forget to write down that Love Alice has credit—"

"I already did." Will'm is holding the cub and his shirt with one hand, pouring tinned milk in a pan with the other. But his eyes are on me.

"There's so much to be done—the hole to fill in. I'm too tired to sort all this out tonight, Wing."

"Then come and let me take care of you both. There's no harm in one night."

The greater part of me wants him to go. I should be putting thought into Phelps' warning. But with Wing sitting in my kitchen, running his thumb over a crack in my tabletop, the whole idea of a threat slips away. I have no idea what I feel about Wing. One minute I'm one thing, the next something else. I shake my head.

"Well then," he says, getting up. "You want me to stop by Doc's, check on Ida?"

"I'll go down first thing in the morning."

He nods. "If you need anything. Will'm, Olivia."

I look at Will'm's face, sulking the way Pauline used to. I'll have old molly hell to pay when Wing walks out the door.

53

In the morning, Will'm's still mad at me. But I leave him with the store, start the truck, and drive down to Doc's. Lights are on in the kitchen and in the tiny back room that he uses for overnight stays. It's where Doc took Pauline's tonsils out.

"Come on in, Olivia." He holds open the door.

Ida is laid out on the cot in the back room, all right, and Doc is in the middle of changing her dressings. Her flesh is terrible to look at, puckered and red-black where she's burnt, the rest of her old and wrinkled. And she's so small. With fresh bandages on, she looks like a child playing at war, a soldier returning. Poor Ida. What an awful life she's had, at least after she married Pap. Maybe he should have let her go on riding her donkey and preaching the gospel. I wonder if, back then, she was sane, if God really held her in the palm of his hand. But I know that's wrong-thinking. God holds us all, Ida says, and she's no different. What could her soul have been thinking when she volunteered for this body? Maybe it was birthing me that sent her over the edge.

"Olivia," Doc says. "She hasn't come around. Seems like she's sunk inside herself. Shock victims do that."

If things were different, I might weep. But I've been angry with

Ida so long, I don't know anything else. Even now the only reason I wish she'd wake up is so I can ask her where she buried Pap.

"I can't keep her in the house with me, Doc," I say. "I'd go plumb out of my mind."

"Nobody's saying you ought to, Olivia. I think you should consider putting her where she'll get the kind of care she needs."

"Where would that be?"

"An institution," he says.

Although the sun is bright, the room feels full of damp. "What kind of institution?"

"Well, there's the sanitarium . . ."

He means the asylum where Ida was a long time ago. "The crazy house."

He makes a face, like I've said a bad word. "They'll take care of her burns, too."

I have never been to the place myself, but I've heard tales. A long time ago, I put those stories away from me, but I've always wondered how doctors deal with the mind. How they ever managed to put Ida back together—at least for this long.

I'm embarrassed to say: "I can't pay for her care."

"I can make a call."

Then, behind me, Wing says, "If you like, I'll drive you over there, Olivia." I did not hear him come in.

"Morning, Wing, Olivia," Doc's wife says, coming in.

Wing looks me straight in the eye. He hasn't slept a minute more than I have.

"Woman," he says in a squared-off voice, "you can get mad all you want, but the way I see it, you need help. You're too stubborn to ask for it. So I've been up to the highway and filled the station wagon with gasoline."

"I—"

"I guess Will'm's minding the store—when he closes, he can go up to Molly's. I'll fix it with Marta."

Molly's—a new hiding place, if his being there hasn't set that whole family in danger.

"That's a good idea, Wing," Doc says. His eyes are watery, his face like crumpled paper. "Olivia—listen now. You were a tyke when I came around with that buggy. Tate and I drove her over there. It was the only thing to do. And I'll tell you the truth—I was surprised she ever came home."

Had he been reading my mind? I look at the floor, at the enamel cabinets and tongue depressors, wanting someone to take all this away from me. I've ignored Ida, hated her from the moment she came. I prayed that God would send her back. Now Doc says I can do it myself, and I don't understand why I'm not jumping at the chance.

"You're a grown woman, Olivia. You make the decisions, but I'm telling you plain. At least go and look."

"All right," I say.

Wing nods.

"Don't be surprised by the place," Doc says. "And let me know what you decide."

54

I've arranged for Will'm to spend the evening at Molly's," Wing says.

In the front seat of his green station wagon, I look over at him.

"Don't worry. Marta and her husband will see to him. Molly's got two sisters—they'll love him."

I remember Molly, the incessant chatter that delighted Will'm, how she had him under her thumb. "It's not *that* I'm worried about."

Wing laughs, and I'm embarrassed that maybe he remembers.

The asylum is actually Stipling State Hospital, surrounded by a high brick wall with broken glass imbedded on top. A gatehouse keeper takes my name, looks over his list, and waves us through. The building itself is a granite box. I count six rows of grilled windows, stacked like gray milk crates. We park and get out.

I do not take Wing's arm, though he offers it. The door is unlocked and we go into a lobby with a glassed-in office, and a woman gets up and hurries away through an inner door. Wing touches my arm, says why don't we take a seat over here.

Victrola music plays somewhere, whining and thin.

An egg-shaped man steps out of the office. He's dressed in a brown suit, with a fringe of pale hair and unpolished shoes. Even his skin is colorless.

"I'm Dr. Baird, from Evaluation and Assignment," he says, shaking Wing's hand and then mine. He carries a clipboard. "Dr. Pritchett phoned from Aurora and said you were in need of quick placement."

"For my mother," I tell him, lest he think it's for me, or for Wing.

"Well," he says, "we'll have to accommodate her, of course. We're a state institution. Although we're understaffed and badly funded."

It sounds like something he says all the time.

"Ida Harker. I understand she had a mishap with fire. A number of patients come to us that way. Scorched hair, chopped off fingers, gangrenous toes. She'll be in our infirmary until she recovers or passes. I suppose you'll want to see the place."

He's the most plainspoken man I've ever met.

"We'll take care of her medications," he says. "Three meals a day."

"She's picky about her food," I tell him.

"They all are." He leads us down a hall. "And should she reach levels One or Two, we have activities to keep her busy."

I can't picture Ida involved in activities.

"We have four psychiatrists on staff," he says. "They see patients as often as they can. Along here are our kitchens, and the cafeteria. We bring One here for their meals. Levels One and Two do their own laundry."

"How many patients?" Wing asks.

"Five hundred and fourteen at the moment, although we're set up to accommodate two hundred and fifty. The state mandates that we take the overflow."

"How many go home from here?" I ask him.

"Staff meets quarterly, releases twenty-five each time."

Twenty-five people, ready or not.

Baird looks at the clipboard. "Ida Harker was young when she was here. The younger they are, the better chance they have."

I recall how Pap labored to pay the bills.

"We have five levels here," Baird is telling Wing. "Miz Harker was on Two, then we moved her to Four."

"I'd like to see those, please."

He sighs. "All right. Come this way."

Is he wondering, *How long before we must accommodate you, too?*

He takes us down corridors, punches a button. Baird pushes back grillwork and we step into the elevator. The walls and ceiling are canvas and padded. When it stops, he takes a key from his pocket and unlocks the door. "Three is our sleepers. This is the men's side."

A long corridor opens before us, with cots lined up, and mattresses between. The place is old, and a lot of the plaster is gone from the walls. The antiseptic is so strong it makes my stomach hurt. At least fifty men lie here, stiff as corpses, though few are sleeping. Eyes are lost in dark sockets; jaws sag, most with no teeth. The sheets are thin with constant laundering, and the arms bone thin and spotted with purple. Nurses glide up and down on rubbery shoes. The snoring is terrible. I find Wing's hand.

"Some are comatose," Baird says. "A few catatonic. Most fade in and out. We take their dentures so they won't choke on them."

"I want to see Four."

"Miz Cross," he says, "that's a bit premature."

But Ida might live here the rest of her life, and right now I'm in a foul mood.

We get back in the elevator and go up one floor. Immediately opposite us is a thickly grilled screen, and behind that, a radio's playing.

"This is the dayroom," Baird says. "As you can see, we've cut down on size to accommodate more cells."

Cells.

In the dayroom, patients sit stiffly on straight-backed chairs or shuffle up and down in pajamas or bathrobes. An elderly man rushes to press his face to the screen. His eyes are milky, the pupils like pinpricks. His head is shaved, and there are purple ink marks on his temples. "Why am I here?" he asks me.

Baird says, "Mr. Franks asks everyone that. He knows why he's here."

"Why is he?" Wing asks.

Baird sighs. "He strangled his wife with a nylon stocking, then tucked her in bed in the spare room and left her for three weeks. By the time police found her, he'd bought her eighty-one pairs of stockings to compensate.

"The women's dayroom is on the other side. And down there are the ladies on Four who can't get along."

Down there is a narrow hall with equally narrow doors with low, slotted openings. I wonder what the slots are for.

Behind almost every one I see papery skin on a skeleton face. The racket is deafening. It's amazing how much they look alike—terribly old, even the young ones. Fingers poke out. Two put their lips to the space. One blows a kiss.

Down the hall, an orderly turns a key in a lock. I hear shrieking, then a tired argument.

"Bath time," Baird says with a sigh.

I try to imagine Ida being here while Pap and I bound torn paws and peddled brown jugs. While we grew corn and beans and ate flapjacks with syrup so sweet it made our teeth ache.

Orderlies have pried the screaming woman from her cell. Inside the bathroom, some tubs are covered with rubber sheets. An old woman shakes violently in a trough full of ice, and a nurse jams a twist of something in her mouth. Along the far wall are leather swings with leg holes like the kind they put babies in. A woman sits on a toilet. She wears a canvas coat with long, strapped arms—a straitjacket, I think. To my right is a staircase.

"There's another level?" I say.

Down the hall Wing is asking about staff—how many of this, what number of that. From above comes a wailing such as tomcats make. I go up, turn at the landing, and listen. Screams and keening in a dozen pitches.

Here are rows and rows of metal wire runs, each holding maybe twenty women—these ladies' chins are wet with spittle, noses crusted. One has no eyes, just lids sewn shut, and I look away. Without exception, their faces are bone, some heads shorn, a few with long, matted hair, but not for long, I think. They'll be bound and bathed and shaved and God knows what else.

Most wear sacks with holes cut out—or nothing at all. Their faces aren't vacant like the sleepers on Three or the walkers on Four, but wrenched into grins, or twisted with a personal terror that came and stayed. Their screams fill cracks in the plaster and bounce off beams. When a dozen stop weeping, a dozen more pick it up, and they move all the time, like a pot of something alive and stirred. Their eyes are dark holes filled with splintered glass.

Inside the cage, someone shrieks, "Lucy, come back here! Lucy?"

One woman slaps; one bursts into tears. "I can't dance to this music!"

"Whatta you mean, charge too much? I never charged a penny more—"

A young girl squats on the floor.

Like a circus monkey, a thin one climbs the wire to the ceiling. "No more babies, Albert! I can't, I can't!"

An orderly comes with a bucket and a mop. He slaps at the cage.

They bang their heads as if their skulls need emptying, and perhaps that's it. Or maybe they've hurt someone, or forgotten things like how to bake bread or milk the cow. Then there was nowhere to put them except on Five. All my life I've been afraid of insanity, and now I'm looking it in the face. It looks like Ida. Phelps. Me.

One of the nurses hurries over. I wonder if she'll snatch my pocketbook and the pins from my hair and toss me a blanket, lock me away. More, I hope there's a commode so I won't have to squat on the floor.

What if this sickness runs in a family? Maybe Ida got it from her ma'am, and her ma'am before her. What an unholy waste of generations. I wish I could find the first woman who bore a child and then walked away from it. Maybe she wasn't the Judas I've always thought her to be. Maybe, in her head, something just broke.

Inside the cage, a woman spins on the balls of her feet, her head cocked as if she hears something I can't. I hook my fingers in the wire, and the ladies come like ducklings to crumbs. Their hands are pale, rigid claws, but they have calluses and broken nails just like me. A bit of a girl with tangled hair sits on the floor, elbows out, rocking. She looks up and sees me. Says, "Mama wants me home right now."

Another murmurs, "That's Bernice, rocking her baby...."

I wonder if Bernice's infant died. Or maybe she put it down and forgot where she left it.

"Don't wake the baby!"

"Olivia," Wing says, taking my shoulders. He turns me gently. I hear him inhale, like he's going to say something, but no words come out.

Mama wants me home right now.

I'm too anguished to cry. "Oh, Wing, I see now—even though we grow to be women, we're still little girls. We never stop wanting our mamas. I've always hoped Ida'd come to her senses, act like she loved us. But she couldn't. She probably wanted her own ma'am—or someone—to tell her she was gonna be all right."

Wing draws me into his soapy smell. My teeth are on his button. I feel his face in my hair.

"That's what Pap used to tell me. And, oh, how I've ached for those words. If I'd known about this place, how bad it was, I could have made things easier for Ida."

"Olivia, you were a child. You weren't responsible for her. And not one day in your life have you been anything other than what God made you, which is wonderful and precious and beautiful."

I rest my forehead on his collarbone. "But I didn't do my best or anywhere near it."

"Olivia, doing our best every minute would exhaust us. Whatever we do—it is what it is."

"How do you know it's enough?" I say, looking at him.

His grin is crooked. "God told me."

"The way he told you to play the trumpet?"

Wing buttons my cape. I think of the night Will'm and I sat folded together, listening to the ragged breathing of the tiny wolf cub.

Dr. Baird says, "Miz Cross—shall I send someone to pick Miz Harker up, then?"

Wing lifts my chin and looks in my face. Life is given to us, and we do what we can. Ida cannot.

"Tomorrow morning?" he says. "Around nine?"

"Yes," I say.

The nurses cluck like hens on a cold morning. Wing leads me down flight after flight of stairs to the street. My breath turns to frost. I'm amazed it's still winter. I love the sight of his station wagon. We get into it and drive away.

55

The Kentuckian is quiet. There's no one here but Wing and me. He gives me a flowered room on the second floor. The one with a front window and velvet drapes.

"When you get settled," he says, "come downstairs, and I'll put on the tea. I made apricot buns this morning—they're still fresh."

I lay out my nightgown and hairbrush. It's been a long time since I've spent the night away from home. Thinking further, I once camped out at Reverend and Miz Culpepper's when Pap was away on business. Whiskey business. Pap used to love saying that. And I've stayed over at the Hanleys'. Truth is, I've never slept in another white person's home.

I go down for tea. Wing has set out silver spoons and napkins, and a china teapot. Two enormous fruit buns are fixed on a plate. He pours tea. I eat little; I'm overcome with the strangeness of things—state hospitals and empty graves, Ida gone from her cabin, and Alton Phelps on something worse than a Klan rampage. And now I'm drinking tea from Wing's best china and sleeping upstairs in his place. I can only blink my eyes and look into my cup.

"I think I know how you feel, Olivia," he says. "Life takes the damnedest turns."

As Love Alice would say, that's a truth. I open my mouth and begin to talk. I tell Wing about my quilts, and how I plan to rebuild the outdoor stall in spring.

He talks about the hotel, and his plan for a dining room, his gift shop window, and that he thinks—no, he *feels*—good things will come to Aurora before long. He's been to the cemetery and removed the dead flowers from Grace's grave. He'll put up a stone. And that brings me to Pap and the problem I face. I may never know where Ida has laid him.

"Crazy old woman," I say. "There's no telling what she's done. It was so long ago."

"We'll take one day at a time," Wing says, as if we're partners. "Fill in the holes."

There's more meaning in that statement than I am able to fathom. Thirty years of not speaking has left great gaps in what we know about each other, what we feel.

Out in the lobby, the telephone rings, and Wing gets up to answer it.

"That was Marta Havlicek," he says when he comes back. "Will'm and the cub are settled in just fine, but the new snow's closed the bridge and the road to their place. They think he ought to stay a couple of nights."

I look up.

"I told her I'd ask you," Wing says. "But the phone lines will probably go down soon, so if it's not OK, I need to call her back now."

I'm grateful that Will'm is out of reach. I nod and push back my chair. "If you don't mind, Wing, I'm going to bed."

" 'Course I don't mind," he says. "You want another blanket? Extra pillow?"

"I don't need a thing."

He nods. "Just sleep."

"That would be good. And, Wing—"

"Mm?"

"I don't know how to thank you—"

"Don't," he says. "It all evens out. I'll drive you up to Doc's around eight. We'll have breakfast first. That all right?"

Yes. Makes me wonder how I got through these years without anyone else. I must not, now, become dependent on him. Until all this is past I must keep some distance.

When I have brushed out my hair and gotten ready for bed, I punch the electric light button and the room falls into darkness. I can't resist going to the window and looking out. Below, everything sleeps in the white of a new snow. It drifts down, thick and lazy. Through the fat flakes, I see that a truck is parked in front of Ruse's. There's someone behind the wheel—a man thick of body and wearing a stocking cap. Buford.

My stomach rolls and settles in a hard knot. My chest aches with each rise and fall. Phelps has sent him to keep watch on me. He probably thinks Will'm's here, too.

God bless the storm and Molly. God bless first love. I have mixed feelings about that last, for my own first love is sleeping not twenty feet away.

56

The snowfall has lightened by morning, but the sky is the color of old dishwater. The truck is gone from in front of Ruse's.

Wing scrambles eggs and makes a pot of coffee, toasts cinnamon bread, and we eat without saying much. Then we bundle up, Wing starts the station wagon, and we head out.

Someone's had the foresight to shovel Doc's driveway, and right now, Doc's wife is sitting with Ida. Miz Pritchett tells me Ida's fading. Her mouth is open and her breath comes and goes in quick puffs. It reminds me of the breath of Will'm's dying cubs. On one hand, I'm sorry he's not here to say good-bye to his great gran. On the other, I'm glad he can't see her this way. Her soul has already taken flight.

Doc brings me creamed coffee. Wing says no thanks, and Doc goes about his business. A half dozen patients are in his waiting room, and I'm sure that, by now, they all know what's happening. After a while I go outside and walk up and down the drive.

Before long, a panel truck with a bright-painted red cross pulls up. I hurry in, to the back room. Miz Pritchett, probably thinking I want a moment alone, scuttles out. I touch Ida's shoulder, shake her a little.

"Ida?"

I'm glad there's no one to hear me, for although maybe I should say good-bye, or tell her she'll be cared for, there's something else I've got to know. "Ida, *tell me what you did with Pap!*"

Two men in white uniforms come in. One has a folded sheet, the other carries a stretcher. They lift Ida, slack-jawed, arms dangling. The one with the sheet snaps it open, tucks it around her. Doc's wife hurries to cover her with a blanket, and there's a paper for me to sign. I follow them out.

Love Alice is there in the road, and she comes to stand with me. We watch as they lift Ida up, the light snow falling on her colorless lashes. In that instant, her eyes pop open, and she stares straight at me. Then she snaps them shut, and they shove her inside.

"Ida!" I shout and scramble in after her.

But they reach for my arms, mistaking this for grief.

"Ida, you tell me! You tell me now!"

"Lord Jesus," Love Alice says, and her voice rises sweetly, with some distant hymn.

The doors slam shut, and I stand there watching while the pure white truck with the painted cross moves along the pure white road toward the highway. The clouds are as dark as a pan of burnt biscuits.

Ida has played the last hand. Is she faking? Or is it possible, as Dr. Baird said, she's fading in and out? Maybe, at Stipling, she'll keep her eyes open, go to Four and spend the rest of her life in her nightgown, wandering. Not a life so different from what she's had. Right now I'm so angry, I hope she ends up on Five. One thing's certain—she won't make it below Three, because they'll never get her to fold laundry.

Love Alice looks past me to the ditch. "I know about losin' thangs, O-livvy."

I put my arms around her tight.

She croons in my ear, "That li'l girl of mine—I calls her Baby— she the reason I see my truths. She gave me that."

Oh, my precious Love Alice. I never knew. I wonder, wrapped in the miseries of my own life, what else I have missed.

Wing comes, then, and puts his arms around both of us.

57

It was good of you to take me home."

"You keep doing that," Wing says softly.

"Doing what?"

"Letting me get close, and then—turning polite." After a few minutes, he says, "Don't worry about it. You're going through a lot right now."

"So have you been," I say. "These last few weeks. Few years, I guess."

He nods and gives his glasses a nudge. Turns off Doc's road and heads toward town.

"Wing, I've got the store to mind, and the goats. Eggs to gather."

"Olivia, on this I am firm. One more night. You've earned it."

It's hard to argue when I'm damn near hostage in his car. My mouth's open to say, *Then take me up for an hour. While I do a few things.* But I don't because I remember the surprise Will'm and I came home to the night before last. If there's more of that, Wing will ask questions.

How close, exactly, is Wing to his guests?

He pulls in the alley beside the hotel and parks the car. "You rest today, then tonight we'll go over to Ruse's for supper."

Wing sends Junk to milk the goats and scatter corn. Other than that, my house stands empty and ripe for more vandalism while I sit drinking tea and watching Wing roll out sticky buns. He coats them with cinnamon, sprinkles on pecans, and shoves forty-eight at a time in the big oven. While they bake, he checks on the bread he's set to rise. His shirtsleeves are rolled up and he's got flour from one end of the kitchen to the other. He beats the bread dough and turns it in its bowl. Then he pours himself coffee, but the timer goes off and he leaps up to pull out the buns. While they're piping hot, he spreads on brown sugar icing.

He glances up. "Olivia Cross smiled," he says. "I believe the world will stop turning. Take these pot holders, will you, and carry this pan."

He takes a second tray, and in short order we're headed across the street. "Come on, woman!" he shouts over his shoulder. "Ruse has got folks lined up for these."

And he does. This is quite a business Wing's started. He needs to add a coffee shop to the hotel. I help him scrub down the kitchen, and at noon he slices hot bread to eat with pieces of fish he's fried in corn meal. While he works he tells me that Sampson's boy, who's nearly sixty, goes ice fishing up north. He brings back more halibut than a body can wrap in waxed paper and bury in snow. "I've got to get three rooms ready," he adds. "Guests arriving late tonight. They'll need sandwiches and coffee, some pastry—"

"I'll help."

"Good. But you've done enough for now. Why don't you turn on the radio and listen to Ma Perkins or whatever it is that you women like?"

As it turns out, I fall asleep on my bed, and Wing has to wake me for supper. I wash my face and tuck my hair in its braid. I argue with him that, all day, I've done nothing but eat. Still, he puts his arm around me, and once more we hustle across the street, coatless, to Ruse's where he orders steak and potatoes and pecan pie. We sit at the corner table, leaning on our elbows and speaking in hushed voices like we've been doing this for years. Wing tells me funny things about folks in town. I confide that I miss Will'm. He tells me about Saturday night when Will'm stayed over, how he fed the cub thick cream whipped with egg yolks. I think—no wonder the furry little devil's growing. I'm embarrassed for such a wastefulness of good food, but Wing laughs. I wonder if he knows how the cub came to live with us, the way its brothers died of hunger or loneliness, and that Ida shot its ma'am.

We go back to the hotel, and, although it's eight o'clock and near my usual bedtime, Wing slices bread and spreads mayonnaise. I lay on thick slabs of ham and roast beef, cut the sandwiches crosswise and arrange them on a platter. He makes coffee.

I'm setting out squares of buttered gingerbread when the lobby door opens and a great convolution of wind and people rushes in. Wing goes to welcome his guests. His seems to be a pleasant life. I don't know whether it's the warmth and elegance of the hotel, or having someone, today, to share the workload. Maybe it's that Wing doesn't have to worry where his next dime'll come from.

Out in the lobby, voices boom, raucous men pumping Wing's hand, slapping his back. Telling baudy jokes in cigar-raspy voices—every one of which I heard Saturday night in Alton Phelps' barn. The hunt club is back. This time, they aren't here to snipe at my wolves and take home ears. Apparently the warning they left in my house was not enough. I scan Wing's kitchen for a place to hide, but even if I slipped out the back door, they might spot me from the hall. They must have seen us, Elizabeth and me, must have posted a guard. And if they have now come for me, what have they already done to Elizabeth?

The elevator wheezes open, and Wing takes them upstairs. In minutes they'll come down, wanting this supper that I've helped prepare—and my cape's up in my room. I round the corner to the hall, slip into the first bedroom and open the wardrobe, looking for one of Wing's old coats. Empty. But there, folded on the bed is the pink rosebud quilt that I gave Grace Harris. I wrap it around me, hurry through the lobby, and step out onto the icy sidewalk. A fine sleet burns my face as I slip into the alley, hurrying between buildings, then cross over at the next block and head for the bridge. I pull the quilt up over my head. Was it just this morning that I watched Wing at his baking? Now I'm slogging through the frozen night, coatless, not knowing what's ahead. I'm ashamed of myself that, once more, I wonder if Wing is a Cott'ner.

58

It's good to be home. Climbing the steps, I am glad I locked the back door. I feel for the chain hanging over the table, and pull. Nothing happens.

In the dark grocery, I hear the clang of the cash register, and my heart lurches. Alton Phelps draws back the curtain, stands in the doorway. I recall, now, that of all the voices I caught in the lobby at Wing's, I did not hear his. His rifle is propped in the corner, by the stove.

"Get out of my house."

"Why, Olivia, that's not friendly," he says. He's wearing a sheepskin coat. He takes up the gun. A big-bellied man steps out of the larder. In his hand are three boiled eggs that he cracks against the sink, and he stands there, peeling them.

"I hope you'll excuse my cousin Doyle Pink," Phelps says smoothly. "He may be the sheriff, but he's short on manners."

Fear crawls up my arms, puckering the skin. They must not see that my heart's lodged in my throat.

I muster a shaky politeness. "Alton, you-all go on down the road, now."

Phelps holds the gun, pointed easy at the floor. He whistles like that's the stupidest thing ever. "When you was out to my place Saturday night, my missus and I weren't near this inhospitable."

Poor Elizabeth. My stomach does a turn.

He gestures with his hand, and Pink produces a rope. "Was I you, Olivia, I'd sit down in that chair."

I do, and wince when he binds my hands behind me, then my feet.

"You're not as social as Ida," Phelps says. "I thought whores begat whores."

Inside me, a twig snaps. "I'm not going to spend one more night afraid. If you came to shoot me, that's fine. At least tell me why."

"Shoot you?" he says and smiles as if he's just now thought of that. "I told you I'd come for you and the boy, Olivia. You got something I want. Or you know where it is."

Pink crams the last egg in his mouth.

Phelps looks around, says, "Goddamn, Doyle, you're making a fucking mess."

" 'Em niggers wouldn't stand for no shootin'," Pink says. "Findin' her with a hole in her gullet."

Phelps' face darkens. "They'll stand for whatever I tell them to."

I'm remembering what Elizabeth said. "You're so full of yourself, you and your club. So vicious even the Klan denies you."

Phelps takes a step, draws back his arm, and strikes me hard across the face.

It brings tears to my eyes. What is it they're after? Old chloroform? Stitching silk, dog runs, tweezers in six sizes? I lay my throbbing cheek to my shoulder, and hold my tongue.

"I'm askin' you one more time," Phelps says.

My ears are ringing, and I can't think clearly. "For what?"

"We'll rip this place apart if we have to, Olivia, one splinter at a time."

I sit for most of an hour while every damn thing is once again ransacked and shattered, mattresses slit. They pull out the stove, throw cans from the larder. Out in the store, I hear glass jar after glass jar breaking. This must be how death sounds when it's coming, and it wears me down worse than a beating. It wears the sheriff down, too.

"Goddamn, Alton," Pink says. "I'm tuckered out."

Phelps fights to keep himself under control. "What say we hold her trial right here, Doyle?"

"Ain't got no bale of cotton, Alton."

So I'm about to find out what a cotton trial is.

Phelps reaches in his back pocket and snaps out a hank of red fabric, turns two cut holes to the front, and slips it over his head. The very scarlet that Aunt Pinny Albert wouldn't buy. Through the eyeholes, now, he watches my face, gauging my fear.

Pink whines, "Shit, Alton, I didn't bring my hood."

"That's all right, Doyle, you can see better without it. I'm just showin' off a little. Why don't you go on down in the cellar and look around. See if you can find a beam—"

A beam.

Now I know how this will end.

Pink tries the cellar door, but it's locked. He spots the key. "Jesus H. Christ, it's dark down there."

"Well, light a goddamn lamp."

While we wait, Phelps looks around. Says, "Me and James Arnold, we used to come here, take turns with Ida. She was a spitfire—man, that suited us fine."

"I never—saw—James Arnold."

"Oh, he liked the feel of Ida's skin. You don't remember," he says with a grunt, " 'cause you were half dead, over to Buelton."

What?

"Alton, I can't find shit down here!" Doyle calls from the cellar.

Phelps' voice is low. "Don't that come as an almighty surprise."

"It's colder'n hell and all cleaned out. But the beams are solid. I'm comin' up!"

The two of them are too much for me, and there's no getting rid of the stronger one. I wet my lips. "Get Pink out of here."

Phelps steps closer. "What's that, now?"

"Send Doyle away. When it's just you and me—I'll tell you what you want to know."

"Why, Olivia!"

"Do it."

He pulls off the hood, entertains a grin. Steps to the doorway. "Doyle boy," he shouts. "That's all right, you come on up."

The sheriff appears, ears red and sour of face.

Phelps takes a toothpick from his pocket. "You take the truck back to my place," he says. "Me and Olivia are gonna have a talk."

"But we were gonna string her up, have us some fun."

Phelps frowns. "Jesus Christ, what kinda way is that to talk? You go on now."

"I say we put her in the cellar, Alton. Lock this door, take the key."

My stomach turns over.

"—Be some time 'fore they find her. We impound her truck, they'll think she took off. We grab the boy—" Pink's pleased with himself.

Phelps picks his teeth. "Like I said, you take my truck. You're always wantin' to drive it."

"But it's parked clear up the road—"

"Walk'll do you good. Now go."   .

When he's gone, Phelps says, "I don't trust you one almighty inch, Olivia. But just to see if your heart's in the right place—" He comes to me, leans, puts his lips on my hair. "Untie me," I say.

"That'd be pure foolishness."

"It's the only way I'm gonna tell you—what you want to know," I say. "Otherwise, I'll die without talking. I mean what I say."

He grins and moves around behind me. I hear him set the rifle down, feel him work the knots loose. I rub my wrists.

"The way I see it, Olivia, I can't lose. And you can't win."

He's come around and is directly in line with the cellar doorway. With my feet still bound, I fly at him, claw his face, get in one long rip before he bellows and grabs me. He catches my wrists, shoving. I land hard on my back. He comes at me, but I deliver a foot to his groin. His fist connects so hard with my jaw that I hear my teeth rattle. He sinks to his knees, clutching himself and fumbling for the rifle. "Bitch," he says through his teeth.

Ankles still bound, I struggle to my feet. Work frantically at the knots.

He groans, grabs my boot, and I hit the floor with my shoulder. I reach for the leg of Will'm's bed, the potato bucket, the door frame. But his hand covers my nose and mouth, squeezing the bones. I bite down and swing the bucket. Connect.

"Fucking bitch!"

I hear my dress rip and scramble away.

He comes after me. "This one's for James Arnold—"

He slaps me hard. I crash against the alcove's corner, the back of my head going warm and wet. My knees give out, and I slide down the wall.

Phelps' face is dark, the eyes so black the sockets seem empty. "I'll tell *you*, little girl! Tate Harker kilt my brother, all right, but it wasn't the night you think it was." He's on his knees, lifts the rifle. "Couple months later your old man came home. Caught James Arnold with his drawers lying right where you're sittin' and his hand up Ida's twat, that's what."

I can't breathe. I can't *breathe*.

"That's right, Miss Holy and Righteous Olivia Harker. Your pap shot my brother deader'n hell."

59

"You hear what I say, Olivia?" Phelps shouts like there's a great distance between us.

Pain shoots down my arm. The air's thick as grease.

"It was a clear goddamn night," he says. "Sound carried to the highway. Folks came just to gawk at James Arnold, him bleeding his brains out on this very floor."

"Pap—died in that—crash."

"Like hell he did. Ground was so hard, Ida couldn't a buried a chicken bone. Not to say she wasn't meaner'n a boar hog in heat." He cocks his head like he's told a joke and expects a laugh.

I get to my knees. "Why—why are you—saying this?"

"Because Olivia Harker couldn't do any wrong. This town had you and Tate on a goddamn pedestal. You lived in ignorance, little girl. That night—shit, I wanted Tate to run. Just so I could hunt his ass down."

"Someone—would've told me."

"Bullshit. They all knew. Ida had the whole town by the balls. Too bad I gotta kill you. Like to see you stand up to them lyin' niggers now, look 'em in the eye."

Pap with his rifle, one clean shot. Love Alice. Junk, digging when they all knew we'd find nothing. Ida, in flames.

Phelps is on his feet. He wobbles closer. My nostrils are full of him.

"What—what happened to—"

His grin is ghastly. The rifle's in his hand. "What happened to your pappy? Goddamn, I waited a long time to say this. He's in prison, in Kingston. Been there all this time."

"Kingston." I gag on the word.

"Always knew I'd be the one to tell you. You're just too much like him. Gotta kick a dead horse." He presses himself to me, shows me the hardness in his trousers. "You smell real good, Olivia. Like whorehouse soap."

"I—"

"I'll bet you had a fine time last night with that Wing Harris." His mouth's on my ear, his hand on my arm. "You're a strong woman, the kind me and the boys like. Bet you're a fighter, the way Ida was." He cups my breast. "You know, Olivia, we can set all this right—"

I deliver spit to his cheek, feel my head snap back. His fists are solid. Blood fills my mouth with the taste of old pennies. It runs down my chin. I fold over and butt with my head, catching enough of his kneecap that he yells and closes his eyes, twists his lips. I grab hold of the rifle, shove the stock upward, hear some part of him snap. He swears and swings wide with an open palm, but I'm on my feet and run hard at his belly. His eyes go wide as he scrambles for a hold and passes, backward, through the cellar doorway. He screams once and cracks several steps as he falls. Then lies at the bottom, arms and legs bent in impossible ways, head tilted back like he's looking for something.

Everything's changed, and everything's wrong. My hair's come loose, and my dress flaps where it's torn. I stumble out to the truck, get in, turn the key wrong, then again. Not a sound. I

slide out, hug my elbows, more snow's coming down. I stumble
through the field, down the hill, cross the bridge where even the
ice on the river deceives. On Main Street every familiar thing is
washed black and purple and streaked with red. In front of
Ruse's, I stand screaming, "You-all come out here! You fucking
tell me the goddamn truth!"

Nobody comes. Not even Wing. Not the Ruses, or any of hell's
Cotton Club. They're waiting for Phelps to show up with my ear.
What a joke—Tate Harker's alive, and Olivia's dead.

I look up through the bare winter trees to Rowe Street. I plow
through the snow, climb up on a porch, beat on doors.

"Liars! You let me think he was dead! Pack of stinking
Judases!"

Now I'm beyond words and chunk a rock through a window,
shatter the next with my fist. I'm bent over with pain, cannot lift
another boot. Surely if I look down I'll see a great hole where my
heart was. I'll watch my life running out, blood from the lifetimes
I spent up here, loving and learning and playing with babies.

In the name of this earth I baptize you . . .

Traitors. Judas bastards.

There's only the sound of snow falling and falling. Somewhere
a door opens, and a woman comes out. Love Alice, and her hands
burn where they touch. Miss Dovey in a shawl. Old people, black
skin. Teeth gone. Liars.

I'm dying. "Don't touch me."

Junk, wrapping me in his arms. "Come in, Miss Livvy. Tell us
what happened."

"You lied, that's what happened!"

"Sweet Jesus," says his mama.

Love Alice, crooning. I sit on a chair. They're pinning my

dress. I look at the floor, scrubbed and knotholed. "Phelps told me."

"Mr. Alton Phelps did this to you?"

"He's dead. In my cellar."

"Oh, Lordy. You sure?"

"No."

Feet skid on wet porch boards, then hurry away like I'm contagious. Quarantined in my skin. Shivering. More whispers. Doors open and close and open again. Somebody cleans the blood from my chin. So many people, and they're all talking, but not to me. Hands pull me up, wrap me in something; we go outside. Snow falls on my face while they hustle me along. Where are they taking me? I wish I could think; I'm glad I can't.

Then, suddenly it's warmer. I smell sweat and wool, and the breath on my face reminds me of supper. My stomach turns over.

A door closes and I hear Junk announce, "He was there, all right. We carried him out."

I think it's Miss Dovey who says, "Lord knows what's next."

"Longfeet," Junk says, "you go down and tell Mr. Wing to keep the boy hid."

They know where Will'm is? They know everything.

Will'm. So Wing's not involved. But he didn't come out, did he, when I was in the street....

Reverend Culpepper says, "Miss Olivia, he bring someone with him?"

"What?"

"Mr. Phelps. When he came to your house, was he alone?"

"No. The sheriff."

Somebody chuckles. "They knowed it would take two growed men to deal wit' you."

"Sheriff's gone now," Junk says.

There's silence while they take in what that means. All around me, faces are drawn so that I can see the shapes of their skulls.

"What Mr. Phelps tell you, 'xactly?"

I close my eyes.

"No, O-livvy. You talk to us, now."

I say, "Love Alice. Don't look in my eyes."

"I won't, baby girl," she says. "But you go on and tell what you know."

"He said Tate Harker's in prison. That he shot James Arnold. And all of you knew."

The silence is so deep I think I have drowned.

"—For your own good."

"—That Ida Mae. We was afraid what she might do."

"What she might *do?*"

"Junk," says the Reverend. "Tell her the truth."

Junk shakes his head.

"Yes, sir," he says. "You tell her now."

Junk turns sorrowful eyes on me. "Miss Olivia—we promised your pap."

"You promised—"

"Ever' one of us owed him that much."

That's more than I can think about. "Is Phelps dead?"

"Yes, ma'am, he is now."

There's just enough space for that in my head. "But, up there at my place—was he dead?"

"That not an'thang you need to know."

"I do! I have to know if I killed him!" I am out of the chair, have Junk's shirt in my fist. *"Don't you lie to me anymore!"*

I see where I am. In the African Methodist Episcopal Church. It's packed full of people, and they're all looking at me.

"I can't say." Junk's eyes are on the floor. "But he sho' is now."

I back away. "Don't come near me, and don't any of you talk to me, not ever again."

It's a damn good thing nobody says a word.

There's a frown on Junk's face. He lifts his chin, sniffing, and we all turn our eyes to the tendrils of black smoke that lick the dry ceiling. The church around us bursts into flame.

60

Icould not collect my wits, if I tried. In minutes, doors are gone, and the front wall collapses, bringing down part of the roof. Beyond the windows, flanks of white men run with flaring torches. They jab and thrust and shout obscenities, their flames making neon streaks in the dark.

I cough. "They want me."

"You are wrong about that," the Reverend says. "They want *us*. They have always wanted us."

The congregation fills the tiny back kitchen, the Sunday school rooms, the choir benches. Babies wail. Overhead, timber screams and falls. Junk's mammy stumbles. He lifts her in his arms, carrying her tenderly the way he did Ida.

Sweet Jesus. Why does fire always bring the end? Ida ignited herself so I'd stop digging. And now the church on Rowe Street. I wonder if they've already set a torch to my place; if they haven't, they will. I figure they'll let us burn, then come in the morning and cover our bodies, or stack us in a wagon, put us all in one grave. Strike another match.

Junk shouts, "We gotta get these folks out of here!"

But there's nowhere to go. We're stuck in this crematory. Beyond it, there's only bitter cold night and cowards in hoods.

The Reverend's smashing windows with his elbow, picking at the glass, pushing folks through. Lambs of God tumble out on the snow. "Get them up!" he shouts. "They'll catch their death!"

He thinks life's an option. I picture Cott'ners standing outside, grinning and waiting to pick us off.

Out in the snow, Miss Dovey's wearing her Sunday hat with the veil and pink roses, and a wool cardigan buttoned over her dress. Over the crack of flames, she shouts, "They gone for now, Reverend! Mark my words, they be back."

More windows shatter with the heat. Junk hustles me over the sill.

"We got no place to go," Wellette says.

"Stay together," Junk tells them. "We be safer that way."

Maybe, but I doubt it.

Love Alice is looking straight in my eyes. "You c'n help us, O-livvy."

How can she look to me after the hurts I've dealt her? Even now I want to reach out and strike her. "Don't you do that to me, Love Alice."

Aunt Pinny Albert's few teeth are chattering. "Reverend, it ain't twenty degrees. We can't last but a few minutes."

"Stay close," the Reverend says, and they cling, elbows knotted, babes to their breasts.

Above us, the sky is nothing but black. I imagine the Cott'ners are at Wing's, drinking coffee and warming their hands. Surely Wing knows. How can he not?

How could I not?

Junk sent him the message: *Keep the boy hid.* I pray to God that Will'm's at Molly's.

Junk's mammy asks, "What we goin' to do, Miss Livvy?"

Phelps is a greater danger now than when he was alive. These men are vengeful in ways we can't imagine. This one thing I know: We're not going to be allowed to live through the night.

Meanwhile, how can these people look to me? I'm not the hero Tate Harker was. But that's wrong, too. He was never a hero—after the accident, it was two whole months before he shot James Arnold. Then, for thirty-some years, he's cowered behind bars, and if he'd wanted to see me, even Ida could not have stopped him. But that's fine. In the meantime I've learned to think for myself—or have I? Didn't I work through years of troubles—or did I just collect them till now they're a mountain? Makes no difference. I cannot, *will* not, face Tate Harker. God*damn* him!

But my head won't stay focused, and I keep going back, wondering what Pap would have said, back when I thought I knew him.

Run, Olivia?

Stand and fight?

It's insane to take on God knows how many, who've committed God knows what crimes. All my miseries are rolled into one, ignited and roaring beneath my rib cage and in the timbers behind me. The one who contrived the lies, the only one who might know what's happening here, is fifty miles away, over roads that have frozen into slabs of dark ice. And my truck won't start.

I look around at what's left of the church, the fire burning low, their silhouettes drawn against the rubble. "Reverend, I need to borrow your car."

"Ain't no gasoline in it, Olivia."

"Then the bus. I need the church bus."

"Only Longfeet can run it," Junk says, his teeth clattering. "Go on and fetch it, then, Longfeet. Take us to Buelton."

Miss Dovey's speech is jerky and slow. "One a them Buelton churches will he'p us."

I cannot let this happen. "No one in Buelton is going to help you! Everyone's either involved or afraid!"

"We got us no choice. We can't stay here."

The bus is parked in the Reverend's side yard, and Longfeet is already loping across the field. Miz Culpepper's wash still hangs on the line, and an abandoned stream of smoke rises up from a barrel in somebody's yard.

I hear the bus cough. Then it lumbers up the hill toward us. Longfeet brakes. The door wheezes open, and they climb on.

The Reverend sits directly behind Longfeet. It's one of the few occasions when I've seen the Reverend without his hat. In fact, the only other time was the night he came to get me from Silty's, and I wouldn't go. They move about in the bus, finding seats on this trip to—where? I'm the only one standing out in the snow.

Junk reaches down for Love Alice's arm.

"Lord Jesus will save us, O-livvy," she says.

I shake my head.

"You're bad hurt, Olivia," the Reverend calls down. "You come on with us now."

Blood still trickles into the corner of my mouth. I taste it on my tongue. My cheekbone hurts, and a dull ache has settled behind my ear.

"I can't. I won't leave Will'm."

He nods.

I call up to him, "They'll come after you-all, no matter where you go. You know too much. Pap knew, and they set him up to find Ida and kill James Arnold."

Till I spoke these things, I had not truly thought them through. Hadn't Phelps said he wanted Pap to run, so he could hunt him down? I watch shadows flicker on the snow and recall the way Phelps rolled over and over down my cellar steps. The Cott'ners will want revenge for his death. When that's done, they won't even miss him. I thought Alton was the leader, but now I know the club is far bigger—so big, in fact, that several times a year it meets openly in the Phelps barn, and in all these years nobody has stopped them.

I see, too, how this will play out. They'll threaten Pap to get all they want from me. Then they'll torment Will'm. Around and around, angles and dealing while they use up our lives and work on our fear. I am dazzled by the blindness of Olivia Harker Cross, who lied to herself and said she could see.

"Reverend," I call up. "You-all drop me in Kingston?"

He nods. "Yes, ma'am."

I climb up. The Reverend pushes over, and I sit next to him, watch Longfeet work the clutch and the gas pedal. We ease forward on the ice. The night is like pitch, and I'm suffocating from the smells—wet wool, babies, and other things.

In the seat across from me, Junk puts his arm around Love Alice. Big, responsible Junk, who carried me home and ate my bread and jam. And now, like the rest, he's running away.

Love Alice is leaning across her husband. "You right, O-livvy. Us runnin' for our lives."

I look away to the dark window and wonder if the only truths I ever knew were the ones Love Alice gave me.

The bus sluices on the ice and stalls. Longfeet swears. Tries the ignition again. The engine roars. We creep forward again.

I twist in my seat and even in the dark I wish I hadn't. As far back as I can make out, they're bunched together on metal seats, on the floor, in the aisle, buttoned in coats or shawls or shirtsleeves. Black faces, lined faces, tired beyond talking. Love Alice pats Junk's hand. He's lucky to have her.

I wonder why, years ago, Doc didn't stitch up his ear, the way I took needle and thread to the wolf's. Same ear, right ear. And then I recall Pap saying, *See if the sheriff don't bring a federal marshal out to your barn on a Saturday night.*

"Junk?" I say softly. "What happened to your ear?"

All the murmuring dies away.

His voice is distant. "I had this ear befo' you was born, Miss Livvy. You ain't ever asked."

"I'm asking now."

"No mo' lies?"

"It was Phelps, wasn't it?"

"Him and his brother."

"What happened?"

He sighs. "We was poor as anything—twelve of us takin' turns at the table and sleeping in beds. I got a job pitchin' manure for their young pappy. One day I was cleanin' out his stable, and I seen these silver spurs hangin' there. Shiniest things ever."

Oh, Junk.

"I wasn't but ten or 'leven, an' I take out my shirttail to polish 'em up. But Mr. Phelps run in, yellin'. *You stealing my spurs, boy?* He fired me on the spot."

It's a pure wonder to me why a white man's so quick to blame coloreds. Perhaps, in their fear, they're easier to blame. And, having placed blame *somewhere*, white men have less of a need to whip themselves or each other.

"The next Saturday night," Junk says, "Mr. Phelps sent his men to my mama's place wit' a rope. They take me to his barn and string me up, jus' like that."

From the back of the bus I hear weeping. Miz Hanley.

"But this old neck, it wouldn't break. A long time they leave me swingin' there, his boys lookin' on. Finally old Phelps says he got to have us all off the place by sunup, on account of his wife's fit to run off. *Good riddance,* he says. But they cut me down."

His voice catches. "Mr. Phelps, he takes out a knife and sets to cuttin' off my ear. But I come to. I jump up and run outa there like the devil had my shirttail. That boy, Booger, whistle to me from the bushes, and I run in there. He hide me till the sun come up and all them men drive off in wagons.

"One day," Junk says, "I tol' Mr. Tate."

Only Elizabeth knew how death came to Booger. I recall the Phelps boys saying he had shot himself. How Pap offered to help bury him, all the time knowing what monsters they were.

"Did they ever come back for you?"

"They come all right. But they take Samuel, my mammy's oldest."

"Were they—wearing red hoods, Junk?"

"Yes, ma'am, they were."

I turn in my seat, see Miss Pinny Albert and her sisters and Miss Dovey. Junk's mama, rocking and holding her daughters, Mettie and Doll, whose husbands ran off—or did they? I see a half dozen children and old men with gray chin whiskers. Mr. Radney Holifield, who is near eighty and a lifetime deacon in the African Methodist Church that is no more. Two ladies with babies asleep in their arms. A dozen more.

The bus is shaking as if it's palsied.

But I need to know. "How many others?"

Mr. Holifield rises partway from his seat. "Yes, ma'am, they hung my brother John. Old man Phelps said he stole a sheep from their field."

Miz Iva says, "My boy Lavelle, when he worked at the bakery. Hung him, then sent word he'd stole bread."

"—My daddy when he rode into town for a newspaper. And my uncle."

A terrible moan rises up from me. "Didn't you ever try to stop them?"

"Yes, ma'am—"

Someone says, "My pap and his buddies, when they come home from the war. But them Phelpses said they caught my pap watchin' their ma through a window. They took him away and brought him home blind in both eyes."

"When we knew they was in town, we'd pray to God, then listen for 'em to drive up in our yard."

"It ain't just our county," Mr. Holifield says. "They brung 'em from clear across the state line. All any family got back was one ear—so's we'd know."

My words are weak and without substance. "Miss Dovey, Miz Hanley. How—how did I not know?"

"You couldn't, Olivia," says Miss Dovey. "You ain't got this black skin."

I look at my hands. If God had answered my prayers back then, I, too, would have dreaded sundown every Saturday.

"You could have told me."

"What for?" Miz Hanley said.

"You-all took the bolt of red cloth from my store, didn't you?"

"We did," she says. "Din't make a dent in what they was doing, but—it was something."

I sigh. "What will happen, now that Phelps is dead?"

"Guess the others'll just carry on."

"Do you know who they are?"

"Ain't nobody knows for sure. Them Cott'ners is deep."

I want to tell Longfeet to hurry. But he's already hunched over the wheel.

61

We arrive early in the prison lot. The others won't leave me. The Reverend suggests we close our eyes and get some sleep—ain't nobody gonna bother us here. Close by are the high turrets of the penitentiary. It's enormous, the white wall going on for miles and it's topped with rolls of razor wire. At eight o'clock the Reverend touches my shoulder, says they'll wait for me, take me with them after I've seen Pap.

I don't argue because I have nowhere else to go and no way to get home. I've thought no further than this. We drive around until we come to a gate where four men in gray uniforms hold rifles to their chests. The Reverend leans across Longfeet and speaks. The guard shakes his head.

"Visiting hours start soon, Olivia."

It's a fair walk to the gate but maybe not so long when you consider the years.

Love Alice gets up to loosen my braid and winds my hair in a knot. She pinches my cheeks.

I step down from the bus, and set off up the road, but by the time I arrive at the gate, I can't remember why I've come. What place is this—granite building after building and small fenced yards. Rows of gray trucks. I should get back on the bus, ask the Reverend to drive away. But now I'm here. *I'm here.*

People stream through the gate. Some have children. The coloreds hang back, to be let in last. I give the guard my name. He asks who I'm here to see. I can't breathe.

"Tate Harker."

I wait for him to say, "Nobody *ever* comes to see him."

But he doesn't, just writes on a card with a buttonhole. Jabs a thumb to show I should button it on my coat—whose coat? Everyone else seems to know what they're doing, where they're going. We walk single file through a chain-link passage. Another guard glances at our cards. One by one they let us into a damp gray room. Although it's not raining, water stains the walls and spreads in puddles on the concrete floor. I follow the others down a ringing hall. Sign my name to a list, sit on a metal chair with bent legs.

I don't know what I feel anymore. I recall being angered that my pap simply wanted his wife to come home. Then when times went bad, he took her side. All these years I blamed him for not surviving the crash. Now all those quarrels seem pale and flat in light of his having lied about his death.

Over a loudspeaker, someone calls names. I am trapped. But when the woman next to me sobs and runs for the door, I see that I, too, can choose to go. I stay. Wait with my hands in my lap and pain in my heart till I hear, "Olivia Cross!"

A guard waits for me in front of a steel door. With a great deal of clanking, the door rolls open. When we step through, the door grinds shut, and there's yet another hall.

The room we enter is long and narrow, a putrid green. A row of windows runs down the center, and on either side are chairs. The guard shows me where to sit, and I see that the window is really two panes of glass with a wire grid between, and a perforated metal plate that, I suppose, allows voices to pass through. A guard stands at each end of the room, and another watches from a balcony.

When all the visitors' chairs are taken, a door opens on the other side. A prisoner comes in. His trousers and shirt are striped, his hands chained in front. The guard snaps the chain to a ring in the counter two windows away, and the prisoner sits down.

"Thirty minutes," he says. On the wall, a big clock ticks off the time.

The woman on my left leans on the sill, puts her hand on the glass, waiting. I look away.

Two more prisoners come.

Then the door opens, and I recognize this man. His hair is white, and he's thinner than I remember. But he walks straight and tall, as Tate Harker always did, and he stands looking at me until the guard gives him a shove. He sits down. *Snap.* He's locked to the counter. I keep my eyes on the stripes. A patch is sewn on his shirt, with the letter M.

I put my hand to my face.

On the other side, there's a terrible groaning, and I worry that the guard will take him away.

After a while he says, "Ida's gone." His voice has not changed. "If you're here, that means Ida's gone."

"She's in Buelton."

After a minute, he nods.

More minutes pass before I force the words out. "I think—I killed Alton Phelps—yesterday."

Through the holes in the metal I hear his sigh. "Aren't we a pair."

"A long time ago—he tried to hang Junk."

"Yes."

"And others—"

"Thirty-four on the day they sent me here."

"Thirty-four! And you didn't say anything?"

"That's right."

I hear laughing, weeping, buzzing talk. I want to climb through this glass and beat him senseless. "You could've told me you were here."

"Ida Mae must have changed a lot."

"She never changed."

"Then you'll understand. If I'd told you, she'd have made your life hell."

I want to laugh at that, make an ugly, sharp-edged sound.

He says, "Whatever she did, she'd have done a hundred times over."

"I slept in a dog run."

"Me, too," he says, looking around.

"The Cotton Club. Tell me what you know."

He shakes his head. "There isn't time."

"Start anyway."

He draws in a breath. "Evil men, evil deeds."

I can't argue with that. I risk a look at his face.

"They're watching me, Olivia. Listening."

I remember the conversation from the bus:

Do you know who they are?

Ain't nobody for sure. Them Cott'ners is deep.

"I can tell you this," Pap says, leaning close. "I witnessed hangings. Went there on a delivery one night and saw into the barn. Boys not much older than you—"

"Tell me who. I'll—"

His elbows are on the counter, hands restless, nails scratching at the paint. I think: *Coward*.

"Why didn't you *do* something?"

He gives me a long look. "With Phelps and the club down the road from you? And then later—who'd listen to a convicted man?"

The guard says, "Five minutes."

That look again. Then Pap drops his eyes, scratches at the glass, looks up. "Who told you?"

I glance up at the guards, lower my voice. By now Pink has told the hunt club everything. I'm as good as dead. "Alton Phelps, just before I pushed him down the cellar stairs."

"God almighty."

"I don't know if I killed him. Junk and some others went up to get him. They say he's dead now."

"Well then, that's that."

"What do you mean *'that's that'*!"

He shakes his head like he's terribly tired. "Olivia, let them do this for you."

I feel hard and cold and sit back in my chair.

"Leave it alone," he says again.

"A lot of people will take the blame—"

He pinches together his thumb and finger. I look at his hands, picking, picking. Their constant movement is giving me a headache. Maybe I'll end up with a nervous disorder like the one Ida had.

"Olivia," he says, "you remember how old Jackson Winnamere used to ride up to our place on his mule?"

I feel like I've hit a bump in the road. "I remember, kind of. He used to wave his hat...."

"You asked me, once, why he did that."

"You said—it was a sign."

He nods. "And?"

"That a body had to learn to read the signs."

And then I see the sign. He's not peeling paint or tracing cracks in the glass—he's holding an invisible pencil, sketching words. What does he want—paper? A letter? He sees that I see.

But I don't, not completely.

He passes one hand from his right to left, idly, as if he's brushing things away. Passing the potatoes, turning a page.

I've seen him do that with his doctoring books, flipping pages, writing some more.

I hear Phelps' voice, *I know what you're doing, and I want it stopped.*

What I'm *doing* is figuring it out. Like Pap did, a long, long time ago.

He says softly, "All of it, Olivia. Every single bit."

I stammer a few words, piecing, piecing, and then, in a glorious unfurling, the truth explodes in my head as the books and the hoods and the hay slide into place. It's all I can do not to scream it out.

And they think I know. They think Pap told me.

On the other side of the glass, he shakes his head. *Shh.*

I can hardly sit still, shove close to the opening. "We'll hire a lawyer, Will'm and me! Wing will help."

"That's useless talk, daughter. I killed a man."

"So did I!"

"What's done is done, Olivia."

He says, do I see this insignia, the letter *M*, on his shirt?

Yes.

He's a medic. He helps inmates, calms men. Now I, myself, must settle down and think clearly. I breathe in and out.

"Pap, did you love Ida—in the beginning?"

"I did."

"And she loved you?"

"I believe so."

He answers the question I can't ask. "Sometimes, Olivia, she loved you, too. In those moments we were as right as apple pie."

The guard bellows, "On your feet!" He unlocks the prisoners and leads them away.

Pap shuffles through the door without looking back.

62

I've seen a ghost.

Who told you, Olivia?

Phelps told me.

Not really. The unraveling began when we dug by the outhouse and found nothing, no coffin, no bones. I felt it the moment Ida ignited her gown. Now I'm choking to death on all that I know—and all that I don't because I haven't yet found what I'm looking for.

I need help, right now, and I bang on the guard's window. "Excuse me, please! I have to make a telephone call!"

"We got no public phone," he says.

"This is an emergency!"

"They're all emergencies. There's a pay phone down the road, that intersection."

I run for the bus, step up, hear the doors wheeze shut. I see them, in their seats, wrapped against the cold, faces waiting, hopeful, babies being soothed and rocked.

"Longfeet, start this thing up. I've got to get to the pay phone."

I reach in my pocket and count the change. "I need twelve cents!"

They dig in their trouser pockets and handbags and pull out

nickels. Then I can see the highway, and Longfeet grinds the bus to a stop.

I step down, and into the booth, pick up the receiver and wait for the operator, but nothing happens. Seconds go by. Sweet Jesus, how far to another telephone? I clutch the nickels and watch through the window as a shiny black car comes down the highway, turns the corner. Two men are inside, their eyes shaded by the brims of their hats.

"*Operator.*"

"The marshals' office in Nashville, Tennessee."

"*Deposit ten cents, please.*"

Another car! This very booth is where I'm going to be slaughtered, and after that every colored man, woman, and child in Aurora.

"Marshal Evan Quaid's office."

"This is Olivia Harker Cross," I wrench out. "I live on Farm Road One in Aurora, Kentucky, and I have proof of thirty-four lynchings in Pope County."

"Ma'am—hold on a moment."

The cars pull in behind the bus. "I can't—"

Marshal Quaid comes on the line. "Miz Cross?"

"We're on a bus at the crossroad in Kingston. We need help right now."

"How many of you?"

Car doors open. They're going to kill us, and they have plenty of reason.

"Maybe thirty. Mr. Quaid, I know where the bodies from the cotton trials are buried. I know—"

"Stay where you are. We've got a landing strip in Kingston."

They're going to fly here? "We can't—"

"Then you-all head this way. We'll intercept—"

"No money for gasoline—"

"Can you-all make it back to Aurora?"

"Maybe."

"We're on our way."

A third car pulls up. The telephone goes dead. Have they cut the line, or did Quaid hang up?

Men I recognize stand outside, talking. Deciding the best way to take us.

I drop in the last nickel.

They won't murder us, but will follow us and force us into a ditch, watch as the bus rolls down, then shoot us as we tumble from the shattered windows. Maybe, like Ida, we'll go up in flames.

"Kentuckian Hotel. This is Molly."

"Molly, put Mr. Harris on. Hurry."

"Yes, ma'am."

They're moving toward the telephone booth now—French, the sheriff, a couple of others. They don't look like killers, but now I know the color of their hearts.

Wing's sweet voice comes on the line.

"It's Olivia. I—"

"Olivia? Where are you?"

"Kingston. Wing?"

"I'm here."

"I've always loved you," I blurt. "Back then, being angry when your folks died, and when you married Grace, I was selfish and childish, but—"

"Olivia, honey—"

"Wing—" I pare the words from my throat. "Is Will'm with you?"

"He's here."

"Take care of him."

I can hear Wing's fear. I drop the phone. Before the door is closed, Longfeet has us moving. The Cott'ners bang on the side of the bus, then race for their cars.

"Help's on the way," I tell Longfeet. "But we have to go back."

Two cars have come alongside, another behind. The Reverend turns from the window and shouts for everyone to get down. "There's only God's help for us now," he says. "Longfeet, take us to the Methodist church."

The bus pulls into traffic.

"No! You can't jeopardize people who have nothing to do with this. Listen to me, I can prove the Cott'ners murdered those people—your brothers and sons. But we've got to go home!"

They look so tired.

I say, "Reverend Culpepper, God helps those who help themselves."

He sighs and rubs at his face. "We'll take a fair show of hands."

"Way I see it," Junk says, hunkering down with his arms around Love Alice, "I'd sooner meet Jesus on the road home as any other."

Miz Hanley speaks up. "Ain't no need to take count, Reverend. If Tate Harker says go home, we go home."

Longfeet finds a wide place in the road and turns the bus around. It wheezes mightily, coughs, and dies. He grinds the gears and starts us up again. I hold on tight and watch the gravel and brush race by my window, duck my head when the cars begin to pass and pull ahead. Coming around a turn, I see that a black sedan barricades the road ahead.

"Hold on!" Longfeet says, and he stands on the gas pedal.

My last thought before we hit broadside is that I hope nobody was in that car. Junk and the Reverend catch me as I topple. With a great screaming of metal and the stink of burnt rubber, we shove the car off to one side, and it disappears. In the mirror I catch Longfeet's toothy grin. Behind me there's sobbing and weeping as we barrel along toward Aurora. Any minute, we'll be surrounded again. The bus rattles so hard, I fear for its parts. No one closes an eye, not even the children who are tucked into laps and under the seats. A great deal of crying has been replaced by prayers.

The only destination I can think that will hold us all is Wing's hotel. On the other hand, Will'm is there, and I'd be bringing the Cott'ners right to his door.

63

We turn off the highway. This old tank won't run on fumes. When it stops dead, the Cott'ners will appear out of nowhere, pry open the door, and swarm the bus. I figure they'll beat us all senseless, then fling us through the ice on the Capulet. Then I see the last rise in the road before town.

Somewhere behind is Phelps' righteous club—Judas Iscariots who admired sighted silver-faces and then shot for sport. Worse, they donned robes, tried men, and snapped necks. And Wing, in his innocence, has bedded them down. If we go to the hotel now, the Cott'ners will destroy the place, and all Wing's work will have been for naught. What's left of Grace Harris's memory will be nothing more than a pile of kindling.

For now, the Cott'ners are keeping their distance.

"Take us to my place," I tell Longfeet.

He pulls off onto Farm Road One.

"Turn up in the driveway, will you?" Then I tell him the rest of my plan.

Longfeet listens and nods.

The Cott'ners' cars haven't come into sight. Maybe they're making telephone calls, finding guns, digging graves. Telling their wives they'll be late getting home.

God, *where is our help?*

The temperature must be rising because the snow has turned to a thick layer of slush. We pull up in our side yard, and Longfeet stops the bus by the outbuilding, the old toolshed where Pap once worked the still. I open the shed door. Longfeet and I move sacks of feed, a couple of barrels, a half dozen crates. Junk helps. He catches hold of the iron ring in the floor and raises the door. Below is the tunnel Pap once dug. Smells of mold, and decay, and rotting earth rush out.

Longfeet and the Reverend are helping folks off the bus and into the shed where they cry out and balk, and I run for the lantern on the porch. But when the back door opens and Will'm comes out holding the cub, I'm near tears, near the end. I have saved nothing.

Junk looks at the slush. "Tracks lead right to us."

"I'ma close the door, cover it over," Longfeet says. "Miss Livvy right. I gon' pass by the barn, that old cabin, drive 'round and 'round. When I see 'em comin', I lead 'em down the road. Maybe they follow me, maybe not. But you got to hurry."

The Reverend holds his daughter in his arms as she pleads, "Longfeet, if they catch up with you—"

"Don't you worry," Longfeet tells his wife.

"All right, then," Junk says. "Reverend, you take this lantern and lead the way down. Love Alice and I will come last with Miss Livvy."

Where are the marshals?

One by one, the Reverend and his flock disappear into the hole. Across the yard, Junk and I drop into the muddy grave we began digging three days ago. Junk has the shovel. I scrabble with my hands. In a few more minutes it'll be our turn to follow the others through the trap door. I wonder, now, if Pap dug it not so much for convenience, but in case he needed to get away from Phelps.

Then Junk strikes something with his shovel. He gets down on his knees in the muck, works his hands. It's the first time I've ever heard Junk swear. With a sucking sound, a tin box pulls loose, and he passes it to me.

Longfeet shouts, "You-all got to hurry! I got to move this bus!"

We scramble from the hole. I take Will'm's hand. Through the winter trees to the west I see the highway. A long line of dark cars slow to make the turn.

Into the shed, then three steps, four, into the belly of the earth. Six, seven. My heart bangs in my throat, and I imagine I can't breathe. Will'm is behind me. With the ninth step, I am standing on the plywood floor, but it's soft and splintered, and water rises. The braces have rotted, and the walls are pure mud. There's a great deal of moaning and some in front of us cry out. I try not to think about the soil overhead, how it crawls with vermin and seals us in. The Reverend once baptized me in the name of this earth. I'm counting on it to save us now.

Even in the muck I pass the word to sit down. If we don't, many will soon faint, and we must not make a sound. Will'm and I sit, and Miss Wellette, next to me, folds herself into the slop. I know so many old feet and legs and knees are cramping, and I wonder how the children are so quiet. I send along word, too, that the other end is only plywood and if worse comes to worse they might push through into our cellar. What comes back along the line is not spoken. They'll die here before they'll hang in Phelps' barn.

Junk and Love Alice scramble down the steps. Longfeet closes the door and stacks things to cover our hiding place. We hear the bus rumble and fade away, locking us in with mildew and our prayers. Love Alice is in her husband's arms.

There are murmurs and static bursts of sobbing, but then they are still. I can hear them breathing, and wonder how long it will be before the Reverend's lantern goes out. I put my arm around Will'm, hold him tight.

Miss Wellette lays her hand on top of his head. A last blessing.

"We'll be all right," I say.

Truth is, we'll run out of air and freeze. We're in here for life, and probably for death. In this belly of the earth, I wish I could see Will'm's gray eyes. I know he has tucked the cub under his shirt, against his heart.

"Gran? When the marshals come," he says softly, "will they know we're down here?"

I pull him into this coat that isn't mine, and button it around us. The air is hot and syrupy. He tucks his head under my chin, and I close my eyes. I never could have asked for more. I'm going to heaven, rocking Will'm.

64

The first to arrive were Misters French and Andrews, and that fat-faced Doyle Pink, who once swore to defend and protect us. They were followed by a dozen or so more, and by the time they got organized and ripped up the trap door, Junk was ready. He launched himself at them. With his fists he bloodied the first four or five before they wrestled him to the ground.

Even as Will'm was losing consciousness, he now swears he could hear sirens out on the highway.

I have no idea how many deputies Marshal Quaid brought, but they drove into our yard and surrounded the Cott'ners who had dragged some of us, unconscious, from the hole. That was their mistake. They should have left us there.

Now Junk and I stand looking down at the hole near the outhouse, where I once thought we'd find what was left of Pap's bones. Love Alice is beside me—flanked by three federal marshals in yellow rain gear, for it's been pouring, but now the sun has come out.

"Let Marshal Quaid take you to the hospital, Junk," I say.

"Hush, O-livvy," Love Alice says, holding an umbrella.

Wing is here, too.

We go into the house. I lay the tin box on the table and lift the latch. Inside is an oilcloth wrapping, and inside that are the two black binders I remember as Pap's doctoring books. Marshal Quaid watches as I lift out the first one, open it, and turn the pages. In Pap's webby script are dates and accounts of the hangings he witnessed. He wrote about the Phelps boys shooting Booger. The inductions that went on in the barn, the trials. The pages are filled, front and back—victims and judges, and who acted as jury. Name after name of the men who were involved, and, to my surprise, a few women, including Elizabeth Phelps. Sketches of coloreds with their necks in nooses, standing on their toes on tight bales, while hooded men kicked the cotton from under them. Here are maps of their graves in Phelps' north acreage, the same field Sanderson Two protects from coyotes.

With an enormous sigh, I give the books up. Wing puts his arms around me. Quaid wraps the books gently in the oilcloth and lays them back in the box. He hoists it under one arm, and shakes my hand. Then he reaches down and shakes Junk's, too.

Then, blessing of blessings, the marshal tips his hat to Love Alice.

She looks in his eyes and tells him he's having too much pecan pie for supper. And *that*, she says, grinning, is one almighty truth.

65

Although I'm exhausted, I can't stop talking. I've told Wing about Alton and James Arnold Phelps, and about death dealt out by the Cotton Club. How they chose victims at random and did such a thorough job, locally, that there are no young colored men left in Aurora. Along with names I've given, Pap's records are enough to convict more than a hundred men. I suspect that, by now, a lot of them are dried-up old codgers.

Wing says he wished he'd known. Just so he could save me. I love him for that and don't mention the uselessness of such a thought. He had his hands full.

Quaid says his office has been investigating the cotton trials for a long time. Too bad, he adds, my pap didn't know that.

So far they've found no trace of Elizabeth. Phelps probably drowned her in the Capulet where enough folks were baptized to sanctify her for eternity.

Will'm is happy he didn't "miss all the important stuff." I wish he had, and before long we'll talk, he and I, about our time in that tunnel. I'm glad he saved the cub.

For hours, Wing listens. I don't point out that Cott'ners bedded down in these very rooms. Wing's eyes are already heavy with sorrow. As best I can, I replay the scenes with Alton and

Doyle Pink, the truth about Pap, the fire at the church. I tell him about the ride to the penitentiary. When I tell him about seeing Pap, Wing closes his eyes. I don't know whether he's picturing it all, or if the enormity of it is just too much. I talk on, coming to the part about phoning him. He says it was a gift.

"Feels like I owe somebody a nickel," he says.

I reach for the brush that he's using on my hair.

"Oh no, you don't," he says, pulling back. "All these years I wanted to take your hair down. Like that might shake loose all the hurt between us."

I bite my lip. I'm right out of the tub with the gilded claw feet, the one next to the pull-chain toilet I demonstrated back when the hotel opened. I can't think why Wing would want to change a thing. He turns me to him. We're sitting on my bed in the velvet-draped room. He lifts my chin, puts his mouth on mine. We've crossed rivers of time, and our heat is so powerful I can't breathe in the face of it.

No matter how hard we try, we can't get close enough, but hold each other so tight, it's a miracle one of us doesn't break. Wing sheds his clothes and lays me back, settles himself, easy, on top. He kisses my neck, hides his face in my hair, and lifts my nightgown.

A vision of us, naked in the woods at fourteen, makes me smile. It's been so long since I've felt his hands that I'm trembling like some heroine on the rack over at Dooby's.

Funny how a body leans into this need. I part my legs and bend my knees. Lift myself to him.

"Oh God, Olivia. I love you, I love you."

Afterward, I want only to lie between his legs, my head on his chest. Slide in and out of sleep. Sometime in the night, his hands caress me.

"Shh," he says against my hair.

In the waxy moonlight I see the muscles in his shoulders, the pleasure on his face. Was there ever a night when we didn't do this—work for breath, try new kisses, find places to touch. I shift slightly, inviting his body, his loving. Heat rises until I cry out for him to fill me again, but he lays a finger on my lips, and won't hurry. I wonder if God is instructing him in that. In any case, Love Alice is right about the pecan pie.

Epilogue

Will'm turned twelve the following month. I gave him Saul's rifle. He blew out his birthday candles at a party given by Miss Dovey, who had just celebrated her own birthday. On the night of the fire, she was eighty-two.

When Evan Quaid's boys arrested Henry French, the hardware closed down. Smooth as pouring gravy, it became the new African Methodist Episcopal Church. French's niece, Eloise, didn't protest.

On Easter Sunday, the folks at Stipling called Doc Pritchett and said Ida had died. I hope next time she'll choose an easier life, if such things are chosen. We buried her in the Methodist churchyard, not far from Alton and James Arnold Phelps. I was right—all things come around.

When summer arrived, there was talk of a new highway being laid closer to Aurora, and it woke us all up. Maybe folks stopped being afraid. One of the Nailhow boys reopened the old bakery, and another the bank. Eloise French is putting in a beauty parlor; she'll charge three dollars for a permanent wave. Will'm will graduate from high school a year early. I wonder if Molly will be on his arm—or maybe a gaggle of girls will covet him, the way they did Wing. He reads a lot and talks about installing a coal furnace and adding two rooms and a wide front porch. Occasionally, but not often, we hear a wolf howl high up on the mountain.

On a more precious note, Love Alice's niece passed over last winter, and left a brand-new infant named Roseanne. Love Alice and Junk are taking the train from Paramus tomorrow, bringing the baby home. I picture a sweet darkling in pink bonnet and booties, her hand no bigger than the end of Junk's thumb. Heaven will be in Miz Hanley's eyes; a baby will rest on her bosom.

I don't know if Wing and I will ever marry. But he's already sold the hotel and is building us a house on Cooper's Ridge—a fine brick place with a real furnace and a grated road winding up to it. We'll live there together. I am less shapely than ever, and he is plagued with rheumatism. However, none of that matters when we make love, when we sleep curled together in the same four-poster where Pauline and I were born.

Most of all, Wing and I drive to Kingston to see Pap every Sunday—in seven weeks he'll be coming home, paroled in exchange for being the state's witness. When we pull up our chairs and Pap looks at me through the double glass, this resurrection is the third greatest blessing I've ever known.

Big Ruse died in March, when snow collapsed the roof of the restaurant. Little Ruse had the place rebuilt. On our way home from Kingston, Wing and I stop there for supper—pot roast, sausage, or corned beef and cabbage.

Alas, in Aurora, there's still division between coloreds and whites. I'm equally to blame. A long time ago, Love Alice said it right—what we think to be so, often isn't. It's not that I pretended—I just didn't see. Maybe, in the next hundred years, we'll at least know the difference.

Sweeping Up Glass

A Novel

Carolyn Wall

A Reader's Guide

The Birth of Sweeping Up Glass

by Carolyn Wall

I was teaching a group of writing students in my living room, and the subject for the evening was "following the heart." I used baseball as the metaphor. "When the mind sets up chatter," I said, "the heart can't remember its name, let alone watch the ball."

At the time, I'd sold several hundred articles, short stories, columns, and reviews, and as a wife and mother of four, I had become more subservient to the Texaco bill and the electric company than any elusive chamber of the heart.

But that night, I swept my class out the door and, still revved from the emotion of my own lecture, I went to the computer and fingered the keys. Out fell a scene from *Sweeping Up Glass*, the one in which Olivia has just told Percy that the baby is his. He shoves her out of his car, and she lies on the side of the road, the broken blue sequins of her dress making her think the stars have fallen. With the baby ready to make its exit, Olivia, stunned with gin, listens to the wolves calling down the night and waits for Ida to come out and fetch her. I had no idea where that scene came from.

Still, I knew how to be a stubborn child, so I backed up and let Olivia boil over. I knew what it was like to adore a father, and experience hellfire with a ma'am, so much of this book is culled from my life. The first character to be spun from thin air was Love Alice. Her name, and its reason for being, burst in my head like a kernel of corn popping.

Love Alice was the first chirping robin of spring, and she had this *gift*, could look in another's eyes and know his Truths. Only in subtle ways could Love Alice tell us how she saw herself. Afterward, I briefly considered writing a book from her viewpoint, but she was too profound, too accepting, and I'd never be able to sustain her for that long. Love Alice was the perfect friend.

Junk was enormous fun to write, and at the end of each scene, I had trouble leaving him. He became Love Alice's soul mate, Olivia's rock, and a baptizer and pillar of the community. Because I wanted this book to also be about "overcoming," it seemed only right that he, too, had been badly hurt.

In my stories, I love to harbor, then expose, secrets. Not all of them, when let loose, bloom as deliciously as my hotelier and trumpet player. I fashioned him from sweet fantasy— comfortably handsome, close to his God, and sexy to the core. Every woman should experience one Wing Harris.

Although my face is that peachy color we folks call white, I live in a mostly black community. I love its fluid movement, the hum of its language. I was not at all surprised when Olivia prayed to God to change the color of her skin. I began her story upon conception: her refusal to leave her mother's womb, how Ida could not recognize her birth and was trucked off to an asylum. Here's a true story that I almost included in this book. Maybe it'll show up in a later one.

When I was born, we lived over a grocery store in Toronto. My father built crates in an alley for Canada Box, and sold meat pies from the basket of his bicycle. With my mother gone off to a small private hospital for shock treatments, we moved into rooms at the top of Gramma's house.

On Sunday evenings, Dad dismantled my crib, roped it to the top of the car, and threw all the baby things in back. Then he laid me on the seat beside him and drove around Toronto, looking for an aunt and uncle to take me. In a relative's house, he'd set up my crib and kiss me good-bye.

To help support us, and to pay the doctor and hospital bills, he worked three nights a week building radios and record players for RCA Victor. He visited my mother in the hospital and took a Wednesday-night electronics class in the back room of a Chinese restaurant.

After work on Fridays, he'd come to me, dismantle my crib, tie it to the car, toss in my stuff, and drive us home. The next Sunday night, we began again.

My poor aunts must have grown terribly weary of me, sometimes calling Dad to "come and get this kid."

"No matter," he once told me. "When Gramma saw you coming, she'd open her arms wide."

Thus were born Olivia and Will'm. Writing love for grandchildren was a given, and I'm sure I'm not finished. Because I did not want to bore the reader, I wrote what I hope are unique relationships between characters. Something basic happens when two people are in a room together, even if they have not yet met. As each character's face, name, *and trouble* spilled from my fingers, I knew the possibilities were endless.

If there ever is a sequel to *Sweeping Up Glass*, Olivia will feel deeper ties to earth, sky, and water. And, had there been an epilogue to the epilogue, surely Will'm's connections to his mother and grandmother would have impacted the ways in which he raised his own children.

From the beginning, Olivia ached to show readers that when a thing seems to be solidly black and white, *maybe it isn't*. And that moment by moment, she chose her actions and who she wanted to be. I opted for this title because, in the face of tragedy, Olivia reached for her dustpan.

As for picking Kentucky—why does any place speak to us? I wanted to set my people down in a community that was close and passionate and persecuted, and somewhere along the way I'd fallen in love with Kentucky's mountains and their stories. In the saddest places, I saw dignity. And somewhere—I can't remember the exact spot—I heard music.

My children and their offspring are far more to me than just my blood and bone. The real Ida gave me her creativity and stubbornness. She passed on two months after *Sweeping Up Glass* was sold, never knowing it existed. In its pages, I don't think she'd have recognized herself. Still, she worked crossword puzzles in the newspaper *with a pen* until six weeks before she died. Not much got past her.

My father was a fine speaker. Guests would say "Put on the kettle, Frank, and tell us a story."

Making up tales—for which I was spanked as a child—is now the axis on which my world turns. May that happen to us all.

Know this: *Sweeping Up Glass* is fifty percent truth, and fifty percent based on fact. The other fifty percent (which speaks of my math skills) is flat made-up.

Questions and Topics
for Discussion

1. The wolves provide a connection to the mountain, and therefore to Olivia's past. What in nature connects you to where you live?

2. How do you think you would react if you discovered a massive, life-changing secret?

3. Olivia discovers that her hometown is a hotbed of racist hatred. Have you ever discovered something awful about the place that you grew up? How did you react?

4. Are the people who kept Olivia's secret from her truly her friends? Do you believe they genuinely had her best interests at heart?

5. The last paragraph of the book finds Olivia contemplating that "in Aurora, there's still division between coloreds and whites. I'm equally to blame." Do you think that Olivia is partly to blame for this division? How or why not? Do you agree with Olivia's assessment that "It's not that I pretended— I just didn't see"?

6. How much do you think Wing knew about the Cott'ners? If you believe that he knew about the lynchings, do you think that makes him as culpable as those who carried them out?

Was Olivia right to prevent Pauline from taking Will'm
with her back to California? Was Will'm safer going back to
the uncertainty of Hollywood with his mother, or staying
on the mountain with Olivia?

Sweeping Up Glass examines segregation enforced by society, but also voluntary segregation from society. Can you
see parallels to today in how people can segregate themselves either as individuals or as a community? What goals
can hope to be achieved through such self-segregation?

Do you believe that there is redemption for Tate? Does
keeping the books and leading Olivia to them redeem him
for his actions?

For letting Olivia grow up believing what she did, is Tate
as much an antagonist to Olivia as Alton Phelps?

Do you think Ida knows what she does? Do you see her
as being in control of her actions? Can you see a parallel in
your own life of someone who appears to be out of control,
but may know exactly what she is doing?

The characters of Will'm and Tate are viewed as being
universally "good," whereas the Phelps brothers are viewed
as being universally "evil." Do you think it is that clear-cut in
the story? In real life, are people ever one or the other?

About the Author

As artist-in-residence for the Oklahoma Arts Council, Carolyn Wall has taught creative writing to more than 4,000 children in her home state of Oklahoma. She operates a national prison-writing program, and authored the only literary book written on the Oklahoma City bombing. Her awards include two Crème-de-la-Crème awards from the Oklahoma Writers Federation Inc. and one from the Kansas State Writers. *Sweeping Up Glass* is her first novel; she is at work on her second, *The Coffin Maker.*